Have
You Seen
Luis Velez?

Also by Catherine Ryan Hyde

Have
You Seen
Luis Velez?

Catherine
Ryan Hyde

A Novel

LAKE UNION
PUBLISHING

Text copyright © 2019 by Catherine Ryan Hyde, Trustee, or Successor Trustee, of the Catherine Ryan Hyde Revocable Trust created under that certain declaration dated September 27, 1999

Published by Lake Union Publishing, Seattle

www.apub.com

Amazon, the Amazon logo, and Lake Union Publishing are trademarks of Amazon.com, Inc., or its affiliates.

ISBN-13: 9781542042369
ISBN-10: 1542042364

Cover design by Shasti O'Leary Soudant

Cover photography by Brandon Hill

Printed in the United States of America

Have You Seen Luis Velez?

PART ONE
OCTOBER

Chapter One

Those Eyes

Raymond slipped out the door of his family's apartment and across the hall to the railed stairs. He looked down the long, rectangular stairwell, four floors down to the lobby. At first he saw no one.

It was morning, and a glare of light hit the stairwell from the windows at the end of every hallway on every floor. Still, as there was nothing but another building outside those windows—which hadn't been cleaned—it only looked dank and muted. It didn't match with Raymond's idea of sunlight.

A moment later Andre's face appeared all the way down in the lobby. He looked up at Raymond. Raymond held up one finger in a signal, asking his friend to wait.

Then he slipped back inside.

His stepfather, who had only just arrived home from his night shift job, sat at the kitchen table, drinking coffee. Reading the sports section of the paper. Raymond's youngest half sister, too young for school, sat eating cereal, tapping the bowl with her spoon in rhythm several times between each bite. She looked up at Raymond and smiled.

"Hi, Ray Ray," she said.

"Hey, Clarissa."

Apparently his two other half sisters had already left for school.

Raymond grabbed a granola bar out of a box in the cupboard and slid it into his shirt pocket. Then he stood—as tall and obvious as possible—in front of his stepfather's newspaper.

Nothing.

It should have worked. Tall was something of a specialty of Raymond's.

He cleared his throat.

Still nothing.

Raymond didn't call his stepfather "Dad." Not ever. He was allowed to call him Ed, but he had never felt comfortable doing so.

"Um . . . ," he began.

Ed lowered the paper and looked up at him. Waited.

"I was hoping you could . . ."

"Unless you tell me what, I probably can't."

"Give me some money for school lunch?"

Ed sighed, and Raymond knew he wouldn't get the money.

"How many times do we have to go over this? It's cheaper to eat the lunch your mother made."

"She didn't make me one."

Ed dropped his newspaper onto the table. He rose, walked briskly to the refrigerator, and threw its door wide. That, Raymond could understand. But he did not understand why the man just stood there, letting all the cold out. There was no lunch prepared, waiting in a brown bag. That much was obvious already. Did he think staring would make one appear?

Clarissa dropped her spoon into her bowl of cereal, splashing milk onto the table. She wrapped herself in her own tiny arms, as though suddenly thrust out onto a frozen Alaskan tundra in her jammies.

"Brrrrrr," she said.

Ed grabbed a package of baloney from a refrigerator shelf. The mustard from inside the door.

Raymond sighed. He would have happily made his own lunch, but when he did his stepfather always complained that he used far too much meat and cheese.

"I'll be late."

"It'll only take a minute."

"Andre is waiting for me."

"He can go without you if he's in such a hurry. You don't have to walk with him every day."

"It's his last day."

Ed's hands stopped moving. He had been opening the bag around a loaf of bread, but he stopped. Looked over his shoulder at Raymond.

"What, you mean . . . on earth?"

"I told you," Raymond said, desperately wishing he could transport himself somewhere else. Anywhere else.

"I don't remember."

No, of course you don't. Because you don't listen.

"He's moving."

"So? You'll take the subway and see him. You're a big boy. Big enough to ride the subway by yourself. Hell, you're nearly grown. Old enough to work a job. *I* had a job when *I* was sixteen. You'll go see him."

Ed had an uncanny ability to work the getting of jobs into every conversation.

"He's moving to California."

"Oh," Ed said. "I guess that does sound familiar."

He swiped a knife across one slice of bread, spreading far too much mustard around. Then he dropped a single slice of baloney on the mustard and slapped another piece of bread onto that. He slid it into a plastic sandwich bag. Grabbed a sad-looking orange from a bowl on the counter. Dropped both into a brown paper bag that looked as though it had made twenty or more trips to school and back.

"On his own?" Ed asked as he handed it to Raymond. "Or with his family?"

Of course with his family. He's not even seventeen yet. Where's he going to go on his own? And if you say, "In my day we . . ."

"With his family."

"Tell him I said bye."

"Right. I will."

Raymond grabbed up his book backpack from the hall on his way to the door. Slung one of its straps over his shoulder. He threw the door wide, and almost bowled Andre down on his way out. He grabbed one of his friend's arms to keep him from tipping over backward. When he was sure Andre had steadied himself, Raymond let go, and they just stood that way a moment. Even though they both knew they were late.

"Oh," Raymond said. He looked down at his friend, who was a good two heads shorter. "You're here."

"Thought you forgot all about me, man."

"Nah. Sorry. I was trying to get lunch money from you-know-who."

They ran down the stairs together, taking them two at a time.

"Don't tell me," Andre said. "Let me guess. He made you a sandwich."

"Right."

"Like, one that's hardly anything to eat at all."

"Pretty much."

They touched down on the third-floor landing. Gripped the railing to spin a tight turn. Hit the stairs going down again.

"And then he told you that when *he* was sixteen, he worked a job."

Raymond felt himself smile. It stood out to him, because it was something he didn't feel often. At first he liked the feeling. Then it hit him how much he would miss Andre when he was gone.

They descended toward the second floor in silence.

Raymond was having that experience of feeling his physical self from the inside. That was the only way he knew how to describe it. Sometimes he was bizarrely aware of feeling too tall. Other times he thought he could feel his Adam's apple protrude. Or he couldn't take his mental eye off the slump of his own shoulders. Or he was so aware of his own facial expression—the set of his lips, for example—that it almost felt as though he were viewing himself from the outside.

All the way down to the second floor it felt like all of the above, plus a sadness in his eyes. It was always an uncomfortable sensation, because he never liked any of what he could feel.

As they spun on the second-floor landing, Raymond heard an older woman's voice call out to them.

"Hello?"

Raymond stopped in his tracks. Andre kept going.

Raymond looked down the hall to see an old woman standing in the doorway of her apartment. A very old woman. Raymond thought she looked ninety. She was wearing a faded housedress printed with flowers. White terry-cloth slippers. Her snow-white hair was pulled back into a braid. Her eyes seemed to be turned in the direction of the stairs, as though she was looking at him. But she wasn't. Not really. There was no focus there. She seemed not to see him, even though he was standing right in her line of vision.

It gave Raymond a creepy feeling. As if something wasn't right in the old woman's head.

Andre turned around and came back to get him. He grabbed the cuff of Raymond's long-sleeved tee. "C'mon, man."

"Hello?" the old woman said again, as though she couldn't decide if there was someone right in front of her or not.

Yeah. Something not right.

"Just. Keep. Walking," Andre whispered.

"Is someone still there?" the old woman asked.

"Yeah. It's Raymond. Jaffe. From the fourth floor?"

Andre dropped his face into his hands and sighed.

"Do you know Luis Velez?" she asked. "Have you seen him?"

"Nah. I mean . . . no, ma'am. I don't know him."

"Oh," she said. "Oh dear."

Andre grabbed his arm and pulled hard. "Come *on*, man. We're *late.*"

It broke Raymond out of his trance, and he moved again.

"Sorry," he called over his shoulder as he and Andre trotted down to the lobby together.

"What d'you think that was all about?" Andre asked as they spilled out into the cold, gray morning. Down the apartment-house steps to the street.

"Don't know."

"I think she's crazy."

"Why do you think that?" Raymond asked, wanting to defend her for reasons he could not have explained. Or even identified.

"Those eyes. What was with those eyes? I mean, we're either right in front of her or we're not. You know?"

"Yeah," Raymond said. "I noticed that, too. I guess that *was* a little strange."

They walked in silence for a time. Half a block, the long way.

Raymond was having that problem again. Too much awareness of his own physical self. First he hooked his thumbs into his backpack straps. But he could feel his elbows sticking out too far. Then he let go and shoved his hands deep into his jeans pockets. But they still stuck out. Even when he walked with his hands at his sides, he could not stop being aware of his elbows. No matter what they were doing, it never felt like the right thing.

Worse yet, he wanted to say something to Andre on this last day. Something simple. *I'll miss you when you move.* But he just couldn't force it out.

Finally he took a big, deep breath and forced out the word "I . . ." He figured once he'd said that much, he'd have no choice but to finish. ". . . wish you didn't have to go to California."

"You and me both," Andre said.

Raymond looked down at his friend as they walked. He was so much smaller than Raymond, but in more ways than just height. He was more compact, with finer features. He looked like all his parts fit together correctly, and each part knew exactly what to do at all times. He was more athletic. His skin was darker. Andre was all one thing, in a number of different ways. He fit with himself. Raymond envied that.

He quickly looked away again.

They drew level with the abandoned building at the end of the block.

"Nope," Andre said. "No way, man. We're late."

"I just have a little thing of tuna. I was just gonna leave it."

"Leave it on the way home. He won't die."

"I think she's a she. Actually."

"Okay. She won't die."

"But she'll be hungry."

"She was a lot hungrier before she met you."

"Yeah," Raymond said. "I guess that's true. Besides, it does take me a while to get her to come to me. I could just leave it, though."

"And then what if some other cat gets it? Or the rats and mice?"

"I guess. Yeah."

But he couldn't help looking over his shoulder. All the way across the street. Until they turned a corner and the building fell out of sight.

"Just think," Andre said. "If you hadn't bought the tuna, you'd be able to buy a school lunch."

"Not really. Tuna's cheaper."

"Still. What happened to that money your real dad gave you?"

"Spent it."

"On tuna?"

"No. Well. Partly. Well. Yeah. Pretty much."

———

They walked home from school together. Slowly. Slower than they had ever walked before. At times Raymond thought it might be slower than anyone had ever walked before—that they were setting some kind of new world record. Gold medal in the mosey division.

Neither commented on why. Then again, they didn't need to.

As they pulled level with the abandoned building, both knowing it was Raymond's jumping-off place, they had to slow even more. And the only way to do that was to stop. So that's what they did.

"I know you wanna . . . ," Andre said. He didn't finish, or mention the cat. It went without saying.

"Right," Raymond said, realizing he was in prison. That his inability to express what he was feeling had formed such a tight and inescapable box around his being that he could barely breathe. It wasn't a complete surprise. But the walls were definitely closing in. "Well," he added, still in no way equipped for a jailbreak.

"See ya," Andre said.

"Yeah," Raymond said. "Except . . . no. That's the whole thing. You won't."

"No, I will, man. It's all good. I'll Skype you."

"Oh. Skype. Right. Okay. That's true."

"So, no big goodbyes. Just . . ."

"Skype to you soon," Raymond said.

His friend offered a little half wave, half salute and turned for home—a building less than a block past Raymond's. A place that would only continue to be Andre's home for less than another twenty-four hours.

Raymond stood perfectly still on the sidewalk and watched him go, and his self-awareness—or maybe better to call it self-consciousness—ran out of control. He could feel the set of every muscle in his face, and not one muscle felt natural. He seemed to be leaning forward too far, as if the top half of him were staging some mutiny in which it attempted to follow Andre down the street without the rest of him. Even his cheekbones seemed to have something to say, though Raymond could not imagine what that might be.

Andre looked over his shoulder and waved. Raymond waved back.

Then he broke free of his pose and slid through a missing window into the basement of the abandoned building, dropping onto the concrete floor with a slap of his athletic shoes.

"Kitty, kitty, kitty," he called. "Here, kitty, kitty, kitty."

He sat down on a hard stone bench that, he assumed, had been too heavy for anybody to bother hauling away. It was ornate, in an oddly affecting way. It had leaflike curls of stone where the legs met the bench. That made it special to Raymond, because nothing else in his life was ornate, especially for no reason in particular. Just for its own sake like that.

The cat jumped up on the bench and mewed to him. She was a tiny cat. Not a kitten, but young and small. Long bodied and skinny. An orange tabby with a thin little cry, like a mouse would make. Or something else not even one-tenth her size.

"I know," he said. "I'm late. I'm sorry I kept you waiting."

He dug through his backpack and pulled out the treat he'd bought for her. A little individual half-sized can of tuna with a ring-top lid. He opened it and set it on the bench.

For a moment—just the count of two or three—she didn't go straight for it. Instead she lobbied for one extra moment of affection. She rubbed her long body against Raymond's side, and when he ran his hand down her back, her tail end rose up into the air. Her tail itself stood straight up, like a furry antenna. It quivered in the air.

Then she dug into the tuna.

But that one moment. That one moment when she chose him over food. It was so sweet. It almost made Raymond want to cry. Or maybe that was his friend moving away. Or a combination.

He didn't cry. He never did.

"Guess it's just you and me now," he said.

The cat raised her head and looked at him earnestly, licking her lips. Then she returned her attention to the food.

———

He climbed the stairs slowly, using the bannister to pull himself up. He felt drained, almost completely devoid of energy.

Just as his head came level with the second-floor landing, he saw her again. And heard her. She was wringing her hands in front of her flowered skirt.

"Is that Raymond?" she asked. "From the fourth floor?"

Once again those eyes seemed to search a spot Raymond did not quite occupy. Almost, but not precisely.

"Yes, ma'am," he said. "It's me."

"I was just thinking . . ."

Raymond stepped up onto the landing and walked a few steps down the hall in her direction. A voice in the back of his head told him not to. If Andre were here, Andre would have told him not to. Maybe that's who the voice was, in the back of Raymond's head, giving unwanted advice. But it seemed silly to fear her. She was so completely ancient. If Raymond felt the need to get away, he could turn and vault up the stairs two at a time and be safely inside his apartment before she could even reach the stairwell. The way she seemed to struggle with her vision, he might be safe inside before she could even locate the stairs.

"Yes, ma'am?" he said when he was as close to her as he cared to go.

"Thank you for stopping. Most people don't stop. Most people hurry by. When I ask a question, they hurry faster. I wonder sometimes why we're all so afraid of one another. Or . . . actually . . . no, I don't really wonder. I know why. But I reflect on it. And I think it's a shame."

Raymond noticed a trace of an accent as she spoke. Nothing obvious. More like some speech pattern she had mostly left behind long ago.

Raymond wasn't good at identifying accents, but it sounded vaguely European to him.

"I'm sorry about this morning," he said. "I was late for school."

He was staring into her eyes, but she didn't seem to notice. They had a rheumy look about them, those eyes. Cloudy where most eyes looked clear. It dawned on Raymond that the problem might be confined to those eyes. That her mind might be sharp and clear, and maybe it was only the literal mechanism of her eyes causing malfunction.

"I understand completely," she said. "I was just thinking . . . You live with your parents? Up there on the fourth floor?"

"Pretty much. My mother and stepfather."

"Maybe they know Luis Velez? I know it's not a likelihood, because people come and go from this building and never speak. Look at *us*. We never said a word to each other before this morning. But I just can't help thinking . . . for more than four years he came here to help me and check on me. Three times a week, at a bare minimum. Maybe someone else who lives here might have seen him."

"I don't know," Raymond said. But he agreed, silently within himself, that it was unlikely. "I'll ask them."

"I would very much appreciate that. And you'll come tell me if they know anything?"

"Sure."

Raymond turned away and walked back toward the stairs. Just as he reached for the bannister and lifted one foot to step up, he heard her voice again.

"You're a thoughtful young man," she said.

Raymond froze. Set his foot back down. Focused on the feeling her words created as they settled in him. It was very much the same feeling as in that brief moment when the cat chose him over food. Other than that, it felt strangely foreign. Welcome, but mostly unfamiliar.

"Thank you," he said. "That's a nice thing to say."

Then he climbed the stairs again to his fourth-floor apartment.

——

"Pass the butter, please," his stepfather said.

Raymond heard him, but only in a distant way. He didn't think to connect much relevance to those words. He definitely didn't realize the man was talking to him.

"Raymond," his mother said. "What's with you? You look like you're sleeping with your eyes open like you used to when you were little."

"Sorry," Raymond said.

He picked up the butter dish, which was more or less in front of his plate, and passed it to the left. His ten-year-old sister, Rhonda, the oldest of his half sisters, took it from him without comment and passed it on. Raymond watched and waited to see if she was laughing at him on the inside. He couldn't tell. He never could tell. Rhonda and the eight-year-old Wendy had been inscrutable to Raymond almost since they had learned to talk. They talked incessantly to each other, but rarely to him. Only the baby of the family, Clarissa, seemed to consistently notice Raymond, and care.

"How was school today?" his mother asked.

But Raymond didn't want to assume she had asked it of him. There were quite a few people at that dinner table.

"Who, me?"

"Yes, honey. You."

"Well. It was Andre's last day."

"Oh, that's right," she said. She ran a hand through her bleached-blonde hair, finger-combing it off her face. She did that when she was thinking.

Unlike Ed, she listened. But then she forgot.

"Well," she said. "You have other friends."

No. Not a one.

"Yeah."

Only the cat.

"I'm sorry, though," she added.

Raymond opened his mouth to say something. But he was still unclear on what the something would be. Part of him wanted to express what a big deal it was. Bigger than her words had tried to make it out to be. But it seemed unlikely that he would say a thing like that. He never had before.

"Do you know someone named Luis Velez?" he asked, looking first to his mother, then to Ed.

"Luis Velez," she said. "That name sounds really familiar. I think I work with a guy named Luis Velez. Oh. Wait. No. That's Luis Vasquez."

"I know a guy named *Jose* Velez," Ed said, which was surprisingly unhelpful. Or it would have been surprising from someone else. Ed tended toward the unhelpful.

Raymond expected them to ask why he wanted to know, or who this Luis Velez was to him. Something that showed an interest, or a connection. Then, a moment later, he wondered why he had expected it. After all these years.

"What about *you*, honey?" his mom said, turning her attention on Rhonda. "How was school?"

Rhonda only shrugged.

Raymond left the table in his head. Thought about finding a phone book or an online directory and seeing how many listings there were for Luis Velez. A couple? A couple dozen? A couple hundred? Then he wondered why the old lady hadn't done the same. Her eyes, maybe? But there was still directory assistance.

He couldn't get a bead on whether there was a logical reason why the old woman wasn't able to solve this problem on her own.

Something she had said earlier came popping up into his brain.

For more than four years he came here to help me and check on me.

Which meant she needed help. And checking. And she had no one helping or checking on her now.

Chapter Two

Tea

He knocked on her door at just after eight thirty in the morning.

He expected her to be afraid to open the door. He thought she'd ask in a wary voice who was out there. Instead he heard the immediate—and strangely rapid for a woman her age—undoing of many locks.

She threw the door open wide.

"Luis? Is that you?"

She was looking right up into Raymond's face when she asked it.

"No, ma'am. I'm sorry. It's just me. Raymond."

"From the fourth floor."

"Yes, ma'am. Sorry. I hope I didn't wake you."

But it was a silly thing to say, he realized. Because he clearly hadn't wakened her. She was dressed in a blue-and-white striped housedress, and real shoes instead of slippers—those solid white shoes that nurses wore. Her hair looked freshly braided, the braid falling forward over one shoulder.

It struck Raymond as a surprisingly youthful gesture, if one could refer to the positioning of a braid as a gesture. The fact that it was pure white notwithstanding, it reminded Raymond that she had once been young.

"Oh my goodness, no," she said. "Even the sun sleeps later than I do. What did you learn? Do your parents know anything?"

"No, ma'am. I'm sorry."

He watched her face fall. His gut filled with a sickening sensation somewhere between guilt and self-loathing. Probably closer to the latter. He had said he would come by if he learned anything. If his parents knew anything about Luis Velez. If he knew nothing more—and he didn't—he should have told her first thing. Maybe even before she opened the door.

"I'm sorry," he said again.

"I think you are sorrier than you need to be," she said. "Especially since you came and knocked on my door. Most people don't. Most people hurry by, and the more I try to reach out, the faster they hurry. 'Oh, no,' they say, not with their lips but with their hurrying. They say, 'You are not my family or my friend, you are not my little tribe. You are a *them*, you are not an *us*.' And I know that the very fact that I would speak to them across those well-recognized dividing lines makes them feel they were right to be afraid of me all along. This is how people are these days, I'm afraid. You are welcome to come in, Raymond from the fourth floor. But I must ask that you not move anything. If you pull out a chair, later today I will fall over that chair. Everything must stay exactly where I expect it to be."

They stood a moment, silent and still. Raymond did not go in. He was not quite ready to be in.

He looked past her, into her apartment. A hand-crocheted afghan lay carefully folded on the back of her faded sofa. There were lace doilies on the arms of it. And more doilies on the round antique wooden dining table.

"Here's why I came by," he said.

"Yes," she said. "Tell me. You came because you are a good young man, but probably there is something more specific than that."

"I got to thinking about something you said. And then I couldn't stop thinking about it. You said Luis used to come help you and check on you."

"He did," she said. "For more than four years."

"And now he's gone."

"I am sorry to say yes."

"So now there's no one to help you. Or check on you."

"You are correct. And you are a very decent person, Raymond. Which I knew all along. I'm a very good judge of human nature, you know."

Raymond shifted his weight back and forth from one foot to the other. It was his way of processing being ill at ease with her kind words. He liked them. But the very fact that they felt good as they settled inside him brought its own sense of unease.

"What did he help you do?"

A woman came down the stairs. Fortyish. Dark haired. Her forehead knitted into a careful frown, though Raymond couldn't imagine over what. She looked up and saw him there, talking to the old woman. And saw the old woman there. She cut her eyes away and hurried faster down the stairs.

Wow, Raymond thought. *I see what you mean.*

"He walked me to the bank and to the market. I know it sounds silly to say."

Raymond opened his mouth to speak. But she just kept talking.

"I have a white cane. And I know how to use it. Even though I haven't been blind all my life, I'm good enough with the cane. It's everybody else I'm worried about. Once upon a time people saw that white cane with the red on it, and they respected that. Everybody knew what it meant. The cars would stay far back. People would be careful not to get in front of me. Total strangers would stop what they were doing to help me cross the street. Now, either nobody knows or nobody cares. Or maybe they just don't pay attention. They are too busy looking at their cellular phones. Last time I went out on the street alone it was more than four years ago. Someone cut right in front of me and tripped me, and I fell and broke my wrist. It was miserable. My right wrist. I couldn't hold things or open jars. I could not sign my monthly checks. I could only just barely feed myself. That's when the program sent Luis as a volunteer. Then the program ran out of funding and closed its doors and was no more, but Luis kept coming to help me. I haven't been out on the street alone since then. I am afraid to go."

"So . . ." Raymond had so many questions. It was hard to single out just one. ". . . how long has Luis been . . . missing?"

"Seventeen days."

"So do you have any food left in there at all?"

"I have one-half of a can of condensed soup. Chicken and rice. I started it day before yesterday. It's the last food I have, so I've been forcing myself to eat only one-fourth of it each day."

"That's all you've had to eat? For the past two days? A quarter of a can of soup a day?"

"I wasn't sure how long it would have to last," she said simply. "But now I feel so weak I'm not sure I can walk there. With help, even."

"Well, get your white cane. And your purse. Here, I'll give you my granola bar. And then if you feel up to it, we'll go to the store."

"First the bank, or I can buy nothing at the store."

"Okay. First the bank."

The old woman pressed the palms of her hands together. Brought them up in front of her face. She squeezed her cloudy eyes shut and turned her head up, as if gazing at the hall ceiling, but with her eyes closed. Then again, with her eyes, what difference did it make?

"Thank you for the answer to my prayers," she said. Then she turned her face back down to the approximate location of Raymond's. "And thank you for *being* the answer to my prayers, Raymond from the fourth floor. I will go get a few things, and we will be on our way."

—

"Here's something I don't get," Raymond said as they walked away from the bank.

He held his left elbow out. Exaggeratedly so.

With his right hand, Raymond dragged her little wheeled grocery cart.

"Ask away," she said.

The morning air felt cool and crisp to Raymond. It smelled of car exhaust and sewer grates, but also some kind of curry cooking. The day had a new feel to it.

"You're completely blind?"

"Almost completely. If you were to walk across my line of vision right now, right in front of me, I would know you had. I would see a general shape of you, like a shadow. But indistinct. But only because we are out in the bright light, so that I have the advantage of contrast."

"So, when I came up the stairs yesterday . . . after school . . ."

"Yes. I remember."

"You knew it was me."

"I did indeed. Not all footfalls sound alike, you know. You can tell a lot from the way a person walks. Which is not to say that I might not confuse one person for another if their footsteps were much the same, and some are. But yours are very distinctive, and I'll tell you why. You have a squeak in one of your shoes."

"I do?"

"You do."

They walked along in silence for a moment. Painfully slowly. Slower than Raymond and Andre had walked when they knew it was their last walk together. Raymond was trying to listen to his shoes, but the world would not be quiet. All he could hear was the roar of car engines, drowned out by the louder roar of bus engines, drowned out by honking horns.

Half a block later he gave up trying.

Three boys younger than himself flew by the corner at a dead sprint, followed by the sound of a police siren.

"We'll stop here," he said, tugging slightly at her elbow. "We have to wait for the light to change. And when it does, there's a curb right in front of you."

"You're good at this," she said.

"Am I? Doesn't seem there's much to it."

"Oh, but there is. You have to be paying attention."

The light changed. They moved forward.

"I'll tell you when to step down," he said. "Now."

Then they were out in the street. Still moving very, very slowly. Raymond knew they would not make it to the other side before the light changed again. The drivers would simply have to deal with it. They would have to wait.

But before the light even changed, cars and cabs began to roll around the corner, anxious to proceed through the crosswalk. One swung around behind them, even though that put it well across the line into the oncoming traffic lane. A cab pulled up closer and closer to them, in jumpy little movements. Throttle. Brake. Throttle. Brake.

Raymond raised his right arm high, the grocery cart still attached, and threatened the cabdriver with it. Threatened to bring it down on the hood of his cab, which would damage the paint at the very least.

The cab held still, holding the cars behind it at bay.

"Step up . . . now," he said.

Raymond and the old woman stepped up onto the curb, and the cab roared into motion behind them, tires squealing. He looked over his shoulder to see the driver give him the finger as he sped away.

Raymond breathed deeply. He had never been so grateful for something as simple as sidewalk under his feet.

"So, another thing I don't get," he said. "There are places that deliver food. You could have ordered a pizza. If you have a phone. Do you have a phone?"

"I have a phone, yes."

"We order pizza all the time. Well. I never ordered pizza here, to our building, because my stepfather won't pay for it. He says it's cheaper to buy food at the store and cook it yourself. But when I'm at my dad's, we order pizza. I go stay at my dad's every other weekend. And we get all kinds of takeout delivered."

"Your father is comfortable?"

"Comfortable? I don't know what you mean."

"Financially."

"Oh. That. Yeah, he doesn't have to pinch pennies like my stepdad. He lives in a really nice building in Midtown. He does okay, yeah."

"I figured he must be. I don't order restaurant takeout because it's expensive. But I certainly would have in the last few days, if I could have. Can you really not guess why I couldn't?"

"Um . . ." He felt he should be able to guess. She made it sound like he should. But nothing was coming to mind. "I'm not sure."

"I couldn't get to the bank. So I had no money with which to pay."

"Oh. I just figured you had a credit card or a debit card or something."

"I wish now I did. I was set in my ways. I thought good old cash money was the way I cared to go, but now I see the problems with my stubbornness."

They walked together in silence for a moment. Past payday loan places and cheap souvenir stands. Raymond could see the awning of a market at the end of the block. Its doors were opened out onto the sidewalk.

"And I also tried knocking on doors in our building," she said. "Only on my own floor, though, because the stairs frighten me. To navigate them all by myself, I mean. I used to know all of my neighbors. I had friends, but I am afraid I've outlived them. But all the people I know in our building, they have moved now. And three of my very best neighbor-friends have passed away just in the last two months. So strange and sad to be so alone here after so many years. Whatever people live there now do not answer their door for a stranger. Either that or no one lives behind those doors now at all. There used to be a different sort of feel to this neighborhood. I know that from my own experience. But then the mayor wanted to clean up Times Square, you know? So the crimes that he didn't want there he pushed west, and we are the unfortunate recipients."

"How long have you lived here?"

"Sixty-seven years."

"Sixty-seven years!" It came out as something close to a full-throated shout. "That's before my parents were born! That's before my *grandparents* were born! That's . . ." Then Raymond stopped himself, and felt ashamed of his thoughtlessness. "I'm sorry," he said.

"You spend a lot of time being sorry, Raymond from the fourth floor. But most of the time I don't know for what."

"That came out kind of rude."

"If you think I don't know I am old," she said, "you can put your mind to rest on that score."

———

"Which of the cookies are the ones with the lemon vanilla wafer on the outside and the dark chocolate between the layers?"

"That's these," Raymond said, taking a package of them off the shelf and placing it in her cart. "I like these, too."

"Good. I'm glad you do. Because when we get home, you're going to come inside and have tea and some cookies. And I'll have no argument about that. It's just the way it's going to be. Unless I would make you late for school."

"It's Saturday."

"Is it? Funny how when you don't work anymore you stop keeping track of such things. So if it's Saturday, then you have no excuses."

"I promise not to move any of your things," he said as they walked to the coffee and tea aisle.

Raymond didn't like tea, but he had every intention of drinking a cup of it. And keeping his feelings about it to himself.

"Thank you," she said. "I trust that will be true."

"Yes, ma'am. I get why it would matter to you."

"You don't have to call me ma'am. It seems so formal."

"I don't know your name."

She stopped suddenly, and Raymond had to stop, too. Because they were walking arm in arm. Just as well, because they had reached the selection of teas. A few more steps and they would have passed it.

"That's right. You don't. I'm so sorry. I have been very rude without meaning to be. My name is Mildred Gutermann."

"So what do I call you?"

"Mildred is fine, or Millie. Luis called me Millie. Or . . . calls. I'm not sure. I keep speaking of him in the past tense, and then I correct myself, because I don't know for a fact. But I have a bad feeling. He would have phoned me, or come by. If he could. I just know it."

"Didn't you have a phone number for him?"

"Yes. I did. I had the number of his cellular phone. And now, suddenly, at the same time he is gone, the cellular phone is out of service. I just have a bad feeling about the whole thing."

"Did you ever try to get a listing for him? Maybe he had a landline, too. Or a new cell number."

"He told me he did not have a landline. I called directory assistance many times, in case there was a new number. I got many listings. Every Luis who answered was not the one. At some of the numbers nobody was ever home. I tried for many days and got exactly nowhere."

They stood in silence for a moment. Arm in arm. Raymond said nothing because he had nothing encouraging to say. It did sound like a bad sign.

"So we go next to the tea," Mildred said.

"We're right in front of the tea."

"Oh. Good. I like a strong black tea. English breakfast. Or Irish breakfast."

"There are two or three brands. Which one do you like?"

"I like best the one that is cheapest," she said.

———

He stood beside her in her kitchen, staring into the bare shelves. She had opened all the cupboard doors, and they stood in front of the task together, breathing slowly. As if mentally preparing for a marathon run.

"It's very important where everything goes," she said. "I need to know so I can find it all again."

"I can imagine."

"Cookies there," she said, feeling for a jar on the counter, "but not until we've had some. Lettuce and of course the other salad vegetables go in the crisper drawer in the refrigerator. Chicken thighs and ice cream in the freezer. Although . . . ice cream in the freezer I suspect you would have figured out on your own."

"Right," Raymond said, and set about working on that.

"Salad dressing and milk on the shelves inside the refrigerator door."

"Check."

"Oh, and before I forget to tell you—when we go sit down at the table, please take the chair nearer the window. That was Luis's chair. You'll see that there are marks on the carpet, made with tape. They show you exactly where to place the chair again when you're done using it."

"Got it," Raymond said.

"You don't have to put all of this away yourself. You can just hand me one item at a time and tell me what it is. Unless it's obvious, like the ice cream. Then the item itself will tell me what it is."

"We'll work on it together," Raymond said.

———

They sat at her round dining table together, Raymond running one finger over the intricate lacework of a doily. He picked up his cup of tea, closed his eyes, and took a tiny sip.

"Wow," he said. "This is good."

"I'm glad you think so."

"It's sweet."

"Yes, I put in two spoons of sugar."

"Does it have milk in it?"

"Yes. It's what my mother used to call cambric tea. I don't know why it's called that, only that I was taught that it is. She used to make it for me anytime I needed comforting or cheering up. After a time it grew into something that could make me happy. Or at least more happy. Depending on where I'd started out."

Raymond took another, longer sip, and did seem to feel a little bit better.

"I didn't think I would like it. I thought it would be bitter, like coffee."

"I didn't brew yours very strong. Not like mine."

They sipped in silence for a minute or two.

It was dim in Mildred Gutermann's apartment. No lights had been turned on. Which made sense when Raymond thought about it. The only light came from the avenue-side window, and it had to make its way through a filmy curtain.

Raymond had expected the apartment to be dirty inside. Or at least dusty. Nothing could have been further from the truth.

"So what about you, young one?" she asked, knocking Raymond out of his thoughts. "Tell me what it is about your life that is making you so unhappy."

"I didn't say I was unhappy."

"You didn't need to."

He struggled inwardly for a moment, floundering in the embarrassment of having been seen. It struck him odd that he'd had to come to the home of a blind woman to be seen clearly. At long last.

"Well . . . ," he began. "Lot of things, I guess. Hard to put my finger on just one."

"Then tell me two or three."

"I just feel like . . ." Raymond paused for a long time. Or at least it seemed long to him. He closed his eyes and listened to the traffic outside. "I guess I feel like I don't fit anywhere."

"You must fit somewhere."

"I don't think so."

"What about up on the fourth floor with your family?"

"That might be where I fit the least."

"Tell me how this is so," she said. "Because I cannot imagine such a thing."

"Well. For starters . . . they're all white."

It struck him, in the pause that followed, that she had not known anything about his color, or lack of same. He wondered if she minded, now that she knew. He wondered if he had ever before met someone who got to know him a little before absorbing that information. Probably not.

"You are adopted?" she asked.

"No. My dad is black and my mom is white. But then they got divorced. And then my mom married my stepdad, who's white, and they had three more kids, all girls."

"You must feel their love for you, though, across whatever differences you think you have."

Raymond sat quietly for a moment, sipping his cambric tea.

"You're not saying anything," she said.

"I was just thinking."

"You do think they love you."

"That wasn't the question, though. The question was whether I *feel* loved. Not usually. Not so much. I think my baby sister loves me. My other two sisters, I don't know. I'll bet they do, in there somewhere. But they have funny ways of showing it. They sort of keep to themselves. I don't think it's about black and white. Or not all about it, anyway. Could be because they're both girls and I'm a boy. But my stepfather. He definitely doesn't love me. He doesn't dislike me. It's more like he just accepts me. I came along with the deal when he met my mom. He loves his girls, because they're . . . you know. His."

"What about your mother?"

"She's just kind of busy. Raising four kids. Working full time. But, you know what? I shouldn't be saying all this. It's probably just me. It's probably a normal sort of a family thing, and I'm just not feeling it right."

"I doubt that," she said. "You're not having cookies."

"Oh. I forgot about the cookies."

He took three, and laid them on the small fine china plate she had set down at his place at the table—a blue floral design that he guessed was very old. Maybe the plates had been passed down to her through generations. They looked like that kind of china.

"Children always feel they are the ones at fault," she said. "They think they are defective somehow, if everything is not just as it should be. But usually not. If there was a lot of love going on all through that house, I think you would feel it. You would know."

Raymond took a bite of cookie and chewed carefully before answering.

"Did you have children?"

"No. I have no children. But I *was* a child, so that will have to do. Tell me this, my young friend. It should not fall to you, but still I will ask if you give love to them. In a big sort of way that they can feel. Because it's entirely possible that you might have to be the one to start this ball rolling. Somebody has to go first. It's unfair that it should be you, but that may be the case all the same. Life is not always fair."

"I never even thought about that," he said. But her advice didn't quite seem to fit in the moment. He agreed most with the idea that it was unfair that it should be him.

"Well, you think about it and let me know."

He ate two cookies while he was thinking. Or trying to think, anyway. Somehow his mind just kept coming up blank.

"I'm not sure I would even know how," he said after a time.

"Well, that is a problem," she said, "yes. Ideally the parents get the ball rolling, so then the child recognizes this emotion and knows how to give love in a real way, so it can be felt. But a lot of parents don't know such things themselves, and they can't very well teach you what they don't know, now can they? I'm sorry you are having trouble being happy right now, Raymond. We all take turns, I think. Yesterday I was very unhappy, but today I feel well. And do you know why? I'm sure you do."

"Because you have food."

"Yes. Because I have food. And because I see now that food was something I had grown to take for granted. And now I know better than to take it for granted again. Or at least, it's my job to remember. We'll see how I do. But also I'm happy because I met you. And not only because you walked me to the store. Someone else might have walked me to the store, and so I would be happy to meet them, but maybe only for that reason. Depending on who it was. You I am happy to meet for a number of reasons."

Raymond felt blood rush to his face, tingly and hot.

"Every time I say a nice thing about you, you get very quiet," she said.

"I'm not used to it."

"That's a shame."

With that, they seemed to run out of things to say. Or things they were willing to say. In that conversational direction, anyway.

A minute or two later he asked, "What would you have done? You know. If I hadn't come by?"

"I guess sooner or later I would have called the police, and said to them, 'I don't know who it is who can help a person like me, but I need them now.' Almost anyone *can* help, I suppose. It's more a matter of who *will*. But I would have called the emergency number. The 9-1-1. Because you can't just sit in your apartment and starve to death. If you have no food, you will die, and that is an emergency. But I wanted so much not to do that. I kept thinking if I could hold on a couple days more, maybe Luis would come. I didn't want to wake up in the morning and admit to myself and others that I had given up on that. I wanted the subject still to be open."

The apartment fell quiet again at the mention of his name. A deep, resonating silence, like that surrounding a eulogy or a prayer.

"I should get back," Raymond said, swallowing the last bite of his last cookie. "I didn't tell anybody where I was going. But I'll come back and check on you."

"That's good of you. Thank you, Raymond. Who knows? Maybe Luis will come back. Maybe he will show up at my door. I have dreams about that. Both when I'm awake and when I'm asleep. He tells me different stories of why he couldn't come sooner. But it's no matter in the dream, because he is back."

She stopped talking. Abruptly, he thought. As if she'd meant to say more, but the more had gotten stuck.

Raymond watched her wring her hands the way she had done that first day in front of her apartment door. It had only been the previous day, but it seemed like a far more ancient history.

"I'm just worried sick about him."

"I know," he said. "I know you are."

Raymond didn't say out loud that he would pitch in and attempt to locate this Luis Velez. If indeed Luis were a person possible to locate. But that was the moment when he knew he would.

———

On his way up the stairs to the fourth floor, he heard it. He hadn't even remembered to listen for it. It was just suddenly there.

On every step with his left shoe, Raymond could hear a light but consistent squeak.

Chapter Three

Out of Here

Raymond dropped through the missing basement window of the abandoned building at the end of the block. It was early the following morning. Sunday. Light, but only barely.

He took a few steps across the basement floor, opened his mouth to call the cat . . . and nearly ran into a living, breathing person.

Raymond heard a little shriek escape him. He stood still, trying to calm his heart, but it hammered in his chest.

"You scream like a girl," the person said. "I thought you were a girl."

It was a young white man not much older than Raymond. Maybe a year older. Not as tall, but bigger on balance. Heavier. Far more dangerous. Then again, who wasn't? He wore a letter jacket, wool with leather sleeves, the kind all the high school athletes wore. Also, Raymond knew him. Vaguely. Because they went to the same school. But he didn't know the boy's name. Or maybe he was a man. Maybe he was eighteen. Raymond knew only that he feared him.

"I know you," the guy said.

"You do?"

"Aren't you in my chem lab?"

"Yeah. Maybe."

Raymond felt his breathing settle. Some, anyway. It was seeming likely that he would survive this encounter. It appeared to be morphing into something like a normal conversation.

"What're you doing down here?" the guy asked.

"Oh. That. I wanted to see if I could get that . . ." Raymond made a sudden, instinctive decision not to mention the cat. ". . . bench. That stone bench. I kind of liked it. I was gonna see if it was too heavy to carry home."

The guy turned away, and Raymond breathed a sigh of relief. They had been standing close to each other, nearly nose to nose, and the stress of that closeness had been wearing Raymond down.

The guy walked to the bench. Reached down and tried to lift one end. It didn't budge.

"Yeah, good luck with that," he said.

"What are *you* doing down here?" Raymond asked. Then he immediately wished he hadn't. His heart took to hammering again.

"Looking for that cat."

Raymond didn't answer. While he wasn't answering, he felt a cold sensation rising up around his ears.

The guy kept talking.

"You know. There's a stray that goes in and out this open window. I see it. I think it lives down here. I was gonna see if I could catch it."

"What do you want a cat for?" Raymond asked. He could hear his voice tremble. He hoped the other boy couldn't.

"I don't. It's for Mason. You know Mason?"

"I don't think so. What does he want a cat for?"

"Hard to say. But, knowing him, I'm glad I'm not the cat. Some kind of evil genius experiment, I'm sure. So . . . have you seen it?"

"The cat?"

"Yeah."

"Yes. I did see a cat. Just as I was coming down here. It was in the alley outside." It hurt Raymond to call the cat an "it." But he didn't want to let on that he knew much about her. "I think I scared it. It ran out to the sidewalk and then made a right. You know. Toward school."

"Thanks," the guy said. "I'm on it."

He jogged to the missing window, pulled himself up in one smooth movement. He rested his belly on the open window sash, then swung a leg out into the alley. Just like that, he was gone.

Raymond walked to the bench and reached his hands down to brace himself. To help himself sit. His legs felt shaky. Something that normally filled the inside of his gut seemed to be missing. He settled on the cold stone bench and worked to calm his own heart rate and breath.

His eyes fell on an open cardboard carton full of . . . well, junk, really. His first thought was to dump it all out and use the box. But it looked water damaged and weak. Ready to fall to pieces.

Sitting right on top was an old pillowcase, frayed at the open edge where it should have been neatly stitched.

He rose, testing the strength of his legs, and walked to it. Picked it up. It felt solid. It had no holes that he could see. He turned it over and over in his hands, but it continued to look up to the task.

He heard a tiny cry. A thin little mew.

"Shhh," he whispered. "Yeah, it's me. Don't say anything."

He walked to the place from which he had heard the sound. Got down on his knees. He looked into a space between two wall studs, where the drywall was missing. The cat had made a little nest there out of loose insulation.

He stared in at her. She stared back.

"We have to get you out of here," he said.

She looked at him in a strange way, Raymond thought. Almost . . . knowingly. She didn't know what the problem was—she couldn't. But she seemed to understand that there was a problem. She was aware of Raymond's fear.

She did not come out to greet him, as she normally would have.

Raymond squeezed his eyes shut, as if praying. But, if he was, he was praying to a skinny little stray cat.

"Please forgive me for what I'm gonna do now," he mumbled under his breath. "Please, please, please."

In one sudden movement he reached into the wall and grabbed the cat by the scruff of her neck, pulled her out, and dropped her into the bag. She flailed wildly and got off one good scratch, slicing the skin on the inside of Raymond's wrist with a single back claw. Raymond could not ignore the pain of it, nor the fact that the wound bled profusely. But he didn't stop moving.

He placed the bagged cat under his shirt, tucked the shirt in, then zipped his jacket over the bulge.

He moved to the window, dripping blood. Wondering how to get out without hurting the cat. Normally he would jump up and rest his weight on his belly against the window sash, as that boy in the letter jacket had done. But he had to find another way, and he had to find it fast.

Meanwhile the cat seemed calmed by the closeness and the dark. She held still. Or maybe she was frozen in her fear.

He ran to the open window and jumped up, grabbing the window frame. Then he used the soles of his athletic shoes to climb up the concrete basement wall. A moment later he was in a nearly untenable position. His hands and feet were almost at the same level, and he had no idea how to propel himself upward.

Raymond moved one hand out onto the concrete of the alley. But there was nothing there to hold. He took a deep breath. Stepped down some with his feet. With every muscle in his body straining at once, he thrust himself up and out through the window, allowing his low belly to fall onto the window sash. He was careful to land on a spot lower than the cat, even though he had to pull a series of muscles to do it.

He lay there a moment, processing the pain. Watching blood drip off his scratched arm onto the filthy concrete of the alley.

"Ow," he said. Belatedly.

Then he scrambled the rest of the way out and to his feet.

He made a left at the street. Because he had told that boy to make a right. But that was the long way home. Still, there was nothing Raymond could do about that.

He broke into a sprint.

Half a block later he was seized with a sudden fear. Could the cat breathe inside that pillowcase? Probably. It was fabric, not plastic. Still, she was also covered by a shirt and a jacket.

He stopped. Stepped into the entryway of a building for privacy. Faced away from the street. Pulled the pillowcase out from under his shirt, smearing blood on his only good jacket. The cat thrashed in fear.

"Shhh," he told her. "Hush. Just hold still. You'll be fine."

He opened the top of the pillowcase just an inch or two. Not enough to let her out. He blew his own breath into the bag. Flapped the opening slightly to push air in. Then he zipped her back into his jacket with the case open at the top, and used his hands to hold her to his chest.

That calmed her.

Raymond ran again.

As he ran, he pulled a piece of the pillowcase out of his jacket and pressed it against his bleeding wrist. Held it there to try to stanch the flow.

Then he was seized with another wave of unease. It was not a clean pillowcase. It was not from his house. It was from a box of junk in the basement of that abandoned building. Raymond's imagination took off, running all the way to an infection so serious he would lose his hand.

He shook the images away again.

He was almost home.

———

He stood in the hallway in front of her door, still using the pillowcase to hold back the bleeding. Because he might as well. It was too late now. He knocked.

"It's me," he said. "Raymond."

A pause. Then he heard her tentative footsteps. The undoing of the many locks. But not as fast as she would have unlocked them if she'd thought it might be Luis.

The door swung wide.

She was wearing a gray cardigan sweater over her red housedress. And a pleasant smile. The smile gave way to a curious look, then dropped away entirely.

"There is some sort of animal with you, Raymond?"

"How do you *do* that?"

"I can smell it. What kind of animal do you have?"

"It's just a little cat."

The old woman looked relieved. Raymond could see and hear her pull in a big breath, then sigh it out again.

"Oh. Good. Cats are very nice animals. I like them. I used to have cats."

Raymond could feel his heart lift up in relief and hope. He opened his mouth to ask his huge favor. But, before he could, she said more.

"Now I can't have them, of course, because it would be too much of a danger. They tend to get underfoot. So tell me about this cat, Raymond. Is it your cat?"

"That's kind of a complicated question," he said.

"Is it really? I didn't think it would be."

They stood in silence for a moment. Raymond's heart was falling again. He felt it sink. He would have to sneak the cat into his room. But she would be discovered. It was only a matter of time. He might have to take her to a shelter. Maybe they could find a home for her. But if not . . .

"You and your cat may come in," she said, knocking him out of his thoughts. "Just don't let the cat go until I'm sitting down on the couch."

"Okay. Thanks."

He stepped inside. He tentatively drew his wrist away from the cloth of the pillowcase to see how the wound was doing. The deep scratch was still bleeding. So he pressed the fabric against it again. He didn't want to bleed on the old woman's furniture or rug. Even though she would never know. It was the principle of the thing. *He* would know he had spoiled her nice things. Nice enough, anyway. Well, he thought, nice or not, these things were all she had.

Mildred Gutermann closed and locked the door behind them. Raymond stood very still and watched her cross to the couch. She lowered herself gently, as if every bone and muscle hurt. Or maybe, he thought, just as if she was very old.

"All right," she said. "Now let's have a look at this cat. So to speak."

Raymond sat on the opposite end of the couch from her, perched on its very edge, and opened the pillowcase. The cat's head shot out. She looked around, eyes wide with fear. Then she launched out of the sack and skittered away.

"Oops," Raymond said. "She took off. I better go see where she went."

"No, she will be okay. Let her explore. You sit here and talk to me. Tell me how she is your cat and at the same time somehow not."

"She's a stray," Raymond said. "I've been feeding her. I tamed her. I got her to the point where she would come to me and let me pet her. But I shouldn't have. Because now she's in trouble, and it would've been better if I'd left her alone. She *should* be scared of people. She was right about that all along. I made her more trusting. And I feel really bad about that now. And if something happens to her because of that, I'll never be able to forgive myself."

"But she is right to trust you, Raymond."

"But what if she's more trusting with somebody else because of it?" He sat in silence for a moment. Mildred Gutermann did not answer his question. "A couple of neighborhood boys are looking for her. I don't know what they would do to her if they caught her. But not feed her and pet her, that's for sure."

"I see," she said. "So you will take her home with you."

"I can't. I'm not allowed to have a pet. I brought her here because I thought . . . Well, it doesn't matter what I thought. I was wrong. I wasn't thinking clearly."

"You were hoping I would take her in."

"Yeah."

"I would if I could, my young friend. But I'm sure you see the problem. You can put tape marks on the rug like I do with the chair, so the cat knows exactly where she should be. But she is a living cat, she is not a chair, so it's likely she will choose to be somewhere different."

Raymond sat in silence for a beat or two, hearing himself breathe. He realized he was just at the edge of tears—that it would be so easy to let them go. It surprised him, because he never cried. But it was something about the cat. She had bypassed a boundary, some wall he'd built to keep everybody and everything out of his vulnerable places. And the idea that someone would hurt her for fun . . .

"Do you have something I could put on a cut? So it doesn't get infected?"

"Oh, yes," she said, and pushed herself up off the couch and onto her feet. "I take lots of bumps and falls. I have everything." She took him by the elbow, wrapping both her hands around it with surprising strength. "Come to the bathroom sink."

"Okay," he said.

And he rose. And followed her.

He felt better. Reassured. He would not get a terrible infection, because she would help him. She knew what to do.

"Where is the cut?" she asked as they walked together.

Surprisingly, *she* seemed to be leading *him*. Then again, it was her house. Her bathroom.

"Inside my right wrist."

They stepped into the bathroom together, and she thrust his right forearm into the sink. Again, with surprising strength. She turned the cold water on and stuck his arm under the flow of it.

"Ow," he said. It was a serious understatement of the pain that surged through him.

"I know. I'm sorry. But we have to take care of these things. Is it still bleeding?"

"I don't think so. I think it stopped."

"Good. Here. Take this." She pulled a tall plastic squeeze bottle out of her medicine cabinet. Handed it to him. "Squeeze some of this onto the cut. And we will let it sit there for a minute."

Raymond took it from her. Opened out the nozzle with one hand. Drenched the scratch with the reddish-brown liquid. There was another sharp blast of pain as it flowed into the wound. This time he saw it coming, and held it in. He expressed nothing.

"How did you cut your wrist?" she asked him.

"It was the cat."

"Oh. She scratches."

"No, it was my fault. I was trying to catch her and put her in a bag. She got scared. I can't really blame her. But if you just let her come to you, she doesn't scratch. She's sweet. She wants attention. If she was here—"

"It doesn't really matter," Mildred Gutermann said, interrupting him. "However I would handle her if she were here. Because, sorry as I am to say so, she can't be here. Too bad you can't train a cat. But you can't."

"Not sure what I could teach her to do, anyway," he said. "Even if you could train a cat. You know, that would keep her out from under your feet."

"Maybe if you could teach her to make noise all the time. Meow wherever she went. Then I would always know where she is. But you can't teach that."

"That's it!" Raymond cried out.

"No, no, it's impossible."

"I could buy her a collar with a bell on it! Then she would make noise wherever she goes!"

"Hmm. Rinse that off now. Turn on the water and rinse it. I'll get you some tissues to dry it off, and then I have antibiotic ointment, and then we'll bandage it up."

"What about what I just said?"

"I am thinking about what you just said."

"What do you think of it so far?"

"I think so far that I am kicking myself for not having a cat all these years, if it's as simple as all that. So now I'm thinking . . . is it really? As simple as all that? And I think part of me wants it not to be. So I can stop kicking myself."

Raymond rinsed his wrist under the cold water and dried it off with the tissues she handed him. He said nothing, because he wanted her to have plenty of time to think.

"You would have to buy a litter box. And litter."

"Right!" he said. Too loud and anxious. "I would!"

"And cat food."

"Oh. I guess I didn't think this out very well. It's getting expensive, isn't it?"

"If you would buy the collar with the bell, and the box, and the first bag of litter, I could probably manage the rest."

"Is that too expensive for you?"

"Not really. I don't do too badly. I get by. I have my social security, and a little pension from a company where I worked as a seamstress for fifty years. But I'll need cat food regularly. So you'll need to come by every few days to walk with me to the store."

"I would have anyway," Raymond said. "Cat or no cat. Just because you needed me to."

"I already know that. And that's why I want to be able to do this for you if I can. So go get the bell, and we will give this a try, and we shall hope for the best. Yes, Raymond?"

"Yes," he said. Breathing for what felt like the first time in a long time. "Thank you!"

———

When Raymond got back from the store, he let himself into her apartment with her keys. She had loaned him her keys so she wouldn't have to cross to the door until the cat was collared and belled.

She was sitting on the couch, and the cat was sitting with her front end on the old woman's lap. Purring. Having her ears scratched.

Raymond pulled a deep breath, sighed it out, and felt deeply grateful. He silently thanked the cat for helping him help her.

"I'm back," he said, locking the door behind him.

"So I hear."

"I'm putting your keys back on the hook by the door."

"Thank you."

"And I'll set up the litter box in . . . I don't know. Where do you want me to set it up?"

"In the bathroom. In the corner under the sink. I can't trip over it there."

While he set the box in place—removed the labels and filled it with litter—Raymond wondered how you train a cat to use a litter box. Or do they train themselves? It seemed to go without saying that this cat would never have seen one before. Or maybe he was wrong about that. Maybe the cat had been owned by someone. Once upon a time. Maybe that was why she came to him in a reasonable space of time and with not too much effort.

He threw away the litter bag in the kitchen trash and joined the old woman and the cat on the couch.

"Does she have a name, this cat?" Mildred Gutermann asked.

"No."

"We shall call her Louise," she said without hesitation.

"Okay."

"It's a very dangerous thing when a young person—when any person—wants to hurt an animal. People pass it off sometimes because it's 'just' an animal. Not a person. But to want to hurt an animal shows a very troubling lack of empathy. Empathy is what allows us to live with each other, Raymond. Maybe you know that. Without it, things fall apart. And the boys who hurt animals tend to become the boys who hurt people. They are practicing. It is not a good thing. Where I grew up there was a boy who killed cats. All the neighborhood cats began to disappear. His parents tried to cover for him. He was never made to pay. But it got worse. Much worse. I hate even to say how much worse. I don't like to speak of such things. But it did not confine itself to animals. I'll just say that and no more."

As she spoke, she continued to stroke the cat's ears. And the cat—Louise—continued to purr.

"The fact that you worked to save her, Raymond," she added, "this tells me so much about you."

"Where did you grow up?"

Something dark crossed the old woman's face then. Even the cat noticed, though not by looking. She just picked up the change in mood. She jumped down and slithered under the couch to hide.

"That doesn't matter for now," she said.

"That's right. You're right. I'm sorry. It doesn't."

"Try not to be so sorry, my young friend. Most of what you regret in this world is not of your own making."

"Okay, I'll try. I'm sorry."

Then a second later he heard himself, as if on instant replay.

"Oops," he said.

"You will practice," she said. "I will remind you."

———

"So do you think you'll be okay alone with her?" he asked. "If I go now?"

It was at least an hour or two later. Raymond couldn't see a clock from where he sat with them on the couch. But the sun outside the curtained window told him it was midday.

"We will keep our fingers crossed," she said. "I will be very aware as I am crossing rooms. If I hear the bell I will stop until I know more. The one thing that could be a problem . . . well, let's just hope she doesn't do it. If she sleeps on the rug right in the middle of a room, that will be a danger. But probably she is too cautious for that. As she gets to know the place, and me, she might do it in one spot, over there by the window where the sun comes through the curtain and warms the rug. But I know that spot. I can avoid it. I hope now that it works out, Raymond, and not only for her sake and yours. I miss having cats. It will be nice to have another beating heart around."

"I'll come check on you more often until we see."

"That would be good. Just come and rap on the door. If I'm fine, I'll call to you. I'll say, 'I am fine, Raymond.' But then if I should take a fall, I'll know someone will be along shortly."

He stood. Moved to the door.

"I don't . . . I don't know how to . . . I want to tell you . . ."

But the words dried up. Because he didn't know how to say them. It should have been easy. *Thank you.* He had said it before. But never about something so intensely important. His gratitude seemed to swell up in his throat and choke him.

"You don't have to," she said. "I know what this little animal means to you. I hear it in your voice when you talk about her. Go on. We will be fine."

Raymond let himself out.

He pressed one ear to the door and listened as she crossed the rug to lock up after him. Just to be sure she made it okay.

"I'm right here," he said as she did up the last lock.

"I knew you would be," she said.

He waited until he was sure she must be sitting again. Then he trotted up the stairs to his own apartment.

Once there, he turned on his computer and searched for phone directory listings. The white pages online. Typed in "Luis Velez." Then "New York, New York." If he was right about the spelling of the first and last name, there were about twenty listings. If not, there were many more. Many variations.

Well, he thought. *I'll just have to start at the first one and keep going until I find him. Or find that he can't be found.*

———

In the middle of the night Raymond woke, nursing a bad thought. He booted up his computer and searched for Luis's name and the word "Obituary." Nothing useful came up.

He breathed a sigh of relief and put himself back to bed.

But before he could get back to sleep he remembered his step-grandmother. Ed's mother. When she died, there had been no obituary, because the newspaper had wanted too much money to run one.

Still, there was nothing he could do about any of it. So he put it out of his head as best he could and tried to get some sleep.

Chapter Four

The Luis Project

"Where did he live?" Raymond asked on his next visit to Mildred and the cat.

"Who? Luis?"

"Yeah. Luis."

His plan was to quietly work her for information. Little bits of it that might narrow down the list. Make his job easier. But he wouldn't tell her straight out about the project. Because he might fail. He didn't want to get her hopes up for nothing.

He watched her brow knit down. She began to wring her hands the way she did whenever she spoke of Luis's disappearance.

"I don't know, Raymond. That is one of the worst parts of the thing. I don't know. He used to live within easy walking distance. Four blocks, he said. But I didn't know four blocks in which direction, because he always came here. Then he moved. Farther away. I kept asking him, 'Where do you live now?' Because I was worried he was coming too far to help me. And he knew I was worried about that. So he never would say. Instead he would dismiss my worries by saying, 'It's just a subway ride, Millie. A simple little subway ride.' He never said how long of one. I wish I knew more. He was such a good friend. But we were not the kind of friends where maybe I would go to his house sometimes. No, it was not like that. He always came here."

"What about a middle name?"

"I never asked," she said, stroking Louise's ears. "Do you know this cat slept on my pillow all night long? Purring. Every time I woke up to roll over I could hear her purring. It was just lovely. Now tell me why you are asking so many questions about Luis."

"No reason," he said. "Just curious."

If she didn't believe him—and she probably didn't—she never said.

—

Raymond stood in his own apartment, in front of the kitchen phone, with his list, staring at the horrible floral wallpaper. It was faded, worn down by children's hands. Almost everything in the apartment was a leftover from the days when Ed's grandmother had lived here. Which meant it was all old-fashioned and just plain old.

He'd made a list of twenty-one men named Luis Velez in the greater New York City area. Addresses and phone numbers both.

Looking at the page, he knew the first question he should have asked the old woman was how to spell Velez. It might have had an *a* in the first syllable, not an *e*. Or how to spell Luis. Maybe he spelled it the English way, Louis. And maybe Mildred Gutermann just used a Spanish pronunciation because Luis had.

He'd started to ask her. At least three times. But it wouldn't have worked. It would have given him away. Nobody asked the spelling of somebody's name out of sheer idle curiosity. No, if Raymond had asked that question, especially on top of asking his middle name, she would have known he was looking for Luis. And he currently had very little confidence in his ability to find the man, so he was giving no clues away for now. Or at least no more than necessary.

Raymond's knees quivered slightly as he picked up the receiver and tapped in the first phone number. Maybe it was just the tension of beginning such a huge task, especially one so important yet so likely to fail. Maybe he was afraid of what he would learn. Or maybe it was simply scary to call a total stranger on the phone.

"Hola," a voice said on the other end of the line. An older woman with a high, vulnerable-sounding voice. Maybe more tentative than Raymond, even.

"Um," he said. "Hello. Is Luis Velez there, please?"

"No, él no está aquí ahora."

"Um. I'm sorry. What?"

Raymond had gotten the bare gist of it, actually. Everybody understands the word "no."

"Lo siento, no hablo inglés."

"Oh. I see. Well . . . I don't speak Spanish. Sorry."

But it struck him hard that he had better learn some, and quickly. The basics, at least.

"Okay," he said, breaking a long silence on the line. "Thanks. I mean . . . gracias."

He looked up to see his stepfather staring at him over the kitchen island.

"That better be a local call," Ed said. Without even giving Raymond a chance to finish his conversation.

"De nada," the woman said, and hung up the phone.

Raymond stood holding the receiver in his hands and stared back at his stepfather.

"How do I know if it's local or not?"

"Easy. If it comes up on my phone bill, and I have to shell out extra for it, it's not."

Yeah. I know that. *Duh.*

"I meant . . . how do I know before I make the call?"

"No idea. But figure it out."

Raymond set the phone back down in its base and hurried out of the kitchen.

My Luis Project is not off to the best start, he thought.

Then he decided that statement might be giving his scant progress more credit than it deserved.

———

He stood in the school library, near the window, squinting under the strong fluorescent lights. There was no one in the room except Raymond and the librarian. He was actually supposed to be in a last-period study hall, but he was cutting. Lately it had been harder and harder to convince himself to sit still for that useless last period. Sometimes he just went home. It seemed to make more sense.

The librarian looked up into his face.

"Raymond," she said. "Where are you supposed to be?"

"Study hall. But you can study in a library, too. Right?"

She gave him a crooked sideways smirk. She was about fifty, with reddish hair and a knowing gaze that always seemed to cut right through him. If he had been guilty of any crime, or even misbehavior, she'd be the last person Raymond would want to see.

"Well, yes and no," she said, still smirking. "Regardless, you're supposed to be where you're supposed to be."

He stood a minute, silently, waiting to see if she really meant he had to leave. She made no moves toward ejecting him.

"I was wondering if there was an English-Spanish dictionary I could check out," he said. "Or even a phrasebook."

"You're learning Spanish?"

"I'd like to, yeah."

"Are you *taking* Spanish?"

"No. I'm taking Latin. But I have less and less idea why every day. Because nobody speaks Latin."

"But it's the root of all the other languages."

"That's what my Latin teacher keeps telling me."

"I agree that Spanish is very useful. And we have three dictionaries. But they're reference only. I can't check them out to you."

"Oh," Raymond said, and dropped his head, telegraphing his disappointment.

"But . . . I don't know. How long do you need it?"

"Just three or four days. Till I get my allowance. Then I'll buy my own."

"Promise you won't let me down on this? You'll bring it back in good condition and buy a replacement if anything happens to it?"

"Yes, ma'am. I promise."

"It's so rare for guys your age to come in here and show an interest in language, and tell me they're wanting to learn something when they're not even being graded on it. It's inspiring for someone like me. So I'm going to quietly hand you one. But the arrangement is strictly between you and me. And it's going to be back in less than a week with no problems. Right?"

"Yes, ma'am. I promise. I won't let you down. Thank you."

———

Raymond practiced on the subway ride. Out loud, but under his breath.

"Me llamo Raymond Jaffe. Luis Velez, está él aquí?"

A Latina woman sitting next to him, bouncing a baby on her knee, glanced over at him and smiled.

"Está aquí," she said. Or, at least, that's what it sounded like she said. Like all one word, really. "Estaquí."

"That's how you say it?" he asked her.

"Pretty much. Otherwise it sounds like you're talking out of a dictionary."

"Well . . . I am."

She smiled again.

"Okay, thanks," he said. "I mean . . . muchas gracias."

"De nada. Or you can be a little more formal and say 'No hay de qué.'"

"But then I might sound like I'm talking out of a dictionary."

"I think you run that risk either way," she said. But her smile told him not to take it as an insult.

Even her baby smiled at him. She was a beautiful little girl, maybe a year old, with curly hair and gold studs in her ears. Raymond smiled back.

The subway train squealed to a halt.

"Oh, this is my stop," he said, and jumped to his feet.

"Buena suerte," she said.

"I don't know that one."

"Good luck."

"Oh. Thank you. I mean, gracias."

He sprinted off the train car before the doors could close again.

As he vaulted up the stairs to the street, two at a time, he wondered how the woman knew he needed luck. She had no idea what Raymond was about to do. Did he really look that scared?

Probably, he figured.

He came up onto the street and looked around.

He was in a part of town he'd never seen before. At least, not as far as he could remember. He wasn't comforted by what he saw. Even compared to his own neighborhood, it did not feel good. A young man stood on a street corner, glancing around nervously. Possibly selling. Raymond, who had never dared to try drugs, wasn't sure he knew the sale of them when he saw it. One in every three or four buildings had its windows boarded up. Kids played in a vacant corner lot overflowing with old cars, couches . . . seas of garbage. Elderly men and women leaned out of open second- and third-floor windows, yelling at the kids in the street, or just watching the world from a safe vantage point.

Raymond almost turned around and headed back down into the subway. But he wasn't sure how he would live with himself if he didn't even try. If he didn't even go to the first address.

Heart hammering—fearful of people under the most familiar of circumstances—he walked along the sidewalk. He kept his head down, his eyes averted. From what, he wasn't sure. Everybody and everything. He tried to convey that he meant no trouble to anyone, and wanted no trouble. He did his best to disappear.

He compulsively glanced again and again at his list until he found the building that matched the first address—as though he could not be trusted to hold four numbers in his head for a few seconds.

He climbed the ten concrete stairs to the front door of the apartment building. Of course, it was locked.

He scanned the directory for 3A. It said "Luis A. Velez." Just like it was supposed to say.

Raymond breathed a sigh of relief and pressed the buzzer.

"Hola," a voice said. It was the same woman he had spoken to on the phone, in what he still hoped was a local call. Raymond would never hear the end of his stepfather's annoyance if it was not.

"Luis Velez, estaquí?" he asked, running the words together the way the woman on the train had.

"Sí," she said.

She buzzed him in.

Raymond stepped into the dim, grimy hallway and smelled something that made his head throb. That made him feel a little dizzy. He started up the stairs slowly, his heart battering around in his chest, and climbed to the third floor.

He stood in front of the door at 3A, poised to knock.

Then, as he had done at the top of the subway stairs, he almost turned and ran away again. But an image of the old woman flooded in behind his eyes. Mrs. G, he had taken to calling her in his head, because he could never be sure he was remembering her last name correctly. In his mind, he saw her wring her hands the way she always did when she was thinking of Luis. When she was wondering what had happened to him.

Which would be worse? Raymond wondered. *If something terrible really had happened to Luis? Or if it turned out Mrs. G wasn't as important to Luis as she thought she was?*

He knocked on the door.

A man answered.

He was huge, but not really tall. In fact, Raymond was a couple of inches taller. But the man was stocky and strong looking, wearing only jeans and a white short-sleeved tee, showing off bulging chest and arm muscles. His feet were bare. He had pockmarks on his face, as if pitted by teenage acne, or some disease that scars the skin. He looked to be about forty.

"Luis Velez?" Raymond asked, his voice too high with fright.

"Who wants to know?"

The man spoke with just a trace of a Spanish accent. Raymond shifted on his feet and pressed the dictionary against his thigh so the man could not read its cover. He was embarrassed now that he had carried it here.

"Just me. I mean, I'm not . . . I don't mean any . . . I'm just . . ." He took a deep breath and started over, forcing himself to focus. "My name is Raymond. Raymond Jaffe. And I'm looking for a Luis Velez, but you might not be the right one. I'm looking for the one who used to help an old woman named Mildred. Millie. She's blind, and he used to come help her get to the market and the bank."

Silence. As if this Luis Velez expected him to say more. As if the man needed more information before he could decide if he were the right Luis Velez or not.

Behind this big man, in his apartment, Raymond watched two boys of about ten or twelve chase each other through the living room, the bigger one trying to get the smaller one in a headlock. The TV was on, the volume up loud, and Raymond could hear cartoons blaring.

"Nah," the guy said. "That ain't me."

"Okay. Sorry to bother you, then."

Raymond turned back toward the stairs and hurried away. When he reached them, he hurried down them two at a time, feeling as though he couldn't get back to the subway fast enough.

He should have just kept calling. That's what he was thinking. He'd come all this way because he thought he'd do better in person, holding his English-Spanish dictionary. But this Luis Velez had turned out to speak English. And it was a long way to come for a thirty-second conversation.

For nothing.

Then he remembered that if he was going to go back to using the phone, he'd have to know what was a local call and what was not. And he'd better not make a mistake with it.

Just as he hit the lobby and set out moving along the flat hardwood toward the door, he heard the man calling out to him.

"Hey. You."

Raymond stopped. Turned around. Watched the man run down the two flights of stairs and up to where Raymond stood with one hand on his dictionary and the other on the door handle. The man, Luis, had put on shoes. Heavy work boots that laced up. Raymond could not imagine how he had put them on so fast.

"I forgot your name," the man said.

"Raymond."

"Right. Raymond. I'm Luis. Oh. You knew that."

Raymond smiled. He could feel it. It felt odd, under the circumstances.

"At least let me walk you to the subway," Luis said. "You took the subway here, right? It's not the best neighborhood."

"Thanks," Raymond said. And breathed. He hadn't realized he'd been holding his breath. But he was keenly aware of the oxygen deficit now.

"Sorry about the smell down here," Luis said. "My downstairs neighbors like to mix up amyl nitrate and sell it."

"I don't know what that is."

"You know. 'Poppers,' they call 'em on the street?"

"Oh," Raymond said. But he still didn't know. "Gives me a headache."

"I tell them to cut it out, and then I tell the landlord. And then the landlord makes 'em stop. And then it all dies down and they're back to mixing again."

They stepped out of the building together and down the stairs to the street.

For the first short block they walked side by side in silence. Luis was still wearing only a sleeveless tee. Raymond thought he must be cold. But, if so, he never let on.

"I *think* about doing stuff like that," the man said.

"Stuff like what?"

Raymond thought he might mean stuff like mixing up amyl nitrate and selling it on the street. But he hoped not.

"Like with that blind lady."

"Oh. Right. That."

"I think about . . . you know. Volunteering. That kind of thing. But it's hard, you know? I have four kids. And I work full time. Sometimes sixty hours a week. I bet this Luis Velez you're looking for . . . maybe he's got no kids. But I shouldn't say, because I never met the man. Does he? Have kids?"

"I don't know," Raymond said. "I never thought to ask."

They passed a young man on the corner, possibly selling. Maybe waiting for a buyer, but Raymond was only guessing. He was younger than Raymond. Fifteen or sixteen, maybe. Raymond could feel the kid's gaze burning into him. Inviting him to look. Waiting to see if Raymond was a customer? Or something else?

Raymond's eyes automatically came up to the young man's face.

"Don't make eye contact," Luis said.

Raymond looked down at the filthy sidewalk again, and they passed without incident.

"'Cause if he had kids," Luis said, still firmly stuck on the same topic, "then I just don't know how he did it."

"Not sure," Raymond said.

They walked in silence for a block more. Raymond could see the subway stairs at the end of the next block. They looked like salvation. Like the end of all trouble and fear.

"How do you know this old blind lady?" Luis asked.

"She lives in my building."

"And are you helping her get to the bank and the store? Until you can find this right Luis Velez?"

"Yeah. I am. I mean . . . somebody has to. So I am."

"Good," he said. "You're a good boy. I don't mean 'boy' like . . . I didn't mean it in the bad way. You know. Just . . . I don't know. Maybe you're eighteen and you're a man. Are you?"

"No. I'll be seventeen next month."

"You're tall, though. That's why I guessed older."

"Yeah. I'm tall."

"Well, you're a good young man, then."

Raymond averted his eyes and fell silent. Just the way Mrs. G said he always did when someone spoke well of him.

They reached the subway stairs and paused. Stood awkwardly together. Raymond stared carefully at his feet.

"Maybe I'll do that," Luis said. "You know. Work at a soup kitchen or something. Couple hours a week. It's just hard. I work hard. Come home tired, you know? But I think about it."

"Thanks for walking me here," Raymond said.

He knew this Luis Velez wanted something from him. Some sense of having been understood. Of being let off the hook. He wanted Raymond to understand *why* he was not the Luis Velez who walked elderly blind women to the bank. But Raymond didn't feel he had the words to help.

"No problem," Luis said. "Good luck finding your guy."

"Thanks."

Luis turned and walked away. Raymond watched and waited. He wanted to get himself underground. But he felt this man named Luis Velez had asked him nicely for something, though not straight out. And Raymond knew he could—and should—have given him more.

"Hey!" he called out. "Luis!"

The man stopped and turned back. He was a quarter of the way down the block now, so Raymond had no choice but to shout.

"Four kids *is* an awful lot!"

Luis broke into a grin, and Raymond knew his simple statement was all the man had really needed.

"Yeah, tell me about it," he said.

Then he walked again.

Raymond ran down the subway stairs and into the pit of tunnel under the street. Under the world as he knew it. While he waited for the train he crossed Luis A. Velez off his list with a pen that was almost out of ink. He had to scratch it out, more than anything else.

———

He knocked on her door with his own geeky—even by his standards—secret knock. It was actually Morse code for the letter *R*. One short rap, then three raps in a row to make up the dash, then another short rap.

He waited for her to cross the room and undo the locks.

When the door opened she beamed up at him, and for the first time in as long as Raymond could remember, he felt happy. From the inside out. Not only was she happy to see him, but he had done something big to try to help her. Even if she didn't know it. Even if it hadn't come to anything.

"Sorry I'm late," he said, but he could feel himself smiling.

"Come in quickly," she said, "so we don't let the cat out."

He stepped into her living room and watched as she fetched her white cane and snugged the strap of her purse over her shoulder.

"Kitty friend Louise," she called, "we are only going out to buy you good things to eat, and me good things to eat. We will be back before you know it."

They stepped into the hall together, and he waited while she locked each dead bolt with a key.

"I'm sorry I'm late," he said again.

"There was no special arrangement for what time you would come."

She hooked her arm through his and they moved toward the stairs, Raymond carrying her folded-up grocery cart under his other arm. He had to reset his internal speedometer to match her pace. He had been running all day. He had forgotten what slow felt like.

"I said I'd come after school, though."

"Well. Is it before school? Or is it after?"

"Oh. Okay. If you want to look at it like that, yeah. Stairs coming up. I'll tell you when it's time to step down. Okay . . . now."

They didn't talk as they navigated the flight of stairs to the lobby. There was too much concentration involved.

"Okay," he said. "Next step you'll be on the lobby floor."

She sighed as she stepped down. It was a sound like air flowing out of a punctured tire, deflating it. It was her tension leaving her. That much was clear. Raymond wondered how it would feel to live in a world where a flight of stairs stood as a massive challenge that could prove to be the end of you on any trip through it. It dampened his rare moment of good mood.

"I just figured you went somewhere with your friends," she said.

He laughed, an embarrassing snort of a sound. "I don't have friends."

"You were with a friend the day I first spoke to you."

"Okay, wait here a minute," he said. "I'm going to go open the door." He did, then let it stand open as he came back to get her.

It was late afternoon, nearly five. Almost sundown. The air felt cold and autumnal, real seasons to experience. Raymond could feel the breeze hit him in the face as he led her out the door, and he knew she could feel it, too. He wondered if it meant more to her, since her other senses had grown stronger. And since she had been deprived of that fresh air for a time.

"That was Andre," he said. "Step down. Good. He moved away. Step down. Okay. One more step. Good. Now we're on the street."

They set off toward the market together. Slowly.

"Already he has moved away? That was only a small handful of days ago."

"That was his last day."

"Oh. I'm very sorry. And he was your only friend?"

"Pretty much. Yeah."

"I can't imagine why that would be, Raymond. You're such a kind boy. Oh, wait. Never mind. Forget I said anything. I just remembered what it felt like to be a child in school. Kindness is not always valued. Children are experimenting with different ways to be in the world, safer and more guarded ways, and they are quick to judge."

"You can say that again."

They walked in silence for most of the block. There was a woman walking in their direction, and she reminded Raymond of the woman on the subway. The one who'd given him advice on the Spanish language. So he looked up into her face, which normally he was careful not to do. With anybody.

She smiled at him. It was a genuine smile. Genuinely felt by her, it seemed, and genuinely meant for him. At first he couldn't imagine why she would do such a thing. Strangers didn't generally smile at each other on the street. Not around here at least. Then her eyes flickered to a spot between Raymond and Mrs. G. Her gaze seemed to land on the place where their arms linked together.

Raymond understood then. She was smiling at him because he was helping a blind woman walk down the street. He might as well have been wearing a badge of good-boy-ness for everybody to see.

He smiled back, but it felt a little strained. Not natural. Maybe because he wasn't used to doing it.

Then she had passed. The moment was over. He could only hope it was a good enough smile. That it had come out the way he'd meant it to.

"So will you still talk to Andre?" Mrs. G asked, bumping him out of his thoughts.

"I'm not sure. He said he would Skype. But he hasn't yet."

"What is this Skype? I feel as though I've heard of that, but I don't know what it is."

"It's a computer application. You can talk to somebody on your computer. Sort of like you would talk to them on the phone. But no toll charges no matter where you are. And it's a way to make a video call."

"Meaning you can see each other?"

"Right."

"Then I do know about this, yes. Luis told me about it. How he would talk to his brother in Minneapolis, and the kids—his nieces and nephews—would come up one by one so Luis could see how much taller they had grown. And I was so astonished. When I was a girl, this was what we had for . . . oh, what's the word for what I mean to say? Like science fiction. This is how the maker of a movie or a television show would predict the future. You would call someone on the phone, and you would see them, and they would see you. And it was so hard for us even to imagine such a thing. Of course, they also told us we'd be driving flying cars, hovering all over the place, and they were wrong about that."

"Maybe just as well," Raymond said.

He watched the traffic and imagined it gaining and losing altitude. Having fender-bender accidents with the upper floors of apartment buildings, or with other flying cars, raining tires and bumpers and headlight glass onto the pedestrians below.

"I agree with you on that, my young friend."

"Curb coming up," he said.

They navigated the difficult crossing without any more extraneous conversation. They had to concentrate.

"So if that really was your only friend," she said as they stepped onto safe sidewalk again, "I am very sorry that he is gone. Is it really so difficult for you to make friends with boys your own age? It's just hard for me to imagine, based on the way you are with me."

"Yeah, it is. They just . . . I don't know. I'm just so different from them." He almost elaborated, but stopped himself. Or, more accurately, the words stopped in spite of him. Came up into his throat and stuck. He hadn't known her that long, after all. "The cat is my friend, though. And . . . I don't know. Would it be weird if I said it feels like I'm friends with *you* now?"

"Not at all, Raymond, not at all. I am honored to be your friend if you want me to be."

"I do," he said.

They walked the rest of the way to the market in silence.

Raymond was exhausted. Not physically, but on the inside. Drained from the intensity of his day. And besides, nothing more seemed to need saying.

———

He barely made it home in time for dinner. And, in his house, that mattered. If you didn't get back in time, you might not eat.

"You're awfully late," his mother said, eyeing him suspiciously.

"I was just out doing a favor for a friend."

"New friend?"

"Yeah. New friend."

"Well, I like seeing you have new friends, baby. But don't cut it so close on dinner."

"Okay," he said. "Sorry."

There it was again. The "sorry." But maybe this one didn't count. Because on the inside of the thing, he really wasn't sorry at all.

Chapter Five

What Would You Think of a Boy Like That?

Raymond stood staring up at the apartment building. It made him feel intimidated, but not for the same reason the last building had. In fact, for exactly the opposite reason.

It was Saturday morning, and he had taken the subway to Midtown. He was only about six blocks from where his father lived. If his father and his new wife hadn't been out of town for the weekend, Raymond could have walked. It was his weekend to be with his father, if his father had been home. They were going away more often on Raymond's weekends, and Raymond blamed the new wife for it. He had a creeping sensation that she was doing it on purpose.

This time he felt as though the building were rejecting *him*. Judging *him* not good enough. As though the whole neighborhood were clutching its figurative purse more tightly under its arm and wondering who this interloper was and what he was doing here. And when he would give up and go away, so everything could breathe again.

To make matters worse, when he looked down he saw a uniformed doorman watching him. The man had not been at his post when Raymond had first walked up.

Raymond shoved the Spanish dictionary into his nearly empty backpack and moved closer to the man, who narrowed his eyes slightly. Almost imperceptibly.

"I'm looking for a Luis Velez," Raymond said. "I need to talk to him for just a minute."

"I can call up to him," the doorman said, sounding skeptical, "but it's up to the residents who I let up and who I don't."

"Thanks," Raymond said.

He shoved his hands deep into his jeans pockets, as if preparing for a very long wait.

"Who shall I say is here to see him?"

"Raymond Jaffe. But he doesn't know me. But just tell him I'm a friend of Millie G. If he's the right Luis Velez, he'll know exactly what I mean."

The doorman stepped behind a podium-like desk, a bellman's desk, and made his call, purposely turning his face away so Raymond couldn't read his lips or hear what was said. A few seconds later he hung up the receiver and stepped out again. But he didn't move closer to Raymond. He walked to the glass main doors of the building, which opened into the lobby. He swung one open and just held it that way. It took Raymond a moment to realize it was an invitation.

"Go on up," he said.

Raymond broke his statue-like pose and stepped up to the doors. He hadn't expected it to go this way, he realized. He had fully expected to be turned away.

Did this mean he had found the right Luis Velez?

"Twenty-second floor, apartment B," the doorman said.

Raymond didn't answer. Just nodded. His heart was hammering in his chest now, his head swimming. He moved to the elevators as if in a dream. A middle-aged woman was waiting for the elevator as well. She had already pushed the button, so he just stood.

When the elevator arrived, and the door opened with a loud bing, it startled Raymond. He stepped on. The middle-aged woman did not. He looked at her questioningly. He even reached one hand out to hold the doors open.

"No, you go ahead," she said. "I forgot something."

The door closed and the elevator moved upward. It was fast, and smooth. And quiet. And something burned in Raymond's chest as he watched the floor numbers light up. Because you might forget something in your apartment, before you go out. But what could you possibly forget in the lobby before you go back up?

The elevator stopped on 22, and Raymond stepped out.

As soon as he did, he saw a woman waiting for him. She was maybe thirty, or maybe in her early thirties. She wore a carefully styled and expensive-looking haircut. Short and modern. Silk lounging pajamas with a silk robe tied over them. It was an outfit that could be worn around the house or into a fancy dinner party. It was that nice. Raymond honestly could not tell if she was Latina or not. Just that she was clearly waiting for him.

Her eyes met his, and she was afraid. And Raymond had no idea why.

It made him more afraid. And he had been plenty scared to begin with.

"Are you Raymond Jaffe?" she asked. She had no accent. At least, no Hispanic accent. Her vowels did carry a slight New York City affect.

"Yes, ma'am," he said, moving closer to her open doorway.

"What do you want to see my husband for?"

Raymond felt something sag in his chest. She didn't even know what he wanted. Why he had come. The doorman must not have told her. The sweet notion that he had found Luis, on only his second foray out into the world, flew away like a shy bird.

"I thought the doorman told you," he said.

"Something about a woman. Millie somebody. And that my hus-band will know exactly what you mean."

"So he did tell you."

He was standing right in front of her now, but a respectful few steps back. Behind her in the apartment sat two massive German shepherd dogs. Black and tan, perfectly matching, and maybe close to a hundred pounds each. Raymond swallowed hard and kept his eyes on them. They looked at him, but made no move. There was a calmness about them, in their eyes. They were not worried about what might happen next. They just watched. Maybe they simply had no doubt about their ability to handle him. To handle anything.

"He told me her name. Not who she was to Luis or anything. So you tell me, and hurry up, please, because this is freaking me out. Who is this Millie person to my Luis?"

The dogs shifted slightly on their haunches, picking up the woman's fear. Raymond took an instinctive step back.

"She's . . . she's this older lady who lives in my building. Over on the west side. Very old," he added, thinking he might know how to put the woman at ease. "Like . . . ninety." He saw her take a deep breath and let it out. He plunged on. "She's blind, and she can't go out by herself. So Luis used to come and walk with her to the store and the bank. To help her, you know? But I don't know if it was Luis your husband. You know. Or some other Luis Velez. Because there are twenty-one of them in the city. Or near it. And even that is only if I'm spelling it right."

The woman pressed her eyes closed. Tipped her head back. Raymond watched her make the sign of the cross against herself.

"Oh, thank God," she said, dropping her head and looking directly into Raymond's face. "I thought you were here to tell me he was seeing some other woman."

"No," Raymond said. "Nothing like that."

"I don't know if he's the right Luis or not," she said, utterly transformed. Her face had softened. Her voice sounded deeper and more relaxed. "Probably not, because I think he would've told me. Although . . . I don't know. He does this thing sometimes where he drops money on people, kind of just because he thinks they deserve it. He never lets them know who gave it to them. And he never used to tell me about it. But then one day I sort of caught him doing it, and I said, 'Why didn't you tell me you were doing that?' He gave me this whole long thing about how it's only really giving if nobody knows. If it's anonymous. He said if you let everybody know you did it, then you're just doing it for the glory. So people will think you're a great guy. Then it's just selfish."

"I don't know," Raymond said, still watching the dogs. "Seems to me then the person gets something nice, and you get to feel good. Two wins instead of one."

"See, I'm with *you* on that," she said. "But I'm being rude. Making you stand out in the hall like some poor relation. Come in. I'll call Luis at the office and ask if he's the one."

Raymond didn't move. Just kept his eyes on the dogs.

"Oh, they won't hurt you," she said. "They like people. But they're trained attack dogs. But they would never do anything I didn't tell them to do."

"You sure?"

"Honey, it's fine. Come in."

She reached one hand out. As if she could take hold of Raymond and pull him inside. He looked at the hand and backed up another step.

"So this thing you say to them when you want them to attack someone . . . you sure it's not a word you could accidentally use in a sentence or anything?"

She laughed. "They're fine. I promise. Come in. Luis is in a client meeting. I'll have to leave a message for him. He might not get back to me until after the meeting's over. You don't want to stand out in the hall that whole time. Do you?"

"I guess not," he said.

But it was sounding like a pretty good idea.

She turned and addressed the dogs. "Bed!" she barked.

The dogs' ears flattened. First out to the sides, then back along their necks. They turned and slithered away, eyes full of the pain of rejection.

Against his better judgment, Raymond stepped in.

"I was just making breakfast," she said as he followed her into the kitchen. It was huge, high-ceilinged. Painted a light lavender. It had an amazing view of Central Park. "Sit down. You want anything? Did you eat?"

While she spoke she rummaged around in her purse and came up with a cell phone.

"I had a granola bar," he said. And sat.

"That's not breakfast."

"It's what I usually have."

"Breakfast is the most important meal of the day."

"There's nobody around to cook at that hour. And I don't really cook. So I just grab one."

"It's not good enough," she said. As though she could make the final pronouncement on such things, and her word was unassailable. She had the phone to her face now. "Yeah, hi, love. Me. So there's this kid here. This nice young guy. He's asking if you know a ninety-year-old woman over on the west side. Blind woman. Millie. I figure probably not, or you would've told me. But I never know with you. You have that anonymity thing going on. So I'm just going to feed this guy some breakfast. Apparently nobody feeds him. When you get out of your meeting, call me and let me know, okay? Because he came all the way over here. I figure the least we can do is get him an answer."

She clicked off the call and leveled him with a direct gaze. Right into his eyes.

"You drink coffee?"

"No, ma'am."

"Tea?"

"Sometimes I drink tea with milk and sugar."

"Coming right up."

—

Raymond stared out over the park as she cooked. Sipped his cambric tea and watched the world go by twenty-two floors below. The smells were making him hungry. The smells were making the dogs hungry, too. They slithered into the kitchen and lay prone at the woman's feet, staring up at the stove. Wagging their tails.

Raymond was still terrified of them. But they had not so much as looked at him since he'd come inside, so it felt silly to be so afraid.

"So, where you live," she said, "do you get what you need?"

Raymond swallowed a sip of tea through a sudden tightness in his throat. "I'm not really sure what you mean," he said.

"I mean like breakfast. Do you have two parents?"

"Yes, ma'am. Three actually. My mom and stepdad. And then I see my father every other weekend."

"Okay. So you have more than two parents. But none of them puts a good breakfast in your belly before you go out for the day? If I had a kid, I'd be covering all those bases. No offense to your folks. But really . . ."

"I think what they do is pretty normal," Raymond said. Though, truthfully, he had no way to know. How do you gauge normal? To do so, you'd have to know how everybody else lives. "I grab a granola bar in the morning, then they make me a lunch to take to school." Except on weekends, he thought, when he had to scrounge something up for himself. "And then they cook us a nice dinner every day. So, pretty normal, I think." But when he was at his father's he ate more. And better.

She was dishing breakfast up onto a china plate now. His breakfast or hers. He wasn't sure.

"You know why I ask. Right?"

"Um. Not really."

"You're so skinny."

"That's just me. I could eat all day and never gain weight."

"Then you should eat all day," she said. "You're a growing boy."

She set the plate down in front of him. On it were two poached eggs, swimming in a golden sauce. Six spears of asparagus, also swimming. Both halves of a split and buttered English muffin.

"This looks great," he said.

"Dig in. Don't wait for me. Don't let it get cold."

He ate in silence while she dished up her own food. Stared down over the park and watched walkers and roller skaters and bikers glide up and down the paths. They looked like ants from this vantage point. The food was amazing. Rich and well seasoned. The eggs were cooked just right, with their whites completely solid, but with yolks that ran orangey, rich and liquid, when he stabbed them with his fork.

She sat down next to him and salted her food.

"Thank you for your hospitality," he said. "It's a lot of hospitality. Most people in the city, they don't even let you in the front door. They figure, they don't know you, and . . . well. You know."

"I have the dogs," she said, and left it at that.

Speaking of the dogs, they both sat at attention, staring. Shifting their gazes back and forth between Raymond and their owner as if watching a ball being lobbed back and forth over the net in a tennis match. Their tails wagged, making a swishing sound on the kitchen tiles.

"Bad boys," the woman said. "No begging. Bed!" The dogs collapsed their ears and slunk away. "So, tell me about yourself, Raymond. That was your name, right? Raymond?"

"Yes, ma'am. But I'm not sure what there is to tell."

"You're in high school?"

"Yes, ma'am. I'm a junior."

"What do you go out for?"

"Go out for?"

"You know. What will it say in your yearbook? You went out for sports? Or you were in the chess club? Or on the debating team?"

"No, ma'am. Nothing like that. I'm afraid the yearbook people won't have much to say about me."

"So what do you do when you're not in school?"

"Well. These days I help out this old woman."

"Millie."

"Right. And before that . . . and when I'm not doing that . . . I like to read. I read a lot. Nonfiction, mostly. I read books about political leaders, and wars, and uprisings, and . . . well, history. But not only history. I like to read about the world. Learn more about it. But it can be the world the way it is now. You know. More like social studies. Like, for example, I'm not really religious, exactly, but I read about different religions. Because that helps you learn more about the way things are. The way people are. And why."

He took another bite of breakfast. It was cooling off fast. But she had been nice enough to serve it to him. If she wanted him to talk, it seemed like the least he could do. He dug into the asparagus. He wasn't fond of asparagus as a rule. But covered in that rich sauce . . . Raymond figured she could pour that sauce on a pile of cardboard, and he'd happily wolf it down.

"I'm Catholic," she said.

"I figured."

"How did you know?"

"Because you crossed yourself when you found out Millie wasn't some woman your husband had been seeing."

"Oh. Right."

They ate in silence for a minute or two.

"You have a girlfriend?" she asked.

"No, ma'am."

"Boyfriend?"

"No. I'm not gay."

"I didn't mean any offense."

"I didn't take offense."

"So you just don't have a girlfriend *now*. But you will. The high school years are awkward. It'll happen for you."

Raymond opened his mouth to answer. But he had no idea what the answer should be. He felt he likely would *not* have a girlfriend later, but he was in no way prepared to tell this relative stranger why he thought so. So why even begin?

He was saved by the bell. Literally.

Her cell phone rang. It was sitting on the table beside her plate. She grabbed it up. Listened for a long moment. Then she spoke into it.

"Oh. Oh no. That's too bad. Yeah, I know how you hate that. I'm sorry, hon. See you in a minute, then."

She clicked off the call and set the phone down.

"Luis will be right up. He's just stepping into the elevator. His client was a no-show. He always turns off his phone when he's about to be with a client, and he forgot to turn it back on until he was just getting out of his car. You know, down in the garage just now. He hates no-shows, so he might not be in the best mood. But don't worry. He doesn't bite."

Raymond finished his food quickly. And silently.

Just as he was swallowing the last bite, he heard the apartment door open. Heard the dogs whimpering in their excitement. Heard Luis Velez greet them with "Hey, boys," and "Good boys."

The man stepped into the kitchen, the dogs winding around his legs in their joy, and looked at Raymond with a withering gaze. As if Raymond should be nowhere on the premises. He turned his gaze onto his wife.

"You just open the door for people you don't know?" he asked her.

Raymond's heart jumped up into his throat.

"The dogs'll take care of me," she said.

"That's true, I guess."

He pulled out a chair and sat close to Raymond, leaning forward on his knees. Inserting himself deeply into Raymond's personal space. Raymond resisted the temptation to push his chair back.

He was a handsome man in his late forties, slight of build. He wore his black hair slicked back along his head. His three-piece suit was clearly expensive, dark material with a very fine pinstripe. He wore a solid-red tie over a silvery-gray dress shirt.

"Now tell me what this is all about," he said. "I didn't even hear the whole message. I mean, I was in the building. So I just came up."

"Okay," Raymond said. His voice sounded steadier than he felt. "I'm looking for a man named Luis Velez who used to come over to the west side to help this older woman who lives alone. She can't go out on the street by herself. She's afraid to. She's over ninety, I think, and almost completely blind. So he used to come over and walk her to the bank and the store."

Luis Velez shook his head. "Sorry," he said. "Not me."

"Oh," Raymond said.

He had known and he hadn't known. But now there was just the one kind of knowing. The final kind. And it was a long fall down to that knowing.

"And how do you fit into all this?" Luis Velez asked him.

"How do I fit in?"

"Why are you over here asking if I'm him?"

"Well. *She* can't. And she's really worried about him. They were friends. I mean, she saw him three times a week for more than four years. She's really broken up about the way he just sort of . . . disappeared. She thinks something terrible happened to him. I'm just trying to help."

The man slid his chair back. Raymond breathed a muffled sigh of relief.

"I see," he said. "You're doing your part. That's good. Especially for a young kid like you. You're just the polar opposite of what everybody expects. Everybody'll tell you the world is going to hell in a handbasket, because they think kids your age don't give a damn about anything, but here you are. Defying expectations. Sorry we couldn't be more helpful. But at least you got a good breakfast out of it, I see."

His wife rose and cleared away the dishes. She stood with her back to them, rinsing off the china plates and loading them into the dishwasher.

"I do my part," Luis Velez continued. "But not like that. I'm a professional. My time is very valuable. So I wouldn't do that sort of thing—walking to the store with an elderly woman. But I do what I can. I give spontaneously. I don't ask for anything in return. Just giving back. Just dropping a little something on anybody I think deserves more than what they're getting. I'm blessed that I can afford to do that."

"Luis is a very successful attorney," his wife said over her shoulder. "One of the three best-known civil litigation attorneys in New York. You've probably seen him on the news."

"I don't watch the news," Raymond said. "I'm sorry."

"Just as well," Luis said. "The world is going to hell in a handbasket."

"Well," Raymond said. "I should get out of your hair. Thank you for breakfast. And everything."

"You tell those three parents of yours that you're a growing boy," the woman said. "They need to feed you."

"Yes, ma'am. I will."

But of course he would not.

Luis Velez walked him to the door. The dogs followed.

"Here," Luis said.

He reached something small out to Raymond. A business card. Raymond took it and held it up to read. It said "Luis Javier Velez, Esquire." And on the bottom was a phone number, email address, and office address.

"If there's anything I can do to help, let me know," the man added.

"Thank you, sir."

"Do you have to go home and tell her you didn't find the right guy?"

"No. She doesn't know I'm looking. For just that reason. So I'm not always having to let her down. But I worry that I'm going to find out she was right, that something terrible happened to him. And then I'll have to tell her. I'm really not looking forward to that. Or that nothing terrible happened to him. That he just stopped coming and didn't bother to let her know. That might even be worse for her."

"Well, you took it on. You'll deal with it."

"I suppose."

"Why don't you just call people on the phone? Wouldn't that be easier?"

Raymond started to tell him about the toll call issue. But he realized it wasn't entirely true. He could have called the phone company and gotten guidance on what was and was not a free call. No, there were more reasons.

He opened his mouth and landed on the most important one. Which felt odd to him, because he had never consciously acknowledged it before speaking it out loud to Luis Javier Velez.

"I was just thinking . . . let's say it's the second thing. He just stopped coming. Didn't even bother to tell her. That's a pretty lousy thing to do to a woman like that who needs a lot of help and doesn't have a ton of options. So if I ask if he's the guy who did that, he might not want to tell me the truth. I wanted to see people's faces when I asked the question."

There was also the looming possibility of a language translation situation at any given doorway, but it seemed less important, so he didn't mention it. Plus, Mrs. G had tried phone calls and gotten nowhere.

The man nodded thoughtfully. Maybe more thoughtfully than the simple statement warranted.

"I guess that makes sense," he said. "Well. Good luck."

Raymond walked out the door, which Luis Velez, Esquire, was holding open. Just for a split second he thought he felt something touch the back of his jeans. Touch his butt, lightly, just over his right back pocket. His backpack was hanging from his left shoulder only. His first thought was one of the dogs. But he whipped his head around and there was nothing there. Nothing at all. Just the door swinging shut behind him.

He stood waiting for the elevator, lost in thought. And yet, if someone had asked him what thoughts they were, it might have been hard to say. He turned around again and looked back down at his jeaned butt. Felt around a little back there. Stuck his hand into his right rear pocket.

There was something there that had not been there before.

He pulled it out just as the elevator doors opened with a loud bing. It was a hundred-dollar bill, new and crisp. Folded over twice.

Raymond stepped onto the elevator, still staring at it.

Apparently Luis Velez, Esquire, thought Raymond deserved more than he was getting.

He shoved the bill deep into his front pocket as he rode down to the lobby.

He crossed Luis Javier Velez off second place on his list.

This time he had thought to bring a fresh pen.

———

He sat in his usual chair, the former Luis chair, gazing out through Mrs. G's curtained window. Gazing down into the street. He could see cars and cabs and pedestrians go by, but only as shapes. Contrast of dark against a lighter, less distinct world. He wondered if that was the way Mrs. G saw the world. He figured she probably saw even less.

The cat jumped up onto his lap, and he scratched behind her ears.

"What would you think," he said, but not to the cat, "if a boy told you this?"

But then he didn't go on to tell her anything.

"A boy like you?" she asked after a time.

She extended the plate with the cookies on it, reminding him he should already have taken some. He was still a little full from breakfast, but he took three all the same. It felt good to be full.

"Well. Any boy. But, you know what? Never mind. Forget I brought it up."

"It's completely up to you," she said, leaning her ancient forearms on her lace placemat. "But I don't know one single person you know. And even if I did, I never tell tales. This I can promise you." She punctuated her promise by stabbing the air with one raised index finger.

Raymond sat a moment, thinking. Or, actually . . . not thinking. It felt more as though he was waiting. Waiting to see what he would decide. But whatever it would be, there seemed to be no thoughts leading him there, or away from there.

"What if a boy told you he didn't like girls? I mean . . . not *like that*. Didn't really feel anything for them, like all the boys around him are feeling. But he didn't feel that way about other boys, either?"

"He just doesn't have those feelings."

"Right."

"Then I would think he just doesn't have those feelings."

"But people think it's abnormal." She didn't answer right away, so he added, "Or they seem to, anyway. Do you think it's abnormal?"

"What is abnormal, though? Normal is just the norm. The norm is just what the average person feels. Most people have those feelings. But some don't. Those who don't are in the minority, so in that sense abnormal. But we don't use 'abnormal' in that sense when we speak. We use it to say 'bad.' It's not bad. It just is. Some people just are. Maybe schoolmates make a thing out to be bad, but only because they don't understand it. People laugh at things they don't understand. It makes them feel safe. But it's a false feeling. They are no safer. They just *feel* as if they are. The world is full of people too foolish to judge the difference."

Raymond chewed a piece of cookie and then dreaded having to swallow it. His throat felt tight and dry. He wondered why he had ever started with this line of discussion.

"They don't laugh," he said. He swallowed hard, against odds. Sipped his cambric tea to wash it down. "Because they don't know. I mean, they notice how I'm not drooling all over the girls like they do. But they just call me a faggot. They just think I'm gay."

"But you're not."

"No."

Raymond took another bite of cookie, wondering how far back in the conversation they had dropped the some-random-boy pretext. Then he decided it hadn't been very useful or convincing anyway.

"But you don't tell them you're not?"

"No."

"So this is another reason why you feel like you don't fit in any-where you go."

"Yeah. One of many."

"Why don't you just tell them they are wrong? Not that it would be a bad thing about you if they were right. But why not say what is true for you?"

"Because it almost seems like . . . it seems worse. Like the truth is worse. There are gay kids at my school. Boys and girls both. I know who they are, most of them. Everybody does. If I was gay, I could just go hang out with them. But who do I go hang out with? I don't know anybody else like me."

"There are others."

"How do you know?"

"Because I have lived ninety-two years, Raymond, and if there's one thing I can tell you, it's that we are never so unique as we think we are. We are all people. Sure, some things will be different from one person to the next. Some people have more of those feelings than others. Some have too much, and it causes all manner of havoc. Some have none at all. But I can tell you this as a human being who's had a lot of experience being one: If you're feeling something, other people in other places are feeling it, too. It's never just us. But don't take my word for it. Explore the world for yourself. Look it up. Research it. In my day we went to the library and had to get up the nerve to tell the librarian what we were looking for. You, you have it easy. You have a computer, yes? So why sit here talking to an old woman when you have all of the recorded knowledge the world has gathered sitting upstairs on your desk?"

"Hmm," he said. And ate another cookie. "I guess I was afraid to look. You know. Afraid what I might find."

"Never be afraid to look, Raymond. It's always better to look. Whatever you're afraid of, turn toward it, not away. Once you're willing to do that, it loses all its power over you. Trust me. I know this. I don't always do it. But I really, truly know."

"Maybe I will," he said.

They sat in silence for a time. It was a reasonably satisfied silence, at least on Raymond's end of the thing. Considering what had just transpired.

"It was so nice of you to bring all that cat food," she said. "But you didn't need to. How much did you bring?"

"A case of the little cans she likes. And a twenty-five-pound bag of the dry stuff."

"You shouldn't have. How can you afford it? I told you I could manage."

"You're doing enough," he said. "You know. Just keeping her here. Besides. I came into some money."

Chapter Six

Por Qué

Raymond raised his hand to knock, then paused. He squeezed his eyes shut and hoped that, this time, someone would be home.

At least, part of him did.

It was the following morning. Sunday. This was Raymond's third door for the morning. His third Luis Velez.

It was hard to admit it to himself, but a sense of palpable relief had flooded over him the first two times, when nobody had come to answer the door. Still, it solved nothing. It meant only that he had to go back to those doors. He had placed a hash mark next to those names on his list—the third and fourth Luis Velez—to indicate that he had tried them once so far.

He knocked.

Immediately he heard a flurry of motion behind the door. The sound of heavy footsteps carried to his ears. A TV that he hadn't consciously realized he was hearing fell silent.

Raymond heard something scrape against the door. A chain lock, if he'd had to guess. He thought someone was undoing the chain. But a moment later the door opened just a few inches, and an older woman's face appeared in the space. The chain had been put in place to protect her from Raymond.

"Is Luis Velez here?" he asked. "I mean, is he home? I know you don't know me, but I just want to ask him a very quick question."

"Qué?"

"Luis Velez, está aquí?"

"Por qué?" the woman asked.

That was a word—or words—Raymond didn't know. He scrambled for the dictionary, which was in his backpack. While he was extricating it, the woman closed the door in his face.

He knocked again.

"I'm sorry to bother you," he called through the door, not knowing if she understood a word he was saying. "I just need to ask him a question. One simple question."

"Por qué quieres saber?" the woman asked through the door.

So there was that "por qué" thing again. And Raymond had not yet managed to look it up.

"Lo siento," he called through the door. He felt more panicky than the situation likely warranted. "No entiendo."

It was the most useful phrase he had taught himself. "I don't understand."

Silence on the other side of the door. Raymond took a step closer and leaned his fingertips against the wood of it. He wasn't sure if that was the end of this visit. If he should go. If anybody inside ever planned on saying another word to him.

He decided he would open his dictionary and quickly teach himself to say "I want to ask Luis a question." He wondered why he hadn't done so right from the start.

Before he could, the door opened again, startling him backward a couple of steps. Again he found himself peering through an opening just inches wide. The chain lock was still solidly in place.

The face he saw this time was different. A younger woman, maybe in her twenties. She wore her amazingly thick, dark hair piled up onto her head, and full makeup. She chewed gum with a snapping sound on every motion of her jaw.

"My grandmother wants to know why you're asking about Luis," she said.

"I'm looking for a Luis Velez who used to help an old woman I know. But then he disappeared. She's worried about him. So I just want to ask him if he's the one."

"When did he disappear?"

"Maybe three weeks ago."

"He's not the one."

The door slammed shut.

Raymond moved in again. Leaned on it with his fingertips as he had before.

"I'm sorry to bother you again," he called, his face close to the edge of the door. As if his voice, his breath, could blow it open. "But do you mind if I ask him? Just to be sure? Just so I can cross him off my list?"

Just so I can see his face when I ask.

The door opened again, and again the younger woman's face appeared behind the chain.

"This is getting old," she said.

"I'm sorry. I'm really, really sorry to disturb you on a Sunday morning. Or any morning. Anytime, I mean. But it'll only take a second. I just want to ask him if he knows this old woman."

"He's. Not. The. One."

"But you can't know that for a fact. Maybe he was helping her, and he didn't tell you. Some people like to keep it a secret when they do stuff like that. They figure it means more that way."

"I know for a fact," she said, and started to swing the door closed.

Raymond almost raised a hand to stop it. But that would have been wrong. That would have been stepping over a line. It would almost have been forcing himself into their lives. Instead he tried to stop the door with his words.

"Wait. Please. Why won't you just let me ask him?"

The door stopped moving.

"Because he's not the one."

"But how do you know?"

The door slammed shut. Raymond could hear a scraping sound on the other side, but he had no idea if she was locking or unlocking.

The door opened. Wide. No chain.

Raymond looked in and saw an older man sitting in a wheelchair, a blanket over his legs, smoking a cigarette. His hair was gray and thin, his eyes distant. He never looked up to see who was at the door. He didn't seem to be the least bit curious as to what all the fuss was about. He never saw Raymond standing there, as far as Raymond could tell.

"This is Luis Velez," the young woman said, clearly at the end of her patience with Raymond. "Nineteen years in that chair. Now do you get it?"

"Yeah," Raymond said. "I get it. I'm sorry."

She slammed the door hard.

"I'm really sorry," he called, feeling something in his belly grow heavy. It was a sickening feeling, as though something metallic were forming in there. Sinking down under its own weight. "I'm sorry I upset you."

No answer.

There seemed to be no method for repairing the situation. Raymond had no choice but to move on to the next address.

He crossed Luis Velez on Third Avenue off his list.

—

Raymond tried one more place, in a rough section of Brooklyn. He thought it might take away the bad taste left by the last encounter. But all he got for his trouble was another no answer.

He walked back down the stairs of the five-floor walk-up. Of course this Luis Velez had been on the fifth floor. It was clear that life had no intention of making this easy for Raymond.

As he descended to the lobby, he thought of his first two Luis Velez visits ever. The doors had opened and someone had been there, ready to talk to him. Actually willing to make some kind of connection, even after it was clear that they had no business with Raymond and could not help him.

Beginner's luck, he now figured.

He had knocked on four doors just that morning. And only one Luis Velez had even been home.

He crossed the lobby and stepped out into the street.

There was at least one basement apartment to the building, Raymond saw as he walked by. A short flight of concrete stairs led down to a sort of recessed patio. On that patio was a sea of . . . well, everything. Mattresses. A kid's big-wheeled plastic trike. Stacks of linoleum tiles. Old floor lamps. And a man, sifting through all of it. As though he'd lost something there. Or as though a careful sweep of the area could turn up something of value.

The man looked up and saw Raymond. "Hey!" he shouted.

Raymond stopped, his heart pounding. The man sounded . . . combative? Angry? *Why is everyone angry this morning?* he wondered. The whole world felt angry. The very air he breathed seemed to tremble with it.

"Yeah?" Raymond asked.

The man was small. Compact and lean. Fairly young. He wore his hair buzzed short. Nearly buzzed off entirely. He wore a soul patch—a little square of almost-beard—under his lower lip. He was heavily tattooed.

"Wha'chou doin' in my neighborhood, boy? I know everybody who lives here, and I don' know you."

Raymond felt his blood go cold. He could actually feel the coolness of it as it circulated. He wanted to run. But first, he knew, he would ask. He didn't think it was the best idea to ask. But he could feel that he was going to do it anyway.

"I was looking for Luis Velez," he said.

"I'm Luis Velez," the man said. His eyes narrowed. He moved closer. Came up the stairs to the street.

Raymond backed away.

"I was just . . . I'm looking for the Luis Velez who used to help an old blind lady over on the west side. Just to make sure he's okay. I didn't mean any trouble for anybody."

Clearly that was not you, he thought. He wisely did not say it out loud.

The man stepped even closer, his energy heavy with threat. His goal seemed to be to intimidate Raymond. And it was working well. Raymond fell into full-on panic mode, the fear exploding in his chest like fireworks. Like electrical charges. He did not run because he thought it might be dangerous to move.

"Do I *look* like a guy who helps little old ladies cross the street?" Luis asked, his voice quiet and steady.

Raymond wasn't sure how a quiet voice could be so scary. But this Luis's voice was. Everything about him was. Fear surrounded Raymond like a cloud that sinks down to the ground to envelop everything underneath it.

Raymond said nothing. There was no safe answer to that question. He just froze there, statue-still. In his head he spoke to a God he wasn't even sure he believed existed. Tried to make a last-minute deal. Then he concentrated on something like beaming himself away. Not that he thought he could. But he wanted—needed—so badly to be gone from here. It was hard not to imagine it happening.

Meanwhile Luis was regarding his face with something like amusement.

Luis leaned in even closer to Raymond, leaving only a few inches between their noses. Raymond could smell onions on the man's breath. He was almost outside his body now with the panic. He vaguely, distantly, wondered if this was what it felt like to go into shock.

"Boo!" Luis Velez said.

Raymond jumped backward. Stumbled. Landed on the filthy concrete on his back, smacking his head on the curb.

Luis laughed.

Raymond scrambled to his feet and ran away.

———

They sat on the hard plastic bench of a subway car together, Raymond and Mrs. G. Close together, because he was still a little bit afraid. He still felt trembly inside from his experiences earlier that morning. He felt as though he were still running in some way. No fight or flight to choose from. Only flight.

He closed his eyes for just a moment, feeling the distinctive rocking motion of the train. He could see the lights flash on and off through his closed eyelids. Then he opened his eyes again.

There were only a small handful of people on the car with them, and each kept his or her distance and paid no attention to Raymond or Mrs. G.

"This is so lovely," she said. "This is so sweet of you to do this."

"When's the last time you ate food you didn't have to cook yourself?"

"In my home, not all that long ago. Luis would bring me takeout every now and again, just for a treat. But in a restaurant . . . I swear I can't even remember, Raymond, it was that long ago. Definitely not since my husband died. When he was alive we would go out to eat on our anniversary. Every year. And he would order a cake or some special dessert and have the waiter or the waitress bring it to our table and sing happy anniversary to us. But he's been gone a little over seventeen years now. So this is some fairly ancient history I'm recounting to you."

"I'm sorry," Raymond said.

"You shouldn't be. You weren't even born, so it couldn't possibly be your fault. We will speak of something else. Tell me. How was your morning?"

"Terrible."

"Anything you care to share?"

"Not really. Just nothing went right. I was standing in front of a brick wall, and I just kept revving up and smashing into it."

As he listened to his own metaphor, he touched the back of his head, gently feeling the spot where he had smacked it on the curb when he fell. A lump was forming there. It was tender.

"I definitely don't recommend that," she said.

"Sometimes it's hard to figure out how to avoid it."

Mrs. G had a watch with a crystal that lifted up, allowing her to touch the minute and hour hands. The hours were marked with raised blue dots. Raymond watched her check the time.

"It's after noon," she said. "Maybe they won't be serving brunch. Maybe they will be serving lunch when we get there."

"They serve brunch all day on Sunday."

"You have eaten there before."

"Yeah. It's not far from where my dad lives."

"You don't have to pick up the check, you know," she said. "I can help."

"No. I told you. It's on me. I told you I came into some money."

"Well, I promise I won't order the very most expensive thing."

"It's a flat price for brunch. But then there are all these different things you can choose from. I already know how much it will cost. I can cover it."

"Well, it's very sweet. I thank you for it."

They rode in silence for a time. Mrs. G was looking up and around, as if reading the ads. But of course she could not have been. Raymond wasn't sure what she was doing. Maybe listening. Maybe watching the changes in the light.

"What does he do, your father, to be able to afford to live in Midtown Manhattan?"

"He's a dentist."

"That explains it," she said. "Yes indeed."

———

Raymond helped her ease into her seat at the restaurant table, while the waiter carefully pushed the chair in behind her. Then the waiter handed them each a menu and hurried away.

Mrs. G set her menu down beside her plate and clapped her hands several times in sheer delight. Quickly. As if she simply could not contain her excited energy. She wore a beaming smile.

"Oh, this is so wonderful!" she said, loudly enough that a couple at the next table looked over and smiled. "It must seem very silly to you. Maybe even pathetic. To be so jubilant about a meal in a restaurant."

"I figured you would enjoy it," he said. "That's why I brought you."

It was half true. That was half the reason he'd brought her. That and the fact that he wanted to feel better about abandoning the Luis Project. He wanted to make it up to her, even though she had no idea he'd ever started looking. Because after his experiences earlier that day, he did not want to knock on even one more door.

He watched her smooth her hands over the starched white tablecloth as if admiring the fabric by feel. There was a tiny bud vase of fresh flowers in the middle of the table, some kind of small purple blooms, and Raymond wished she could see them. Maybe she could smell them, he thought.

"I'll read you the brunch choices," he said.

"I want an omelet. I already know I want an omelet. Just tell me what kinds they have."

"You sort of custom-order it. They have a list of omelet fillings, and you can choose three. And you can choose what you want on top. I'll read you the choices."

"I know what I like the best," she said, her voice still buzzing with excitement. "So let me tell you what I want, and you tell me if it's on the list."

"Okay."

"Spinach? Cheese? Tomatoes?"

"Yes, all of that. They have those. What kind of cheese do you want?"

"I don't mind which, because I like every kind of cheese there is. Is sour cream one of the things I can get on top?"

"It is."

"Good. I'll have that."

"And you can have either bacon or fried potatoes."

"Fried potatoes."

"What kind of toast do you like?"

"Oh my goodness!" she said, as if she had eaten too much already. "This is so much food! I can't eat so much food!"

"It doesn't matter. Just eat however much you want, and then they'll put the rest in a box, and you can take it home for later."

"Yes," a new voice said, "we have doggie bags. And you can also have champagne. It's included with your brunch." It was the waiter, who had stepped up to their table again.

"Champagne!" Mrs. G exclaimed. As though he had offered to set a diamond tiara on her head.

"I'm sorry," the waiter said, looking directly at Raymond, "but *you* can't have any. I'm guessing I don't need to tell you why not. But the lady may have champagne. And just because I'm in a good mood today,

I won't even ask to see your identification, miss. I'll trust that you're old enough to drink."

"Oh my. Champagne! I don't know. Poor Raymond. He can't carry me home. I have to be able to move my own feet. Champagne will go straight to my head!"

"It's up to you," the waiter said.

"It'll be on a full stomach," Raymond added.

"I'll tell you what. Maybe bring me half a glass."

"Coming up," the waiter said. "Coffee or tea?"

"Tea," Mrs. G said.

"Tea," Raymond said.

The waiter disappeared again.

"So, tell me, Raymond," she said. "How are you suddenly so rich?"

"I'm not. I'm not rich at all. This is going to be almost the last of that unexpected money I got. But I just knew this was what I wanted to spend it on."

———

He watched her take the measure of her omelet with her fork and knife, touching the boundaries of it to see how long it was. How tall it stood.

"It is a good thing about the box to take it home," she said. "Because I couldn't eat this much food if you gave me all day to try."

"Eat slowly," he said. "We're not in any hurry."

The longer they sat there enjoying their brunch, the easier it would be to call it a day. To go home without crossing any more names off his list. Ever again.

"I will ask you a personal question," she said, cutting off a piece of egg with her fork. "But you don't have to tell me if you don't want. Did you do the research on your computer the way we spoke about yesterday?"

Then she took a big bite and chewed slowly—almost dreamily—clearly savoring the flavors.

"I did. Before I went to bed last night."

"And are you happier because of what you learned?"

"Yeah. Actually. I am. You were right. There are lots of people."

"Good."

They ate in silence for a time. He was waiting for her to do that typical grown-up thing. The one where grown-ups asked him to mark the fact that they were right, so as to never doubt their rightness again. She never said anything of the sort. In fact, she offered nothing more on the subject.

"It's an actual orientation," he said, surprised to hear himself still volunteering information.

"An orientation?"

"Right. Like, gay is an orientation, and so is straight. And there's bisexual. And there's asexual."

It troubled him to use the word "sexual" in front of her, even if only as a suffix. It didn't seem to trouble her to hear it.

"We are never so very different as we think we are," she said, her mouth still full of omelet. She swallowed. Sipped her champagne. "I'm sorry, I am terribly rude to speak with my mouth full, but I can't bring myself to stop eating because it is too good."

"It's okay," he said.

For several minutes they both seemed to agree to focus on the food.

———

"I want to ask you a personal question, too," he said after a time.

"Go right ahead."

"When you first met me . . . you didn't see me. You didn't know I'm black. What if you had?"

"What if I had? Are you asking if it would have changed anything?"

"I guess I am."

"Not even a little bit."

"Are you sure?"

"I have never been so sure of anything in my life."

"I always figure people have a little bit of feelings about it in there somewhere. Whether they know it or not. Like my stepdad. He never really says or does anything bad, so I don't even know why I think so. He just seems a little uneasy around me. Even after all these years. Probably a combination of things, but . . . I just figure it gets trained into people, and they don't even know it's there."

"This is very true," she said. "It is a thing in their life that has always been there. They are white, and there is much privilege that comes with being so, but they don't see it, because there's never been a day in their life when it wasn't there. So you ask them if ethnicity makes a difference to them, and they say no. And in many cases they think they are telling the truth. It becomes like asking a fish to tell you about the water. It's all around him. He swims in it at every moment. But he will likely say, 'Water? What is this water of which you speak?' So often this is true."

Raymond poked his remaining omelet with his fork. He was feeling like he might not be able to eat any more.

"I thought it was everybody," he said. "But you think it's not true for you."

"Well, I hope it is not. I started out just like everybody else, but the world changed me."

"Everybody else, though?"

"Many, many people."

"What's the difference? How do some people get around it?"

"I don't think anyone gets around it. I don't think it ever bypasses a person completely. But I do think some of us have experiences that wake us up—when we see the horror that eventually comes of such judgments, or when we find ourselves on the wrong end of them, and feel how powerful that hate can grow to become. It can shake you to the very core of your being. And here is the thing about experiences that wake you up, Raymond: You try to get back to sleep, but it's easier said than done. Once you're awake, you're awake. Good luck hitting the snooze button, my friend."

He waited, thinking she would eventually tell him what experiences had awakened her.

She never did.

———

While they were riding home on the subway together, he watched her face. Just observed her in a moment of silence. The fragile vulnerability of her. The wrinkled, nearly translucent skin over her cheekbones. The fine haze of individual white hairs that had sprung loose from her braid. The milky appearance in the corneas of her eyes.

He realized, to his disappointment, that he would not—could not—abandon the Luis Project. Because she was someone he could not bear to disappoint. And because now *he* needed to know what had happened to Luis Velez, too. It was a mystery his mind needed to solve. It was a challenge he had taken on and needed to see through, both for himself and for her.

And he knew if he was going to go out knocking on doors again, it had better be soon. Right away. Right after he got her home so she could safely tuck herself in for an afternoon nap.

If he waited too long he was in danger of losing his nerve.

He dug his money out of his pocket and counted it. He had twelve dollars and seventy-five cents left out of the hundred dollars. Probably just enough for that Spanish phrasebook he would be needing. Because this afternoon he would be knocking on more doors. Seeking out more men named Luis Velez. And he would likely have to do the same the following day. And the day after that. After the dictionary was back at the school library as promised.

Chapter Seven

There's a Saint for That

Raymond stood in another strange hallway, prepared to knock on another unknown door—to talk to another person he didn't know and might soon learn he did not want to know. His heart pounded harder than usual, and he was tired of that. In fact, he was tired, period. He felt profoundly exhausted by these forays into the world of potentially awkward interactions with strangers.

He had been standing there, in front of the door of yet another Luis Velez, for a strangely long time. How long, he could not have said. But for a good minute he held one hand poised to knock, then dropped it, then raised it again. Then dropped it again.

He closed his eyes and said a . . . well, it would not do to call it a prayer, because Raymond was not at all sure he thought there was a God. And even if there was, it would be terribly rude to come to him with a favor after all these years of not speaking. He had done so once earlier that morning, and it had felt entirely selfish and wrong. No, what he said was more of a whispered entreaty to no one in particular. Maybe out into the universe in case there was anything listening. Maybe to some less ruined part of himself.

"Please let this one be easier."

As he spoke those words, he heard the sound of voices and laughter coming from the other side of the door. Many voices, all sounding as though they enjoyed each other's company. Happy family sounds. But they hadn't just sprung up in that moment, Raymond knew. The voices had been there all along. They had simply gone unregistered. They had taken their time breaking through his dread.

He knocked on the door, and while he waited his heart pounded more vigorously.

A woman answered. A Latina woman in her late thirties. Big and round, with a friendly face. She smiled at him, even though she had no idea who he was or why he had come.

"Yes? Can I help you?"

There was an openness in her words. A tentative expectation that whatever he was bringing to her door could be trusted and would prove itself good.

"I'm looking for Luis Velez."

Her smile widened and her eyes lit up. Apparently all one needed to do to make this woman's day was to say that name.

"Yes," she said. "Come in. We're having our supper."

"Oh. I didn't mean to bother you in the middle of . . ."

But then he stopped, because he wasn't sure what he was interrupting. It was about three thirty in the afternoon as far as he knew. Right after his brunch with Mrs. G. Neither lunch- nor dinnertime. "Supper," she had said, but he had no idea if that word meant something different from dinner, or why it would take place so early.

"We have a midday supper on Sundays," she said, as if reading his confusion. "It's pretty much the one day the whole family can get together."

"I shouldn't bother you, then," Raymond said.

"No, it's okay. Come in. Have you eaten?"

Raymond instinctively placed one hand on his belly, almost defensively. He was so full it was nearly painful.

"Oh yes. Thank you. I just had a big Sunday brunch."

"Well, come in, anyway. We'll tell Luis you're here."

He followed her down a hallway and into a dining room with dark paneling on the walls and a long table, suitable for maybe twelve people. Seated around it Raymond saw an older couple. Grandparents, he guessed. Five children. A girl nearly Raymond's age. Maybe fifteen from the look of her. Three boys in varying sizes, starting at around five and working up to ten or eleven. Then a toddler girl in a booster seat. At the head of the table sat a heavy and robust man who Raymond assumed must be Luis Velez.

All eyes came up to Raymond.

"Look who's here, honey," the woman said.

For a moment, nothing. Everybody just stared.

Then Luis said, "I don't . . . I'm not sure who this is."

"Oh," the woman said. "I'm sorry. I just assumed you two knew each other."

So that's that, Raymond thought. She had assumed he was a friend to Luis. Someone Luis would know on sight. That's why she had invited him in. That's why she was being so friendly. And now that false notion was gone.

"I'm sorry," Raymond said. "I wasn't trying to . . . it wasn't meant to be . . . you know . . . coming into your home on some kind of false pretense. I just asked if you were here. I wanted to see you and ask you a question. Maybe I should have said right out that you don't know me. I guess to me it went without saying. But if you want me to go right now, I will. I'm not trying to intrude. I'll leave if you want me to."

Raymond stopped talking. Finally. He stood awkwardly, listening to the sheer volume of his words ricochet around in the small room. Everyone was waiting. No one was even chewing anymore, save for the toddler.

"Take a deep breath," Luis Velez said, his tone soothing. "You don't have to be afraid of us. We won't bite you. Tell me what you came here to ask."

Raymond sighed out a breath he had apparently been holding for too long.

"Please let it be him," he breathed quietly.

It was only a soft whisper. But it was still louder than he had intended it to be. It had been meant to remain a thought in the privacy of his head. He hoped the words had not made it to anyone's ears but his own. He would have been embarrassed if someone else had heard.

"Okay," he began. "Here's the question. Do you know Millie G? The ninety-two-year-old blind woman who lives over on the west side? Are you the one who used to come and help her do her banking and shop for groceries?"

Luis Velez opened his mouth to speak. But Raymond already knew the answer. He could see it in the man's eyes.

"I'm sorry," he said. "I don't know her."

Raymond felt as though he were falling. Maybe off a tall building, or down a deep well. For a brief moment, he had allowed himself to believe that in this friendly, safe environment he had found his Luis Velez. That he would have to go no further. He'd had no idea how much he'd set himself up for a fall. He thought he'd known how deeply he wanted to be done with this project, but there was more to that well of dread than he'd imagined.

"Okay, thanks anyway," Raymond said. "I'll let you get back to your meal."

He turned to walk out of the dining room.

"Wait," Luis Velez said. "Take a seat with us for a minute. You look so tired."

"I don't want to bother you while you're eating."

"We're almost done. There's cake coming. You can join us for dessert."

Raymond stood still a moment, feeling stunned. He had no idea why anyone would choose to be so nice to him, or what had possessed this Luis Velez to want to add Raymond to the one meal his family could enjoy together every week.

But he *was* tired. So he sat.

———

The cake was dark chocolate, with gobs of chocolate frosting. It was hard to imagine putting anything more in his stomach. But Raymond's mouth wanted it. His psyche wanted it. He wanted to eat sugar until he was nearly in a coma. Until he could feel nothing. He wanted to disappear.

He lifted his fork and took a huge bite. His eyes rolled back as if to scan the ceiling. It was that good.

He looked up to the head of the table to see the big, rotund Luis Velez watching him and smiling.

"She makes a hell of a cake, my wife," he said. "Am I right?"

"Luis!" the wife said. "Language!"

"Sorry. She makes a mean cake. That's what I meant to say."

"It's really, really good," Raymond said. "I really appreciate it. I have no idea why you invited me to sit down and eat cake." He wanted to ask straight out: *"Why?"* But he could not think of a way to say it that did not risk sounding ungrateful. "But I really appreciate it. I just don't know why," he added, poking at the question again.

Luis looked to his wife, Sofia, and she looked back. Everybody else seemed lost in dessert.

Raymond had been introduced to everyone while Luis was cutting the cake. But he could remember only that the wife was Sofia, the teenage girl was Luisa, and the toddler girl was Karina. The rest had refused to stick. There was a Luis Jr. in there somewhere, but Raymond couldn't remember which of the boys bore that name.

He waited to see if they would answer the question he could not quite bring himself to ask. At least, not directly.

"You just looked so . . . ," Luis began.

"Dispirited," Sofia added.

Apparently they finished each other's sentences.

"I was going to say discouraged, but yeah. You looked so sad. We couldn't send you back out into the world like that."

Raymond took another huge bite of cake. Because he couldn't stop himself. It was too good. But now he couldn't answer until he had chewed and swallowed. Which he did as quickly as he could.

"I guess it's just . . . ," he began. "I had this really terrible morning. I went to look for a Luis Velez in Brooklyn. And he was . . . scary. Maybe he was just playing with my head, but I thought he was going to hurt me. It scared me a lot. And before that, I got into this thing with another family where I kept saying they didn't know for a fact that he wasn't the right Luis Velez. They wouldn't let me ask him, and I just wanted to ask him. And then it turned out he's been in a wheelchair for nineteen years and doesn't even seem to know what's going on around him."

"That's not your fault," Sofia said. "You couldn't have known."

"I felt bad about it, though."

He took another huge bite of cake.

"And you wanted this to be your last stop," Luis said.

Raymond nodded, his mouth full. He felt himself fall a little deeper. Yes. He had so wanted this to be his last stop.

"How do you know this Millie?"

"She lives in my building," Raymond said after managing to swallow his huge mouthful. "She doesn't have anyone. Her husband died a long time ago. She doesn't have any children. I met her because she was standing out in the hall, asking everybody who came by if they knew Luis Velez, or had seen him. Which was quite a long shot. I guess you know what I mean. But she was desperate. She was down to half a can of soup, and she'd been eating a quarter of it every day. Rationing it. Because Luis wasn't coming by to walk her to the bank, and his cell phone was out of service, and she just . . . she didn't have any options to fall back on. She was so hungry I had to give her my granola bar just so she had enough energy to walk to the store with me. You know. To do her shopping. People should have some options, you know? Why do we leave people on their own like that? It doesn't seem right."

He looked up to see every face at the table staring at him. Even the toddler. No one was eating cake. They were all watching him, transfixed. As if waiting to see what he would say next.

"Did I say something wrong?"

"Wrong?" Sofia said. "*Wrong?* No, everything you said was just exactly right. Why do we leave people on their own like that? I ask myself all the time. They're human beings, they're our fellow human beings, but we don't even act like we care. See, this is what I'm always telling you kids." She looked to the side of the table where her five children sat. Two of the boys had gone back to eating their cake. "Junior! Eduardo! Pay attention when I'm talking to you." Two forks dropped. One hit its dessert plate with a startling clang. "What this young man is saying is just what I'm always telling you kids. You see someone struggling, you help that person. Doesn't matter if they're familia, or even a friend. They're a person. So you help."

Luis Junior rolled his eyes. Or maybe it was Eduardo.

The senior Luis slammed one of his palms down on the table. Everyone jumped. But no one jumped higher than Raymond.

"Junior," Luis said, his voice dense and grave. "You have one more chance to show respect to your mother, and if you can't, you will leave this table. And the cake will stay here."

"Sorry, Mom," Junior mumbled. It sounded sincere.

Everyone went back to eating their cake in silence.

A minute or two later Raymond looked up to see the older girl staring at him. Luisa.

"You shouldn't feel so discouraged," she said. "Maybe the next Luis will be the right one. Or the one after that."

"Maybe," Raymond said.

"But he had a bad experience this morning," Sofia said. "A couple of them, and now it's much harder for him to knock on doors. Am I right, honey?"

She looked directly at Raymond, who cleared his throat and swallowed hard.

"Yeah," he said. "But there's more to it than that. There's even more. I feel like I sort of . . . painted myself into a corner with this. Like . . . I'm not even sure how to say it. Like there's just no good way this can end now. Mrs. G thinks Luis would never have stopped coming without even telling her why. I guess she thinks the best about people. But I don't know if she's right or not. So now I'm trying to think of a good way this can end. And I just don't see it. Maybe she's right, and something terrible happened to him. And that would be . . . well . . . terrible. Or maybe he doesn't care nearly as much as she thinks he does. And that would be a whole different kind of terrible. I keep trying to picture finding out something better than that. But what would it be? Sometimes I think maybe he's in the hospital, and he can't come. But he could call, or send somebody. Or I think about what if he had amnesia or something. But that's one of those silly things that I think only happens in the movies or on TV."

Raymond paused. Took a deep breath. He poked his remaining cake with his fork. He purposely did not look up at the faces. He plunged on.

"So today I decided to stop. Not knock on any doors anymore. But then I looked at her, and she looked so . . . helpless, kind of. I mean, not literally, because she has a good brain. She can take care of herself in a lot of ways. But she just looked so . . . easy to hurt. And I don't want the world to keep hurting her. I mean, if I can help it. Even though I know she's probably pretty strong and she's been taking care of herself since before I was born. So it's probably just me, but I get worried about her. So I came and knocked on another door. But I just don't see any good coming of it at this point. It just all feels so hopeless."

He paused again. Shoved a huge bite of cake into his mouth. He did not look up at them as he chewed and swallowed. No one spoke.

"I'm sorry," he said. "I didn't mean to bring everybody down."

A long pause.

Then the teen girl, Luisa, said, "I want to give him the medal. My Jude medal. Can I give it to him?"

Raymond looked up to see her exchanging glances with first one of her parents, then the other.

"The one your abuela gave you?" Sofia asked. "Are you sure you want to do that, honey?"

"Yeah. I'm sure. He needs it more than I do. Anyway, I've been thinking I shouldn't be wearing it anymore. Because that makes it seem like I'm still hopeless. And I'm not. I'm good now."

Raymond stared at her as she spoke. She was thin and pretty, with straight hair that was so long she might have sat on it if she wasn't careful. She spoke in a high, quiet voice. There was something insubstantial about her. But only on the outside.

He looked to Luis and Sofia to see their reactions. He had no understanding of what was being offered, and that must have reflected in his eyes.

Luis Velez Senior said, "Luisa's grandmother gave her a Saint Jude medal last year when she was sick. She had meningitis. It really looked like we were going to lose her for a while there. But she came through."

A ringing silence. Raymond did not feel he could accept such a gift, but had no words to say so. At least, no words he did not fear would sound ungrateful.

The grandmother spoke up for the first time since Raymond arrived. She spoke in breathless Spanish, one word running into the next. Raymond did not understand one of them. Also, he could not have separated one out from the crowd to look it up in his book.

He raised his gaze and caught Luis's eye.

"I'm sorry. What did she say?"

"You're sorry a lot," Luis said. "And I don't think you need to be."

"That's what Mrs. G always tells me."

It was Sofia who answered his question. "Abuela says it's not a family heirloom. She says she bought it at the store for Luisa, and if she ever needed to, she could go buy another. And she also agrees that you should not wear the medal if your case is not hopeless."

Luisa rose from the table and walked to Raymond, who pushed his chair back slightly and then froze in fear. Why fear, he had no idea. He was simply afraid of people. Afraid to be approached. It seemed to make no sense, but there was little he could do about it. At least, as far as he could tell.

The girl pulled the medal out from under her peach-colored shirt. It was on a heavy chain. A long chain. She slipped it off over her head, and Raymond sat very still as she reached out and slid the chain over his head. One of her hands accidentally brushed against his closely cropped hair, and he shivered slightly, because it tickled.

"There," she said. "Saint Jude is the patron saint of hopeless causes. Now you have him with you."

"Thank you," Raymond said, his voice hushed with awe.

Raymond did not believe in the saints. He did not think that Saint Jude was now with him, helping him with his hopeless cause. He did, however, very much believe in the simple magic of a girl who barely knew him, yet would be so kind. And that kindness, he knew, would stay with him through the end of the Luis Project. However it turned out.

He held the medal in his hand, out away from his chest. As if it had something to tell him, and he could listen by feel.

"That's such a nice thing to do," he said. "I don't know what to say."

"You don't have to say anything," Luisa said, returning to her place at the table. Swinging her long hair out of the way before she sat. "It just felt like the right thing. It felt like it wanted to be yours."

—

They sat in the living room together, a relentlessly spotless area with plastic slipcovers on all the furniture. Raymond's stuffed wing chair squeaked underneath him when he shifted his weight, so he tried not to.

Luis Senior was speaking. The boys and the grandparents had gone their separate ways. Luisa sat across the room and watched Raymond finger the medallion she had given him. The toddler, whose name he had forgotten, stood too close and stared into Raymond's face.

"I just feel bad," Luis was saying. "Because I really want to be the guy who was helping the blind woman do her errands. And I don't just mean because you wanted me to be. I mean I want to be that guy. I always thought I'd be that guy. But then I have all these kids, and we're taking care of Sofia's parents, and we both work full time. But still, I look back over what I've done in my life, and it's good and all . . . but I still want to be that guy."

"You've done a lot with your life," Sofia said, reaching across the couch and taking her husband's hand. "You take good care of your family."

"I try," he said. "Yeah. But most people take care of their family. That's the problem. They give everything they've got to their family and nothing to anybody else. And then this poor old blind woman, she has no family. And she's just out of luck. Nobody figures she's their problem."

"I agree with Sofia," Raymond said. "It sounds like you do a lot, and you shouldn't feel bad."

"Maybe," Luis said. He had huge eyebrows, graying and long. Wild, swirling in every direction. They seemed to join in the middle of his forehead as he furrowed his brow. "But I still want to be that guy. This Luis Velez you're looking for, does he have kids?"

"I don't know," Raymond said. "Somebody else asked me that question. A different Luis Velez. And I don't know. I didn't think to ask. I asked a few questions that I thought might help me find him. But now I feel like if I ask any more, she'll figure out what I'm doing. And I don't want her to know. Not now. Not till I know how it turns out. When I come home and I'm all disappointed, I don't want her to have to take it on with me. And now I'm just feeling more and more like I'll have no way to make her feel better in the end. She's hurting now, because she doesn't know. But whatever I find out, I feel like it'll hurt her to know it. I have no idea what the answer is. I have no idea what to do."

They sat in silence for a time. The baby girl stepped closer and stared up into Raymond's face as though fascinated by his sadness. She leaned her sticky, sausage-plump fingers against the knee of his jeans.

"Honey," Sofia said. "Karina. Give the boy a little space."

The girl did not retreat, so Sofia swooped in and picked her up. The girl fussed and cried at being overpowered.

"I should go," Raymond said. He stood, feeling how full he was. All that omelet. All that cake. "I should get out of your hair. But I want to thank you for talking to me and being so nice. And for this medal. It really made a difference after this morning, and how horrible everything was. It's going to make a difference next time I have to knock on a door."

But, even as he said it, he could feel his overly full belly curdle sickeningly at the idea.

Sofia walked him to the door. Variations of good wishes and luck followed him as he walked down the hall.

"You're a lovely boy," Sofia said to him.

Raymond looked down at his shoes and said nothing.

"Here," she said, and pushed a folded scrap of paper into his hand. "I wrote down our phone number. I know you might forget, and it's okay if you do. There's no obligation. But if you can think to do it, please give a call and let us know how it works out."

Raymond nodded, still feeling as though his mouth might or might not be in full working order.

"Thanks," he said. "Thanks for everything."

"I think you're wrong," Sofia said as he walked out her door. "I think that lady's story *will* have a happy ending. Because no matter what happens with Luis, she has you. And that's not nothing. That's no small prize."

———

Raymond got off the subway on the Upper East Side and tried Luis M. Velez again, one of his "no answer" stops from earlier that morning. Because it was on his way.

There was no answer at Luis M. Velez's door this time, either.

He put a second hash mark by that name and address on his list.

———

His mother was waiting for him in the kitchen when he got home, hands on her hips, her face set into a hard mask of belligerence.

"And where the hell have *you* been?" she asked.

It surprised him. He hadn't expected any trouble.

"Just out," he said. "I told the babysitter I was going."

"She didn't say you'd be gone until *after dinner*. We didn't save you anything. You know the rules. You want to eat, you show up."

"It doesn't matter," he said, one hand on his full belly. "I'm stuffed."

His sister Rhonda stuck her head into the room, betraying the fact that she'd been eavesdropping.

"Raymond has a girlfriend!" she crowed in a singsong voice.

His mother looked first at her, then at Raymond. "Go to your room, Rhonda," she said. Then, to Raymond, "*Do* you have a girlfriend?"

"No."

"Friend at least?"

"Yeah," he said. "I told you. I've made some new friends."

"Yeah. I guess you did tell me that. But you've been gone *so much*."

She crossed the room in his direction, looking at something in the vicinity of his neck. "Hey. What's this?"

She grabbed the heavy chain around his neck and pulled hard. It must have been visible above the neck of his T-shirt. A second later she was holding the Saint Jude medal in her hand.

"If you don't mind," he said, pulling it back again. "That's mine." He stuffed it back under his shirt.

"Did you go and get religion on me, baby?"

"No!" he said. As if being accused of a transgression.

"I'm not saying it's bad if you did."

"I know. But I didn't. Somebody just gave it to me, that's all. *She's* got religion. But that doesn't mean I do."

"Ah," she said, a smile breaking. "A young lady. That explains a lot." Then she took his chin firmly in her hand, hurting him with her long fingernails. He chose not to let on. "But next time *call*."

"How am I supposed to call when you won't get me a cell phone?" Then he could see by her face that he'd made a mistake. "Sorry," he said. "I will. I should have. I'm sorry."

"Ed's not made of money," she said, her voice tight.

Really? I had no idea. He's never brought it up.

As if.

"I know. But Dad would get me one."

"And you know why I don't want him to."

"Yeah. I know. Ed gets upset when Dad gets me nice things. He feels like Dad's lording it over him how much more money he's got."

That seemed to send their conversation into a dead-end street. No one knew quite where to go from there. The only option seemed to be backtracking. Retreat.

"You sure you're not hungry? You could have a snack at least."

"I've never been surer of anything in my life," he said. He realized as he heard it come out of his mouth that he had learned the phrase from Mrs. G. Or something very much like it, at least. "But thanks. I'm sorry I didn't call."

She sighed and walked out of the room, leaving him alone.

The truth was that he hadn't bothered to call because he didn't think anyone would notice or care.

It was a comfort to be wrong on that score.

Chapter Eight

What Happened

It was the time of day when Raymond should have been in his last-period study hall. Instead he had slipped out of school early and gone to the doors of the two Luis Velez addresses he had tried before, but still had not managed to cross off his list. The hash-marked addresses. The "no answers."

He dreaded the addresses down the list, because they would take him to places like Flushing and Newark and Bridgeport and Bay Shore on Long Island. He was postponing these longer trips until he had no closer options.

Luis Rodrigo Velez had been home this time. But he hadn't exactly answered the door. Just yelled through it that he was not the one.

Luis M. Velez still was not home.

Raymond was sitting on an elevated train through the Bronx, most of the way to the Fordham University area—his father's alma mater—when he realized that the next name on his list was also Luis M. Velez. He wondered if that was coincidence, or if they were the same person. Maybe he had moved, and that's why he was never home at the Manhattan address. Still, you would think someone would be. The next person to occupy the apartment at least.

Raymond leaned over and glanced at the watch of a man sitting near him on the bench seat, and the man gathered himself and his newspaper and moved one seat farther away.

It was only twenty after three. But Raymond would have to keep an eye on the time today. He would have to find a pay phone and call his mother if he was going to be late.

———

Raymond got off the train at 183rd and walked to Andrews Avenue. Found the address.

He didn't need to call up and have someone buzz him in, because a youngish couple was just coming in through the door with two bags of groceries each. They looked over their shoulders at him, smiled, and allowed him to come through behind them.

They climbed the stairs to the third floor more or less together, Raymond hanging a step or two behind. Then they walked down the hall in the same direction. It wasn't until they had passed the second-to-last apartment that it seemed to dawn on them all at once. They were going to the same place.

Or maybe the couple thought Raymond was following them. Maybe they were regretting having let him in. They might even have been about to question him and his purpose in the building.

Raymond figured he'd better talk fast.

The couple stopped suddenly and turned to him, fixing him with questioning—and slightly nervous—gazes.

"Are you Luis Velez?" Raymond asked.

"Yeah," the man said. "Can I help you with something?"

He was probably no older than twenty-five, with a short, spikey modern haircut that stuck up like a wave in front, just over his forehead. He had a corner broken off one very white front tooth. His wife—if she was his wife—was strangely tiny, barely five feet, blonde. Not Latina as far as Raymond could tell. Raymond watched her move a step closer to Luis as if for protection.

"I hope so," Raymond said. "I'm looking for a guy named Luis Velez who used to come into Manhattan, over on the west side, and help this older blind woman. Millie, the woman's name is. He kind of . . . disappeared. And I'm just trying to find him for her."

Raymond waited. But no answer seemed forthcoming. He seemed to have stunned them with the question, but he could not imagine why. It was a pretty simple question. *You're either that guy or you're not.*

The woman's mouth had fallen open. Luis glanced over and tried to catch her eye but did not succeed.

"So . . . ," Raymond said.

He was hoping that simple word might prompt an answer. Restart the conversation.

He was beginning to suspect he had found his Luis. How could they be so startled by the question if they knew nothing about the situation? No, his question had seemed to trigger something in them. Something uncomfortable.

Meanwhile the one dirty window at the end of the hall threw a slant of afternoon sun on the three of them. Left their shadows on the plaid hall carpeting. Raymond couldn't help noticing that those shadows did not move in the slightest.

"He used to go help this woman?" Luis asked. As though Raymond hadn't just said so. "And then he disappeared?"

"Yeah," Raymond said. "Right."

"When did he stop showing up?"

"I don't know to the day. But a little over three weeks ago, I think."

Again Luis glanced over to catch the woman's eye. This time she looked back. They exchanged a strangely freighted look with one another. Heavy with something. Raymond had no idea what, but it made his heart pound, and his stomach sagged with the weight of the thing.

"Are you thinking what I'm thinking?" Luis asked his wife, or girl-friend. Or whatever she was to him.

"I'm thinking maybe it was the Luis Velez who got killed," she said.

It hit Raymond like a speeding crosstown bus. He actually felt the physical impact of it. For a split second he was surprised that it had not knocked him down. Then he reminded himself that it was not a real, physical thing. Except to the extent that it was.

"There's a Luis Velez who . . . died?" Raymond asked, his voice sounding foreign and far away. Nearly unfamiliar.

You knew this. You knew. Why are you acting so surprised? You knew all along.

"I'm sorry you had to find out about it this way," the tiny woman said. "I just blurted it out. I wasn't really thinking. I do that all the time. Talk first, think later. It's my curse. I'm really sorry."

"Give us a minute to put our groceries away," Luis said. "And then we'll take you out for a cup of coffee and tell you what we know."

He opened his apartment door with a key, and they both stepped inside, leaving Raymond to wait in the hall. Clearly they did not feel comfortable inviting him in. But it was okay. Raymond understood. People didn't invite strangers into their homes. Raymond had been shocked by the people who *had* opened their doors for him. He was not shocked by this.

———

It wasn't until they were seated in a small, mostly deserted café, their coffee and tea on the table in front of them, that Luis Velez opened his mouth to speak.

They had said nothing to each other on the walk. Not even simple introductions. Just a heavy silence.

If Raymond had been someone else entirely, he might have dragged it out of them on the way over. Screamed at them to spit out what they knew. But Raymond was only who he had always been. And besides, he was no more anxious to hear the details than this couple seemed anxious to tell them.

"It was in the paper just yesterday morning," Luis said.

"Luis reads the Sunday *Times* like nobody I ever met before," the woman said. "I'm not going to say he reads every word on every page, because I think that might take weeks. Do you get the Sunday *Times*? It's huge."

Luis seemed to notice that she was pushing the conversation off track. He pushed it back again.

"It was a story that was kind of buried," he said. "I think that's what Kate is trying to say. Somebody might get the Sunday *Times* and not even see this. It was in the city section, but way back. I don't remember what page. I remember it kind of pissed me off that they buried it back there, because it seemed like a big deal to me. But maybe that's because his name was Luis M. Velez. That's me. Luis M. Velez. It hit me like a baseball bat. Like I was reading my own obituary. Except it wasn't an obituary, it was a story. You know. An article. But he was Luis Miguel Velez, and I'm Luis Manuel Velez. But at the beginning of the article it just said Luis M. Velez. It was pretty shocking, to read your name that way. And the more I read what happened to him, the more I realized . . . that could *so* happen to me. That could have been me. I haven't really stopped thinking about it since. And then today you show up at my door looking for this guy. It's all just really weird."

A silence fell. Raymond waited. Surely Luis knew that when he threw around terms like "what happened," he was talking to someone who did not know what had happened. So Raymond waited. He could have asked. But he was dreading the information and wasn't sure if he wanted to hurry it along.

"So, did you know him well?" Kate asked.

"I didn't know him at all. I never met him. But my friend Millie . . . they were close. Oh my God. I'm going to have to tell her!"

Another awkward silence. It was almost as though they planned to leave Raymond on his own with this. Force him to find a leftover Sunday paper and figure it out for himself.

"So . . . ," Raymond said. "I guess . . ." He felt as though he were walking on partially thawed ice over deep water. Inviting a shocking fall. Knowing it could be any minute. Any step. "Maybe go ahead and tell me what happened?"

"It's bad," Luis said. "It's really bad, what happened. And it could have been me. It could have been you, too. When you hear this, you'll be thinking to yourself, Jeez, that could have been me. Except your name is not Luis M. Velez. That's what was so shocking about it. The name thing."

Raymond threw him a desperate look, and he caught it.

"Right. Sorry. Get this over with. Okay. So, originally, this woman who shot him—"

Raymond's mind left the table for a flash of a moment. Levitated to somewhere near the ceiling of the café. It had never occurred to him that Luis had been shot. He had been thinking in terms of a terrible accident. Well . . . it may have occurred to him. But it hadn't been a thought he'd long entertained.

But Luis was still talking.

"—told the police he was trying to rob her. She even lied and tried to prove it by using the fact that he was holding her wallet when she shot him. She tried to use that as proof that it was a robbery. But there was a witness. At the time there was only one witness. And the witness said no, Luis already had the wallet in his hand before he ever approached her. He was running down the street after her, holding up this wallet. He kept saying, 'Ma'am! Ma'am!' The witness didn't know if the lady dropped it on the street, or maybe she'd left it somewhere, but she said it was real clear that he was trying to give it back.

"But then another witness came forward, much later. I don't know why. Conscience bothering him, maybe. And this guy said the woman who shot Luis, she was digging around in her purse already, for that gun. Luis was walking behind her, and it was dusk. Almost nightfall. And already she was going for that gun. Like maybe just in case, you know. But just in case what? Luis hadn't said a word to her. Hadn't come anywhere near her. But he was this great big guy, and he was walking down the street behind her. You know. Walking While Latino. And she was already going for the gun. And while she was rummaging around in there, in her purse, she dropped her wallet on the street. And I guess she never saw it. She just kept walking. Luis picked it up and tried to give it back to her. But she didn't hear him. It said in the article she wears hearing aids. Not a really old lady. Fifty-six, I think the paper said. But she wears hearing aids. She said she turns them off on the street because of all the background noise. You know. Traffic and all. I guess it sort of echoes or something. Irritates her. So he's following her, yelling to her, and the witnesses can hear Luis, but she can't. So finally he catches up to her and puts a hand on her shoulder, you know? To try to turn her around. Well, she turned around, all right. She turned around and fired six rounds into this poor guy's chest. For trying to give her back something she dropped on the street. And now this guy is gone. Gone. Forever. A wife and three kids. That's what he left. An eleven-year-old and a seven-year-old, and the wife is pregnant with their third kid. Can you imagine anything more tragic than that? What a waste of a life."

A ringing silence fell. Raymond tried to register what he had heard, but he seemed to be temporarily incapable of coherence. He stared out the window at what he thought must be the university across the street. Watched people coming and going from its grounds.

Envied them.

When a thought finally came through, it was only a repeat of this: *I have to be the one to tell her.*

"That could *so* have been you," Kate said, touching Luis's arm tenderly.

Luis paid her no mind. He seemed embarrassed by the fact that she was thinking of Luis Manuel Velez in that moment. Not sparing a thought for Luis Miguel Velez and the people who had hoped to find him alive.

"I'm sorry," Luis said to Raymond. "I know it's bad. I know it's a lot to take in."

"If this happened, like, almost a month ago," Raymond said, "why wasn't it in the paper back then?"

"Maybe it was. Maybe it was in there on a weekday, and I missed it. I don't know."

"But I tried to find an obituary or something for him, and I never found it."

"Oh. Maybe not, then. I think they ran a story about it yesterday because—miracle of miracles—they decided to bring charges against the woman. You know. The shooter."

"Good," Raymond said.

"That's what I think," Luis added.

Then nobody seemed to know what else to say.

"What time is it?" Raymond asked him.

Luis was wearing a watch, but his jacket sleeve covered it.

"A minute or two after four."

"Any chance either one of you has a cell phone I could use?"

Luis produced one from his jacket pocket and set it on the table in front of Raymond.

Raymond thanked him and picked it up. Dialed his home number.

He felt immensely relieved when the call went to voicemail.

"Hi, Mom," he said. "It's me. I'm going to be late again. Just letting you know."

———

Raymond stood in front of the door of Luis M. Velez on the Upper East Side of Manhattan. For the fourth time.

He knocked on the door. But this time he really didn't expect an answer. He had to try, though.

He got what he'd been expecting: nothing.

He turned around and pulled off his backpack. Leaned back against the door and slid down until he was sitting on the carpet in front of Luis's door. *The* Luis.

It struck him that the Luis Project was over. He had been so looking forward to that day—when he could forever stop knocking on doors and talking to strangers. Now he wished it wasn't over. Because what he had just heard, well . . . he would do nearly anything to live in a land where he still did not know it.

He took a spiral notebook of lined paper out of his backpack. Dug around for a pen but found only a pencil.

He braced the notebook on his knees and began to write a note. For Luis's wife, maybe. For whoever might get it.

> Dear Luis Velez's family,
>   You don't know me, but my name is Raymond Jaffe. I'm friends with Millie G, the lady Luis used to help for so long. I only just found out today, just now, what happened. I've been looking for Luis, because Mrs. G is worried sick about him, but now I guess I'm just looking for whatever family he left behind. Here's my phone number, if you want to call me. If you do, I'll really appreciate it. I have to be the one to tell Mrs. G, and I really hate that. I'm dreading that.

Then he stopped writing and realized he might be getting off track. What did Luis's widow care that he had to break the bad news to someone? That was a pathetically small problem by her standards.

He looked up to see a woman standing outside her apartment door, right across the hall. Staring down at him. A large middle-aged black woman with beautifully braided hair and a loose, flowing muumuu of a housedress in a wild print.

"May I help you?" Her voice was deep and comfortable.

"Oh," he said. "I was just leaving a note for . . . Luis's wife."

"Did you know Luis?"

"No. But I was looking for him for someone. Someone who was really worried about him because she didn't know where he'd gone."

"Not *Millie!*"

"Yes! Yes, that's who I was trying to help by finding him!"

Raymond struggled to his feet, pushing his back against the door for support.

"Oh, Isabel will be so happy! She wanted so badly to be able to talk to Millie. To let her know what happened. But she didn't know where Millie lived, and she couldn't remember her last name exactly. And she didn't have her phone number because Luis never backed up his phone."

"Didn't she get his phone back?"

"Oh, darlin', there wasn't much to get back. It was in his jacket pocket. And this son of a bitch who shot him . . . she put one of the bullets right through it. Just blew it all to pieces. All these shards of it in Luis's side. Embedded. But we don't want to talk about that. Do we? It's just too horrible. Anyway, son, Isabel won't be home for quite some time. How long, I don't know. She took the kids and went to stay with her parents. It's just a terrible time for her, as I'm sure you can imagine."

"You . . . wouldn't have any idea how to get in touch with her there. Would you?"

The woman shifted on her feet slightly. Uncomfortably. First one direction, then the other.

"She gave me the number. In case there was some kind of emergency at the apartment. But I don't see as I have a right to hand it out to anybody."

"But you could give her a note. Couldn't you? You could give her *my* number. And if she wants to call me, she will. Right?"

He quickly scribbled his phone number at the end of his note. Tore the sheet out of the notebook.

"Yeah," the woman said, her voice sinking down into balance and comfort again. "Yeah. That I can do."

———

When Raymond arrived home, his mother was setting the table for dinner. She raised her left hand, turned her wrist over, and made a big show of looking at her watch.

"You just made it," she said. "But not with much time to spare."

"Right. You got my message?"

"I did. Thank you for that."

"I'm going to be in my room," he said. "I have to look something up online. You'll call me for dinner?"

"Once," she said. "So keep the door to your room open. Also your ears."

He walked away without comment. He had too much on his mind to want to engage with her.

He sat down in his room, in front of his desk. Woke up his laptop computer. Did a search for the *New York Times*. Entered the term "Luis M. Velez." And there it was. Just like that. Everything he'd been searching for but hadn't seemed to be there at the time. Right in front of him to read. To print. To share. It sank hard into his belly again that he was about to have to tell her.

He clicked on the headline link. It said, "Woman Charged with Voluntary Manslaughter in Fatal Shooting of Fellow Pedestrian."

When the story came up, Raymond couldn't bring himself to read it. Because there on his screen, front and center, was a photo of Luis M. Velez. Raymond just couldn't seem to get any farther than that photo.

He was younger than the man Raymond had pictured. And so alive. He was so alive in the photo that it seemed impossible to think he could be dead. His smile was so infectious that it almost made Raymond smile just to look at it. And there was nothing for Raymond to smile about in that moment. Luis's eyes shone. His hair was dark and a little bit shaggy, his eyes dark. Eyebrows neat and thin. But it was hard to focus on those details, because Luis's smile just kept stealing the show.

The caption under the photo read, "Luis M. Velez, 33, of Manhattan, leaves behind a wife and two children: Maria Elena, 11, and Esteban, 7. His widow, Isabella, is pregnant with their third child."

Raymond's door flew open, and his mother stuck her head into the room.

"I thought you were going to keep your ears open."

"Sorry. Did you call dinner? I didn't hear."

"No, I called in and said someone was on the phone for you. You didn't hear the phone ring?"

"Oh. Sorry. I was busy paying attention, I guess."

His heart pounded, wondering if it was Isabel. He figured it must be, because nobody else ever called him. Mrs. G had memorized his number, but she always waited for him to come by her apartment of his own volition.

He clicked his computer back into sleep mode and rose from his chair. As he walked through the open bedroom doorway, his mother punched him on the shoulder, surprisingly hard.

"It's a *young lady*," she said, her voice all full of happy conspiracy. "Thought you said you didn't have a girlfriend."

"I don't," he said, and ran to take the phone.

Unfortunately, the phone in the kitchen was the only phone they owned.

"Hello?" he said, sounding breathless from the fear.

"Raymond Jaffe?" she asked.

"Yes."

"It's Isabel. Luis's wife."

"Thank you so much for calling me," he said on a desperate rush of breath. He heard a movement. Turned his head to see his mother standing in the kitchen doorway behind him. He covered the mouthpiece of the receiver with one palm. "Excuse me," he said. "A little privacy, please?"

"Fine. But dinner has started. So come straight to the table when you're done. Special dispensation for special circumstances."

She spun away and left him alone.

He took his hand off the receiver and addressed Isabel again. "I'm sorry," he said. "Something just distracted me. I was saying how much I appreciate your calling."

"I was so glad to hear from you. A friend of Millie's! That's what your note said. My neighbor read it to me on the phone. I was so happy because I thought Millie didn't have anyone except Luis."

"She didn't. I didn't meet her until after Luis . . ."

A silence fell. It was perhaps a second or two. Or three. But it stretched out painfully in Raymond's mind and gut and heart, like a bad week you might live through that just never seems to end.

"I'm very sorry for your loss," he said.

"Thank you." He couldn't tell if she was crying or not. Her voice was heavy and dense with emotion, and that emotion seemed to bend the words at their edges. But he wasn't sure about tears. How could he be? They were only on the phone. "So, tell me," she said. "Are you helping her now? Taking her to the store for groceries, and to the bank to deposit her checks?"

"Yes. Both. We go out every couple of days for groceries. And . . . I've been wondering about laundry. Should I be helping her do her laundry?"

"Don't worry about laundry, because Luis talked her into using a service that picks it up and brings it back clean. Well, a thousand blessings on you, then, Raymond, because I worried so much about that. About her. I swear Luis would roll over in his grave if he thought that sweet old woman was home alone with no one to help. Maybe trying to cross the street by herself, which eventually she would have been desperate enough to do. So tell me something else, Raymond. I know you just now found out what happened. That's what you said in your note. So have you told her yet?"

Raymond swallowed hard. Felt a frightened tingling sensation rise up through his belly. Into his throat.

"Not yet," he said. "I'm really sorry. I swear I was going to. Right after dinner. In my family you have to show up in time for dinner if you expect to eat. I had like six or seven minutes to spare. I couldn't go tell her and then just disappear. Leave her alone with all that. So instead I found the newspaper article. I thought I'd print it out so I could answer as many of her questions as possible. I was going to go right after dinner, I swear I was. I'm really sorry. I wasn't trying to—"

"Raymond," she said, her voice interrupting him, but gently. "Relax. I wasn't criticizing. It's just . . . I want to come meet her as soon as possible. So I was thinking, if you want, I'll tell her. Or at least be there with you when you tell her."

Raymond closed his eyes and breathed. Gasped air, really. He'd had no idea he'd been holding his breath.

"Yes, please," he said.

"Okay. Give me your address. I'll ask my mom to watch the kids. But I might have to run their baths first or get them started on their homework. I could be there in maybe an hour. I know it used to take Luis twenty minutes on the subway."

While he recited his address by rote, his mind miles away, he imagined her coming to his door. Meeting his parents. Who thought he had a new girlfriend. And there she would be. In her thirties. And pregnant.

"I'll meet you on the street out front," he said.

———

As he moved toward the kitchen doorway to join his family in the dining room, he heard his mother and stepfather talking about him.

"Well, he's obviously in love," his mother said, clearly talking to Ed. It was not the tone she would take with her children. "When he came home today he was just ruined. Just destroyed. I've never seen him look so down. They must've had a fight. And then she calls on the phone . . ."

"He still needs to get to dinner on time," Ed said.

"No. Absolutely not, Ed. Do *not* do that. You will not put your arbitrary rules on him when he's going through a thing like this. Don't you remember what it felt like to be in love? For the first time, I mean," she added, stumbling and clearly embarrassed by what she had accidentally implied.

"You can stop talking about me now," Raymond said. "Please? Because I'm coming in."

Silence.

Raymond walked into the dining room and sat at his place at the table. Looked down at his plate. It was spaghetti with plain marinara sauce and garlic bread. He sighed as quietly as possible. He never liked the way he felt after eating a meal that was almost all carbs and almost no protein. And he never slept as well.

He took a big bite, then looked up, spaghetti still hanging on to his chin, to see his sister Rhonda smiling at him. But not in a good way. Tauntingly.

A second later Raymond watched a piece of garlic bread bounce off Rhonda's forehead and tumble to the carpet.

"Leave your brother alone," Raymond's mother said.

———

Raymond paced as he waited. And paced. And paced.

It was pitch-dark out on the street in front of his building, but two streetlights shone on the scene. Raymond could see his breath. He hadn't bothered to grab a jacket, and he was cold. But not enough to drive him back inside where he might chance missing her.

Neighbors were coming home from work, walking from the subway. A few Raymond knew by sight, but most he did not. So he looked into the face of each youngish woman and wondered if that might be her.

Then, when it was, he didn't wonder. He knew. And she knew it was him. He could tell. They locked eyes and knew. Somehow their special knowledge was half of a match that identified them to each other, like the jagged-cut playing cards two strangers piece back together when they meet in a spy film.

Her long, dark hair was pinned up in the back. She wore an oversize light-blue down jacket. It did not reveal that she was pregnant. Her dark eyes looked wet, as though she had been crying, or was about to.

They walked closer to each other and stood a stride apart, saying nothing for a time. It seemed almost as though they didn't need to speak.

He glanced again at her belly without meaning to.

"I'm only two months pregnant," she said.

"Oh. Sorry."

Another long, awkward silence.

"She lives on the second floor," he said at last.

"Let's go, then."

They walked into Raymond's building in silence.

"I'm sorry about all the stairs," he said to her as they climbed to the second floor. "Some nicer apartments have elevators. But ours is just a walk-up."

"You don't have to be sorry," she said. "My apartment is a walk-up, too, and so is my parents'. But even if we had elevators, you don't have to be sorry. You didn't design the building, and I'm guessing you weren't even the one who rented here. You live here with your parents, right? You had no choice in the matter."

"You sound just like Mrs. G," he said as they reached the second-floor landing. "She's always saying I need to stop being so sorry for everything. Actually . . . a lot of people have been telling me that lately."

"Then that's probably an important thing for you to think about."

Raymond looked away from her face and saw they were standing in front of Mrs. G's door. It surprised him. It felt as though he had led her there on some kind of human autopilot.

He raised a hand to knock. But for a long moment he did not knock.

"Oh, I hate this," he said.

"Has to be done, though," Isabel said.

He knocked. His special Morse code knock. Rap. Rap-rap-rap. Rap.

He could hear her immediately on the other side of the door. Hear her make her way quickly across the living room. He could hear the bell on the cat's collar as Louise skittered out of her way. At least, he hoped out of her way.

"Oh, good! Raymond!" she called to him through the door. She spoke to him as she undid the locks. "I thought maybe you would not come today. But I'm so glad you did. I've grown so used to having you come by to see me. I missed that, thinking you might skip today."

As she spoke, Raymond could feel a pressure growing in his chest. As though his heart were being compressed in a vise. Or crushed by one of those huge machines that turn junk cars into cubes of metal.

She was happy.

They were about to end all that.

She threw the door wide and looked up at him with a face that gleamed. Her smile reminded him of Luis's smile in the photo, in that it took over everything. Dominated her face until it became the only possible focus.

"Oh," she said. "You have somebody with you."

"Yeah," Raymond said. "I do. I brought somebody. For you to meet. This is Isabel Velez."

For a few seconds, her smile grew even wider and more beaming. Which Raymond would have thought impossible.

"*Isabel Velez*? Is that really you? Why, Luis told me so much about you that I feel as though I know you already! I'm so—" Then she stopped. Stopped talking. Stopped smiling. Stopped beaming. "Oh," she said. "Oh. Oh. I see now. He's gone. He's really gone, isn't he?"

Isabel Velez burst into tears. As literally as Raymond could imagine a person doing. A sob simply burst out of her and then she did not stop sobbing.

Mrs. G did not sob. In fact, she never made a sound. But her eyes filled and then spilled over.

Raymond watched dry-eyed for a few seconds. Then he worked hard to hold back tears. Then he decided it was not a thing worth working for, so he let them have their way.

As he stood, watching the two women and letting himself cry for the first time in as long as he could remember, he noticed something about himself. His self-consciousness, his physical self-awareness—it was gone. It must have been gone for approximately as long as he'd known Mrs. G. She had pulled him out of himself and set him down in a place that was not all about him anymore.

Chapter Nine

The Brooklyn Bridge

"I could tell you a lot more," he heard Isabel say. "If you wanted me to. A lot more detail. But maybe it's better if I don't."

Raymond was in the kitchen fixing cookies and tea for the three of them. He had watched Mrs. G make tea enough times to know how it was done. And he had wanted to make himself scarce while Isabel told Mrs. G what had happened to Luis. Still, he could hear everything that was said in the next room, where the two women sat at the table.

"First I'd want to be sure you really care to hear more," Isabel added. "The details are hard, I know. It's all so hard for me to say, and I can only imagine how hard it must be for you to hear. But one thing I really need to say is that I would've come sooner if I could have. Luis's phone was destroyed in the shooting, and he didn't have his contacts backed up anywhere else. If I'd known where to find you, I would have come right away. Like I said to Raymond, Luis would roll over in his grave if he thought you were here alone, with no one to walk you to the store."

"What I want you to tell me," Mrs. G said, "is how all of this has been for you and your family. How are you getting by? Do you have someone to help look after the children? Are you all right day to day? Is there anything I can do?"

Raymond missed most of the answer because the teakettle boiled on the stove. It whistled when it was ready. Raymond turned off the gas flame and used an oven mitt to pick up the kettle to pour. The handle got hot.

Then he hung in the kitchen a moment too long. The tea was steeping. The cookies had been arranged on a plate. It was time to rejoin them. But he couldn't bring himself to do so. He felt as though the women were enjoying a moment of privacy that he might inadvertently shatter.

"How did you find me now, then?" Mrs. G asked. Strangely belatedly.

"I didn't. I didn't find you at all. Raymond found *me*."

Upon hearing his name, Raymond hurried out with the tea and cookies. As he did, he made a mental note to return Isabel's chair to exactly the right spot at the table when this meeting was over.

Mrs. G turned her face up to Raymond.

"That's right, isn't it? You brought Isabel to my door." Her voice was low and a little shaky, as if she might be right at the edge of tears again. "How did you do this, my young friend?"

"I just made a list of every Luis Velez in New York."

"So did I. Not a written one, but I got the telephone listings. But I could never get my calls answered by the right one."

"I didn't call," Raymond said, sitting down at the table with them. Picking up a cookie. He felt embarrassed for some reason. As if he wanted everyone to stop staring. But it was a foolish thought, because Isabel was gazing blankly through the curtained window, and Mrs. G couldn't see him. "I went to each apartment in person."

"To how many places?"

"I don't remember exactly. If you only count the places where someone came to the door . . . I guess . . . six or seven."

"By yourself you did this? You could have been robbed!"

Raymond laughed. "I have nothing for them to take."

"Or hurt."

An image filled his mind. Luis Velez with the buzzed-off hair and the soul patch. His face close to Raymond's, the smell of onions on his breath. The desperate, helpless feeling of falling, and the thought that Luis might have been more meanly teasing Raymond than genuinely threatening him, and that Raymond's fear might have been too extreme.

"I wasn't, though," he said.

The rest of the experience would stay with him and him only. Safe inside.

"I'm surprised that he found me," Isabel interjected. "Because I took the kids and went to stay with my parents after Luis . . . after the shooting."

"I got lucky," Raymond said, when he was sure Isabel did not plan to say more. "I talked to this Luis Velez in the Bronx who told me about a newspaper article. So then I knew it was the Luis M. Velez on the Upper East Side, where nobody ever answered the door. I went there to leave a note, but while I was there I ran into a neighbor who knew where Isabel was."

A silence fell. Nobody filled it.

"I brought your tea," he added.

He placed the pot in front of Mrs. G's place at the table. In case she wasn't sure where it was. She had always seemed to find it in the past, though. Raymond suspected her hands could be guided by its heat.

"I still can't believe you did that," she said. "You did all of that for me?"

"Well . . . yeah. I mean, you were so miserable. Not knowing. But now I wonder if that was better. You know. The not knowing. If it's a really terrible thing like this . . . was it better not to know?"

Mrs. G sighed deeply. Poured herself a cup of tea, placing her finger just inside the rim as a gauge.

"Right now it is very hard," she said, "but I think in the long run I will tell you it is always best to know. In this moment I'm still caught up in the fact that you did this huge thing for me, and I can't seem to get my words together to tell you how grateful I am. But I will. I promise you I will. My thoughts are all over the landscape. As to the question you asked me, Isabel. If I want to know more of the terrible details. I think I want—or actually need, really—for you to tell me that Luis did not suffer. But of course you can only do that if it's true. I'm not asking you to lie to me just to make me feel the tiniest bit better. But also I want you to say what you can bear to say and not one word more. If you can't bear to relive this, then don't do it for me. Please."

"The medical examiner said he was killed instantly," Isabel said.

"All right, then. I am afraid this will have to be the small favor for which I attempt to be thankful."

———

"Oh, you have a cat," Isabel said after several minutes of sipping their tea in silence. "Luis didn't tell me you had a cat."

"She is new here," Mrs. G said. "Where do you see her?"

She was speaking normally. Almost casually. But her voice had lost something, Raymond thought. It had lost its energy. Its unique brand of aliveness. It felt almost as though Mrs. G's voice had lost Mrs. G, and was now existing on its own, without her.

"She just stuck her head out from under the couch. But then she took one look at me and went right back under again."

"She was wild for part of her life. Not all of it, I don't think. She does not behave like a cat who has never known people. But still she is quite wary. I'm not surprised that she would hide when a new person is at hand."

"I don't think I have to tell you that Luis adored you," Isabel said, turning the conversation suddenly back around. Out of small-talk territory. "Because I know he was not a man who would make a secret of a thing like that."

"The feeling was definitely mutual," Mrs. G said in return. A tiny glimpse of her old self peeked out through those words.

Raymond heard himself let out a sigh of relief. Even though he would never in a million years have welcomed this outcome, he felt deeply relieved that Mrs. G had been right. That Luis really had loved her.

"He told me you were the only person he'd ever met who didn't have one prejudiced bone in your entire body," Isabel said. "Not even one hair on your head with a slight bias—that's what he said. For the first couple of years he kept looking for some of that when he was with you. Some little bit of judgment. He figured, yeah, of course, you were better than most. Better than ninety-nine percent of the people he met. But he figured he'd find some little scrap of something in there somewhere, because he mostly always did with people. But not you. He just stopped looking after a while. He said if there was one thing he could say about you, one big thing that defined you, it's that you value every human life the same. He said if you were a story, your title would be something like 'Every Life Has Value.' He really admired that about you. And it confused him a little, too. He kept wondering how a person gets put together that way, but he never found out. He could never figure out the roots of that."

"I don't think every life has exactly the same value," Mrs. G said. "I think Rosa Parks's life had more value than Adolf Hitler's. But I think that's a different kind of a subject than what you meant."

"I think so, too. I'll bring the kids around to meet you. But maybe when things settle down a little more."

"I would love that," Mrs. G replied. But she was gone from her voice again.

"I always meant to," Isabel added.

Her voice sounded heavy with that special brand of guilt Raymond had heard so much of in the past few days. How many people had told him lately of things they had always imagined themselves doing, but then life had intervened and the things had gone undone? And with that weighty tone of regret.

"I always meant to bring them and come around. Luis and I talked about it all the time. We wanted you to meet the whole family. I have no words for why it didn't happen. No explanation. We were busy with the two kids. Then I got pregnant again. But that's no excuse. There's no real reason why we didn't. We just made the mistake of putting it off. We thought we would lose nothing by putting it off. We thought we had plenty of time. I guess that was our key mistake, right? We thought there would always be more time. Why do we do that? I mean, not just Luis and me. Everybody. Why does everybody do that? Think we'll always have more time?"

"Well, *I* don't do that," Mrs. G said. "But that's a different story. When I was a young girl I had an experience that taught me not to take time for granted. And now that I'm ninety-two, I know it even better."

"But we were taking for granted that we would always have more time with a ninety-two-year-old woman. It was a whole wrong way of looking at the world. Like death wasn't real and would never really catch up."

"Oh, it's all too real," Mrs. G said. "That I can tell you."

"I know that now. I know it all too well. Now that it's caught up."

A pause.

Then Mrs. G spoke up suddenly.

"Well. I hate even to say it, because I am so very grateful that you came. But I am just so tired. I feel I have not one ounce of energy left for anything, not even to hold myself upright at the table. And I very much hope it will not sound rude, but if you will assure me that I will see you again, I think I had best put myself to bed. I know it seems very early to you. Seven o'clock or so, I'm guessing. But I am just so tired."

"Of course," Isabel said. "No, that's fine. I'll write down my address and phone number for Raymond."

But Mrs. G was already walking away. Shuffling off toward her bedroom, waving over her shoulder.

Raymond and Isabel sat a moment. They looked into each other's face. Then Raymond quickly looked away.

"Is she all right?" Isabel asked.

"I don't know. I never saw her do that before—run out of energy to sit in a chair. Then again, I don't usually visit in the evening, after dinner. Still, I think the news hit her hard. I'll get you a pen and paper."

But then Raymond was unsure where to find such a thing in Mrs. G's apartment.

"I think I have something in my purse," she said.

She dug around in there for a moment. It was a full purse, a hard place to find anything as far as Raymond could tell. In the middle of trying, she displaced an item and knocked it onto the rug. A sunglasses case, from the look of it. She reached down for it, then froze. Raymond wondered if they were both thinking the same thing. He figured they were.

Who would have imagined that dropping an item out of your purse could be the first act in a cascade of events that could get somebody killed?

A second later she unstuck herself and picked it up.

"I could come by now and again, too," Isabel said. "Not to suggest for a moment that you can't help her enough. I'm sure you can. But now that I know where she is, I would love to have her meet the children."

"Maybe you can come visit her over the weekend. I stay with my father and his wife every other weekend. This weekend is when I'll be there. I might be able to get away, but it's hard to know. I never know if my dad's made plans for us or not. Until I get there."

"Okay," she said. "I'll gather up the kids and come by."

"When is the trial?" Raymond asked as she began to write down her address.

"They think it'll be scheduled sometime next year."

"*Next year?* Why so long?"

Isabel shrugged. "Just the way the justice system works, I guess. Slowly. I'm told that's lightning fast. The DA's office told me a lot of defendants are waiting two and three years for their trials."

She slid the paper across the table to him, and he picked it up and tucked it deep into a front pocket of his jeans.

"And where is that woman in the meantime? In jail?"

"Oh no. They let her out on bail. She's comfortable at home, I'm sure."

She stood, so he stood. They walked to the door together.

It didn't seem fair to Raymond that the woman should be comfortable at home. But there was nothing he could do about it. Saying so out loud wouldn't change a thing.

"Thank you so much for coming," he said. "I'll walk you down. Or . . . to the subway. Would you like me to walk you to the subway?"

"Either way. I'll be all right either way."

He opened the door for her, and realized the flaw in their thinking.

"Oh. Wait. I have no way to lock her in. If I walk with you, she'll be here with the door unlocked."

"Stay with her and work that out, then. Take care of her. I'll be fine."

"Can I ask you a question before you go? Was there anything in the paper about it before Sunday?"

"Not that I know of," she said. "I guess a lot of people die in this city."

"I did an internet search. But I couldn't even find an obituary."

"There *was* one," she said. "But it only came out about a week ago. They charge a lot for that. Did you know that? I had to wait for my paycheck. I thought a newspaper did that like a public service. But no, the family has to pay."

"I did know that," he said. "Yeah. The family has to pay."

She stood up on her tiptoes, placed one hand on Raymond's forearm, and kissed him quickly on the cheek. Then she walked out.

He watched her walk down the hall, feeling that spot on his cheek burning. As if the very skin of his face were capable of embarrassment.

He closed the door again and walked through Mrs. G's living room. Down the apartment's hallway. Not all the way to the open door of Mrs. G's bedroom, because she might need her privacy. But near enough that she could hear him.

"How do I lock you in?" he asked.

"You may come to my room," she said. "It's all right."

He did. Hesitantly. Just to the doorway, where he leaned one hand on the jamb. Mrs. G was still fully dressed, lying on top of the bedspread. She had taken off her shoes, and pulled a crocheted afghan over herself. She looked more than exhausted. She looked helpless and lost. Utterly incapable of facing this moment.

The cat sat in a sphinxlike position on her pillow, purring. She looked up at Raymond with half-closed, contented eyes. Mrs. G's eyes, on the other hand, remained fully closed.

"Take my keys," she said. "Then you can lock me in and come check on me later, please. If you will. Tomorrow sometime, maybe."

"Okay. I will. Are you really going to sleep in your clothes all night? Won't that be uncomfortable?"

"I'm not sure. If I wake up later, and it bothers me, I'll change into a nightgown. Right now it feels like more than I can manage."

"Are you sure you're okay?"

"I'm not sick, if that's what you mean. I heard you ask where that woman is now. Until trial. But I couldn't hear what Isabel said in reply."

"Out on bail."

"Oh. I see."

"It doesn't seem fair."

"That is our system of justice," Mrs. G said.

"But why should she get to be all comfortable in her own home while we're going through this?"

"Oh, I doubt she is comfortable."

"Why would you say that?"

She opened her eyes. But her face lacked the enthusiasm, the engagement, he usually saw there.

"It is a huge thing, Raymond, to take a human life. Which is not to say that I've ever done it. I have not. But it must weigh on a person. Guilt is a terrible thing—that I can tell you for a fact. It tears a person apart from the inside. So I feel a little pity for her. I'm not saying I have no bad feelings toward her; I have many. But also I feel a little bit sorry for her. I would rather be me, home in my bed, having had Luis taken away from me, than to be that woman and know I had been the one to take him away. If she has a conscience, then it's a terrible thing to have to live with. If she has no conscience, then I feel sorry for her because she has no conscience. There is a saying. I think it was said by Mark Twain, but I might be wrong about that. It might have been Will Rogers. 'I would rather be the man who buys the Brooklyn Bridge than the man who sells it.' Words to that effect. You're a bright young man, so I think you know what he meant by that."

"Yeah. I think I do."

"Good. Now, I am just very tired."

Raymond picked up her keys on his way to the door. Then he stopped. Turned back. Realized what he had forgotten.

He hurried to the table and replaced the chair he had used, carefully aligning it with its tape marks. He replaced Isabel's chair as best he could, in against the table where Mrs. G would not trip over it. Assuming, of course, that she got up.

Then he let himself out.

—

He sat in front of his computer composing an email to Isabel.

She had written down her email address as well as her parents' street address and phone number. Raymond wanted to give her Mrs. G's phone number. And by emailing her, she would have his email address, too.

Or at least, that was the neat bundle of reasons he had given himself. As he typed, a greater truth began to emerge.

I'm really worried about her. That was the first thing he wrote.

> She went to bed for the night and didn't even change out of her clothes. She said it was too much trouble, or too much energy. Something like that. I forget her exact words. I know it hit her really hard, what happened to Luis. And I knew it would, so it's stupid to write all this like I'm surprised or something. I guess I just needed to tell someone that I'm worried.

> She even said she's not sick, but

His computer burst into a weird series of tones, like sudden music, and it made him jump. Literally. He shot straight up into the air a few inches and came down with his heart pounding.

Then he realized it was only Skype. The ringtone you get when someone is Skype-calling you. A little round avatar photo of Andre had popped up onto his screen. He clicked the video call button, even though he would have preferred to finish his email.

"Hey," he said.

"Hey," Andre said in return.

Andre was smiling widely. Raymond checked his own face in the little inset screen that monitored his end of the call. He was not smiling.

"So, what's wrong with you, man?" Andre asked.

"Nothing," Raymond said. "Just a long day. Hard day."

"Tell me about it."

"Nah. Not worth it."

Raymond had found himself suddenly drowning in the feeling that he was not the same person who had been friends with Andre. That he had changed into someone Andre would not understand.

And besides, he thought, *we never talked about the really important stuff anyway.*

"How's the new school?" Raymond asked, mostly to change the subject.

"Not sure. It's only been a few days. The first few days are always the hardest anyway. So what about you? What's going on? Where you been, man?"

"Nothing's going on."

"Really? Seems like something is. I've opened up my Skype, like, two dozen times to try to call you, but you're never online. Since when did you get busy? And with what? Or is it a who?"

"I'm not seeing anybody."

This was one of the deeper and more important things they had never talked about.

"What, then? Why the big mystery?"

"It's not. It's just . . ." Then Raymond decided he was being silly. Why *would* he keep it a secret? If Andre didn't understand, then he just didn't. But it was nothing Raymond should be ashamed to say. "You remember that older lady? In the hall on your last day?"

"The crazy one? The 'Have you seen Luis Valdez' one?"

"Velez. And she's not crazy. Not at all. She has a really good mind. She's just blind, and that's why you got that weird feeling about where she was looking."

"Oh. Okay. So she's not crazy. But she's, like . . . ninety."

"Actually she's ninety-two. But she's nice. And interesting. And I've been learning a lot from her and sort of helping her."

"Why?"

A silence, during which Raymond studied the video image of his old friend's face. Andre was not interested in this line of conversation. Raymond could tell. He had that slightly blank look in his eyes, the one he used to get when Raymond had tried to discuss the political or historical books he had been reading.

"Because she's got nobody else."

"But you'll find her somebody. Right?"

"What do you mean 'find her somebody'?"

"Like you can call some sort of county services thing and get somebody to come out and help her. Right? So then you don't have to."

"I don't mind doing it. I told you. She's interesting and nice. I like talking to her."

"But she's ninety."

"I don't mind it. I'm telling you that, and you're not hearing me."

Raymond was growing irritated. He'd tried to keep it out of his voice, but he knew he had failed.

"Okay. Whatever. Whatever you wanna do, Raymond. I don't care. So, at my new school there's this chess club, but it's just so totally different from the one—"

"You know what?" Raymond interjected. "It's been a really long day. And I have to finish this email. Can I Skype you back sometime when I have a little more time?"

"Uh . . ."

A long pause. Andre was surprised and a little hurt. Raymond could tell. It hurt when two friends couldn't meet in the same place they had used to. But if that was the truth, it was the truth. Raymond didn't see the point of prolonging or denying it.

"Yeah," Andre said. "Sure. Okay."

Raymond said goodbye and clicked off the call.

At first he did not imagine himself Skyping Andre back anytime soon. Then, as he sat staring at the application screen, he realized that

Andre had meant no harm by being unable to understand, and that his old friend was alone in a new place.

So Raymond finished his email, and by then he had cooled down enough to call Andre back and be civil. Possibly even helpful.

They didn't speak of Mrs. G again, which was likely for the best.

Chapter Ten

Make for Us This World

Raymond left fifteen minutes early for school, so he could stop and check on her.

He knocked his special knock. Twice. Got no reply.

He let himself in with her keys.

He stood in her empty living room and called to her.

"Mrs. G? Hello?"

"Hello, Raymond," he heard her say.

But the words came to him quietly. She was still in the bedroom, and her voice was soft. She was not doing a good job of projecting.

He walked down the hall and stopped a couple of steps short of the open bedroom door. Reached out and knocked on the jamb.

"You may come in," she said. "It's all right."

He stepped into the open doorway.

She lay on her bed in a soft spill of light that poured through the curtained window. She was still fully dressed, in the same clothes, with the afghan thrown over her. The cat was curled up on the bed between her right arm and her side. Mrs. G was petting her absentmindedly with her left hand. She seemed to be staring out the window, as if fascinated by something specific. But of course that was impossible.

"You never changed into your nightgown."

"No," she said. Simply. Quietly.

"Have you gotten up at all since I last saw you? Can you get up if you need to?"

"I got up once to use the toilet."

"Have you eaten?"

"I'm not hungry."

"I'll make you something before I go to school."

"Oh, I don't know, Raymond. I'm not sure I can stomach much."

"I'll make you cambric tea and toast. Can you eat that?"

"I might be able to eat cinnamon-sugar toast. My mother used to make it for me with my cambric tea when I was unhappy. You just sprinkle a little sugar on top of the melted butter, and then some cinnamon from the spice rack."

"Okay," Raymond said. "I'll be right back."

———

He brought it to her on a polished wooden tray from her pantry, and she sat up with some effort to allow him to place the tray on her lap.

She took one bite of the toast and sighed. Not in a bad way, he thought.

"This was very good of you," she said. "And the way you have made it is just exactly correct."

Raymond glanced at the clock radio beside her bed. He would be late for school, even if he left now. But he was going nowhere until he was sure she was okay on her own.

"Anything else you need before I go?" he asked, sitting lightly on the edge of her bed.

"You can make this world into a place where no one would ever shoot Luis, because they would never have their gun already drawn. Or better yet because they weren't carrying a gun at all. Because why would they shoot? He was only walking on the street with them, and if they had never met him, what cause would they have to judge? Why would they perceive a threat from a man only walking along? If you could make the world into such a place, that would be very helpful to me. Well. Forget me. It would have been helpful to Luis. It would be helpful to everyone."

He sat in silence for a moment, feeling stung. He watched her take another bite of her toast.

"You know I can't do that."

"Yes. I do know. And I hope that was not the wrong way to make my point. All I am saying is that people need a world that no one seems to be able to create. And since it can't be fixed, I think only time will help. I think I need a great deal of time for this thing that has happened to move through me. But the fact that you want to help means more to me than I can say. It means the world, Raymond. That and the idea of those children, his children, coming to meet me and know me. They and you might be the only things holding me down to the earth right now. Oh, and this little cat. She has been such a comfort to me, sitting on my lap and purring. And I'd like you to stop to think which of these things I would have if you had not befriended me. Think about it, Raymond. Everything that is holding me down on the planet right now is something you brought into my life. And speaking of right now . . . aren't you going to be late for school?"

"Yeah," he said. "Getting toward late."

But he didn't move.

"Go," she said. "What do you think will change while you are gone? Nothing will change. I will be right here."

Reluctantly—very reluctantly—he left her and ran all the way to school.

———

He stopped in on the way home, hoping to see that she had moved while he was away.

She had not moved.

She was sitting up on the bed, the cat on her lap. Dressed in the same clothes. Staring in the same direction.

"Have you eaten?" That was the first thing he asked her.

She answered with only a sigh.

"If I make you something, will you eat it?"

"I don't really feel very much like eating," she said, turning her head vaguely in his direction. "I did get up and feed the cat, though. That's the lovely thing about having an animal. You might not want to get up for your own sake, but you will bring yourself to do it for them. But I didn't feel hungry."

Raymond sat on the very edge of her bed.

"But that wasn't really the question, though. Not so much if you felt hungry or felt like eating. I was asking if you *would* eat. If I fixed something and brought it in here, if you would at least try to get some of it down the way you did this morning. Because people need food to live. And the food doesn't care if you really wanted it or not. It nourishes you either way."

They sat in silence for a minute or two.

Then she said, "I feel like I'm letting you down, Raymond. Like I'm holding you back from the way you deserve to live."

For some reason it made his face tingle. Almost a fear response. Or maybe embarrassment.

"I'm not sure why you would say that."

"You want me to be okay. To get up and feel better. And go on."

"Yeah," he said. "And you want me to make the world a place where nobody would shoot Luis, because their gun would still be in their purse when they found out he was only trying to return their wallet. But I'm not taking it on that I can't do that for you. I'm not seeing that as any personal failure on my part."

"Good point, my friend. Good point."

Another silent minute or two.

"Maybe a scrambled egg," she said.

"Coming right up."

"I feel bad having you wait on me hand and foot like this."

"Don't," he said. "It's no trouble."

"What did I do to deserve such a good friend as you, Raymond?"

It might have been a lightly tossed-off comment. Raymond wasn't sure. But he decided to approach it as a genuine question.

"I think you're the first person I've ever known . . . I might not say it right. We'll see . . . who really sees me. And I mean the whole thing of me, not just the part that fits with how they want to see me. And it seems weird to me, because the first person I met who really sees me for all of who I am . . . you know . . . can't see."

"When it comes to seeing what is important about a person," she said, "I think it's possible that what our eyes tell us is only a distraction. Not that I wouldn't take them back if I could. Oh, I would. I miss seeing. But I also like the things I've learned to see without them."

"What if I made you *two* scrambled eggs?" he asked, sensing a slight lift in the mood. Both of their moods. "Would you try to eat two?"

"Yes. For Raymond, at least I will try."

———

When he arrived back at his own apartment, he closed himself into his room and opened his laptop. He found what he had hoped to find: an email from Isabel.

Dear Raymond, it said.

> I think it's hitting us all hard, those of us who knew him well. But this is new information for her, so be patient. It's nice that you're worried about her, but

people take time to process bad news. I'm not even going to try to tell you that worry is not appropriate. Maybe it is. I'm only going to remind you of something you likely already know: that there's not a whole lot you can do to help her with this. You're making sure she has her basic needs met, and that's a lot.

I'll come by with the kids on Saturday, while you're away at your father's.

Should I think about running to the store for her, or will you be making sure she has enough in the house to eat before you go?

Thanks for everything. You're a very sweet boy.

Sincerely,
Isabel Velez

Raymond sat a minute, feeling the way his face burned whenever someone said a thing like that to him. Even in writing. Even when they were nowhere around.

Then he hit "Reply."

Isabel, he typed.

I'll go through her cupboards this week and make sure she's stocked up on everything. It's hard to get her to eat much, but there have to be enough groceries in the house that I can push her to eat a little, which is what I've been doing. You might try

getting her to eat something while you're there.
If it works, I'll appreciate it. Or even if it doesn't,
thank you for trying.

—Raymond

No sooner had he hit "Send" than the door to his room flew open, and his mother's voice bellowed in.

"Get off the line with your girlfriend and come eat dinner," she said. "I can't believe I had to call you twice."

———

His father's wife opened the apartment door. His stepmother, he should probably have called her. But she was less than ten years older than Raymond, so it felt too weird.

He tended to call her by her first name, despite having no idea if she objected to that or not.

"Hi, Neesha," he said.

It was Friday afternoon, and he had no choice but to show up at this door. It was the way his life had been planned out for him. He had no way of influencing the situation. Not that he minded seeing his father; that was generally good. But it was uncomfortable to have to show up on Friday before the man was even home.

"Raymond," she said in reply.

That's all. Just "Raymond." Not "Hello." Not "How are you?" or even "Come in." Just a statement of his name, a random fact. A bit of trivia she probably felt she was doing well enough by remembering.

He stood in silence in the hallway, looking down at her through the open apartment door. His canvas duffel bag rested on one shoulder. It was beginning to feel heavy.

"He's still at the office?"

"Yeah. So what's new?"

She stepped backward out of the doorway. Raymond knew it was the closest she would come to inviting him in. Then again, this was a custody arrangement. He lived here every other weekend by order of a judge. It did not require her permission.

He moved into the living room and stood, still carrying the heavy duffel bag on his shoulder. There were two twenty-dollar bills on the coffee table. He stared down at them, not sure if he wanted to bring them up in conversation. They might have been his allowance. His father often gave him a fairly generous allowance, at least compared to Ed. But he didn't dare pick them up until he knew for sure.

It might have been a test. Sometimes with Neesha there were tests.

"I have my book group tonight," she said when she noticed him staring at the bills. "And I didn't get a chance to cook anything."

It seemed like an odd statement to Raymond, because she never cooked on the Fridays when he arrived.

"So order some pizza for you and Malcolm," she added.

She never called him "your dad" or "your father." Never. She seemed to be in some disagreement about that reality. Or at least a degree of denial.

"You know what he likes on it. Right?"

"Yeah. Same things I do."

Like father, like son. Whether you like it or not.

"I have to go," she said.

She grabbed up her purse and let herself out. Raymond walked into his secondary bedroom and dropped the duffel bag onto the bed. Then he came out and turned on the TV.

He had forgotten to bring the book he'd been in the middle of reading. There wasn't much else to do.

—

His father didn't come home until almost seven o'clock in the evening.

Raymond looked up from his pizza as he heard the door being unlocked.

His father came in with his jacket over one shoulder, despite the fact that it was fairly cold outside. He held a never-lit cigar in his teeth, and Raymond knew he was not allowed to smoke it in the house. He smiled when he saw Raymond sitting on the couch, watching TV. Which was nice, as far as a thing like that goes.

"I started without you," Raymond said, holding up a half-eaten slice of pizza. "Sorry. I was hungry."

"I don't blame you." His father was a big man with a deep, booming bass of a voice. Yet utterly unintimidating. Raymond had gotten his height from his father, but not his thin frame. "I had an emergency. A patient with a lost crown. I can throw a slice in the microwave. It's okay."

"Don't use the microwave. It kills the crust. Warm a piece up in the oven. Or I will. If you're too tired."

His father shrugged. "Tastes fine to me from the microwave."

He disappeared into the kitchen.

Raymond heard the beeping of the microwave oven.

Not two minutes later, his father came out with a slice on a paper plate. He dropped heavily onto the couch beside Raymond and loosened his tie. Clapped Raymond on the knee. Then he kicked off his shoes and put his sock feet up on the coffee table.

Raymond stared at his father's feet for a moment. "Might as well get that feet-up thing out of your system before Neesha comes home," he said, "huh?"

"I'll say. What are you watching?"

Truthfully, Raymond had to struggle to remember. He had to look at the screen for clues. He had been switching from channel to channel, and his mind had been somewhere else most of the time.

"Um. Some kind of mystery about extraterrestrial life, I think. It's not very realistic."

"What have I missed so far?"

"I'm not sure. I haven't been paying very good attention."

He had been mostly worrying about Mrs. G.

They sat staring at the screen together. Raymond wondered if his father was paying any better attention than Raymond was. They didn't speak. They mostly didn't speak when together.

Raymond figured he got along fine with his father. They had no beefs with each other, and never argued. But they went nearly two weeks at a time without seeing each other. And then, when they got together again, neither one of them seemed to be able to think of much to say. If anything.

———

On Sunday, midmorning, they sat in their favorite restaurant together. The brunch place. The one where Raymond had taken Mrs. G.

"I asked your stepmother to join us," his father said. "But she brought some work home that she has to get done by tomorrow."

Raymond stared at his menu, even though he already knew what he wanted. At first he thought he would let the statement go by. Just let it stand, the way he always did.

Then, to his surprise, he shook off the complacency that had always held him down in the past.

"You make excuses for her every time she ditches spending time with us. But she doesn't like me, and I don't know why we can't just talk about that out loud. It's so obvious. It's not like I don't notice."

He watched his father as the words sank in. Watched the dark skin of his face crease and fall.

Raymond regretted having spoken. The idea had not been to hurt the man, but apparently that was what Raymond had done.

"You're misunderstanding the situation, Raymond."

"I'm sorry if I upset you. But I don't think I am."

"In a way you are. I'm not saying she's not closed off to you. Of course she is. But when you say she doesn't like you, I can tell you have a wrong impression. You think it has something to do with you, but it doesn't. She doesn't dislike who you are. She probably doesn't even know who you are. She looks at you, and all she can see is a whole life I had with another woman before I met her. That's her problem."

Raymond said nothing. Just studied his menu. He figured what his father had said was probably true. It certainly had a ring of truth to it. He wasn't sure this new perspective improved the situation, though.

The waiter came to take their order. They both ordered omelets. Raymond ordered tea with milk. There were packets of sugar in the middle of the table. He didn't have to ask for them. His father ordered champagne.

"So you have a girlfriend now," his father said when the waiter had moved off again. "That's big news."

"I don't have a girlfriend. Mom got that wrong."

"Oh."

A pause. Raymond could feel himself stuck in that feeling again. The one that said he was hurting his father without meaning to. So he volunteered more in an effort to make things better.

"I'm just making some new friends is all."

"Glad to hear that. So, other boys, then?"

"No," Raymond said, wishing he could leave it at that, but knowing he probably couldn't.

"So it *is* a girl."

"I don't think I'd call her a girl. She's over ninety."

"Oh," his father said again. In fact, his father said "oh" a lot. Words did not seem to come easily to the man, nor in great quantities. "Why does your mom think otherwise?"

"I don't know. I told her it's just a friend thing, but she won't listen. She just figures I have a girlfriend but I don't want to admit it."

"So you've told her what it isn't but not what it is?"

"Pretty much. Yeah. I don't think she'd understand. It's hard to explain why I like to be around this new friend. I mean, at first it was just because she needed me to be. She's blind, and she needs some help, and the person who was helping her just got killed. But that's not the only thing. I like spending time around her. We talk."

His father nodded a few times but said nothing.

Their tea and champagne arrived. They sipped in silence for another minute or two.

"Since when do you drink tea?" his father asked. As if he had only just awakened and noticed it there.

"Pretty much the last couple of weeks."

"Oh."

Then another silence. But this one was different. His father was trying to fight his way up through it, and Raymond could feel that. Feel his struggle. He wondered how much of the time that was true. How many of their silences were not fully voluntary on his father's end of things.

Maybe they shared more in common than Raymond had realized.

"When I was a little younger than you," his father began, "maybe in my early teens, there was a guy in our neighborhood. Used to walk his dog down to the playground. The dog had a ton of energy, so the other boys used to play with the dog, but I used to sit on the bench and talk to the man. The Colonel, we called him, because he used to be a colonel in the army. Career military, retired. He was an older guy. Fifty, maybe. Maybe even sixty. I liked him because he talked to me like a man, not like a kid. And because he seemed to have more of a handle on life than the other adults I knew. So maybe it's something like that?"

"Yeah!" Raymond said, realizing too late that he was nearly shouting. "Yeah, almost exactly like that. I listen to her talk, and I feel like she understands the world. How to live in it, you know? Then I listen to other people talk, and it sounds like they're just faking it."

Except his father hadn't been faking it. At least, not just now, as he'd told Raymond the story about the Colonel. But Raymond wasn't quite sure how to wrap that into words and acknowledge it.

"I think your mom is capable of understanding that."

"I'd hate to say it to her."

"Why?"

"Because she's one of the people who's just faking it."

"I see. Well, you're a thoughtful young man. You'll work it out in your own way."

Raymond almost asked his father why he'd waited so long to pay Raymond a genuine compliment, but he couldn't bear to see the man's face fall again, so he kept his thoughts to himself.

His father pulled out his wallet and selected two twenties, sliding them over the table to Raymond.

"Thank you," Raymond said.

"Don't flaunt it in front of Ed."

"No. I won't."

Raymond had already decided that if his father gave him money, he would order an omelet to take out. To take back with him at the end of the day. Spinach, tomato, and cheese. Any kind of cheese. With sour cream for the top.

He could warm it up for her in her oven.

Maybe it would be more food temptation than she could resist.

———

"Come in, Raymond," she said through the door.

Raymond opened the locks with his keys. Or . . . her keys, really. But lately they had stayed with him.

She was sitting up on the couch, which seemed like shockingly good news to Raymond. She had changed her clothes—changed into the red housedress with the pinstripes. Her hair was clean and braided.

Then he remembered that Isabel and the kids had visited her the day before. She had probably put herself together nicely for their visit. Whether she had done so again since, Raymond couldn't tell.

Still progress, he thought.

"What have you brought?" she asked. "Something to eat."

"How do you *do* that?" Then he realized the answer was fairly simple in this case. "Oh. Right. Your nose."

"Yes. My nose is telling me all kinds of lovely things, but I'm not sure enough yet, so I will only wait and see."

"Have you eaten?"

"Not today. No. Yesterday Isabel brought pizza. But not yet today."

Raymond shook his head as he walked into her kitchen. "Good thing I'm back, then," he muttered to himself.

"I heard that, you know."

"Sorry. I'm going to warm up part of this in the oven for you."

"All right. Thank you. I hope it's what I think it is."

He pulled a knife from her drawer and cut the omelet into two-thirds and one-third sections. He found a casserole dish with a lid in her cupboard, and placed the smaller portion inside it. Closed the takeout container and found a spot for it in her fridge, leaving the little cup of sour cream out on the counter.

There was leftover pizza in there. And an open bottle of white wine, the cork replaced to keep it fresh.

"There's wine in your refrigerator," he said.

"Yes, there is."

"From Isabel?"

"Correct. She thought half a glass with dinner might help me sleep better."

"Did it help?"

"Hard to say. I didn't sleep all that well. But I suppose it didn't hurt."

"Want half a glass with your . . ." He almost said "omelet." But he wanted to preserve the surprise. ". . . dinner?"

"That would be nice. Thank you."

"Let's hope you don't end up with a drinking problem," he said. He was ninety-five percent kidding, and he hoped that came through in his voice.

To his surprise, she laughed. Quite naturally. As if someone dear hadn't just died.

"Considering I would fall dead asleep after less than one glass," she said, "I suppose I will take my chances with that."

———

He guided her to the table, and slid her chair in underneath her as she sat.

"I was right," she said. "It's what I thought it was! I almost worried that it was too much to hope for."

"Spinach, tomato, and cheese."

"With sour cream?"

"Of course."

"Your father took you to that lovely restaurant for brunch?"

"Yeah."

"How very thoughtful of you to bring me this back." She touched the edges of it with her fork and knife, probably to see how much he had given her.

"It's about a third of it. The rest is in the fridge."

"Still a lot," she said, taking her first bite.

She closed her eyes and sighed contentedly.

"Just do your best with it."

"This I can do. So very kind of you to bring this, Raymond. So delicious. Every bit as good as the first one, even reheated."

She ate in silence for a time. Raymond only sat with her, staring through the curtained window at nothing.

"How was your visit with the kids?" he asked after a time.

She worked quickly to swallow before speaking.

"Harder than I thought it would be. They are like a mirror for this huge loss. They don't completely understand yet. Well, they do and they don't. It's a hard thing to take in at their age. Oh, who am I fooling? It's a hard thing to take in at any age. Even mine." She took a small sip of her wine. "And how was your weekend with your father?"

"Pretty good, actually. Better than usual. I feel like we actually managed to talk about something. You know. Something real."

"Good. Good. Now tell me one other thing, Raymond. I've been wondering about it while you were gone. So I will simply ask. Why are you so afraid for me?"

"Afraid for you?" he asked.

He turned his head to look at her face. For clues, maybe. It was angled toward him as if to help her listen. Slightly tilted, like a dog trying to identify a curious sound. Her fork and knife stood poised in the air, completely still. He could see that he had her full attention.

"Am I afraid for you?"

"It seems to me that you are."

"Well . . . people have to eat, you know."

"People can go many days without eating."

"I suppose. But . . ." And then he felt it. The thing she had asked about. It was there. It was coming up through him. It was about to make its way out of his mouth. Out into the world, where he could not take it back again. Not deny it anymore. "I feel like . . . now that Luis is gone . . . you just seemed to have this really strong will to live, and I guess I worry that you're losing that."

"I see," she said. She set down her fork and knife. Dabbed at her mouth with her napkin. "Well, then, Raymond. Let me tell you more about me, so you will know. Many people I have known died young. And that is all I care to say about that. Were I to see them again . . . and, who knows? Maybe there is an afterlife. Maybe I will see them. Who can say? Do you think I will join them any sooner than necessary and tell them I gave up trying because life took something away from me? That is an affront to those who were not lucky enough to grow old. It's a slap in the face. And even if I never see them, it would be a slap in the face to you."

"Me?"

"Yes, you. It would be failing to recognize that life took Luis away but also brought me you. Life takes something away from all of us. I will tell you something about life that you might or might not know, my young friend. Life gives us nothing outright. It only lends. Nothing is ours to keep. Absolutely nothing. Not even our bodies, our brains. This 'self' that we think we know so well, that we think of as us. It is only on loan. If a person comes into our life, they will go again. In a parting of ways, or because everyone dies. They will die or you will die. Nothing we receive in this life are we allowed to keep. I am not some spoiled child who will take my toys and go home because I do not wish to accept that this is the way things work."

"Good," Raymond said. "I'm glad to hear you say that. I was afraid you might . . ." But he couldn't bring himself to say it.

"Die? Of course I will die. Much sooner than you, I should think, though I thought the same about Luis. Yes, I will die, Raymond, and I can't promise you when. Maybe tomorrow. Maybe when I'm a hundred and six. But one thing I *will* promise you: it won't be because I soured on the idea of living. Living long is a gift denied to many, and so it comes with a responsibility to make the most of it. At very least to appreciate it. People gripe about growing older—their aches and pains, how much harder everything is—as if they had forgotten that the alternative is dying young."

She picked up her fork again and resumed eating. With renewed vigor, Raymond thought. Or at least with a driving stubbornness.

"Besides," she said between bites. "I have to live long enough to learn what happens to that woman when she goes to trial."

PART TWO

APRIL

Chapter Eleven

Fortune Cookie

Raymond's father walked in, surprising him. Raymond had been sitting on the couch in his father's apartment, alone, reading an e-book about the Second World War on his laptop and eating Chinese food.

Raymond looked quickly at the time readout on his computer. It was six twenty.

"I hope you don't mind," he said to his dad. "I got tired of pizza."

"Thank goodness." His father crossed the room to stand over Raymond, throwing his jacket on a chair. It slid down onto the rug, and he left it there. It would have driven Neesha crazy if she'd been home. "I thought *you* were the one who wanted all that pizza."

"Well. To a point."

"What did you get?"

His father sat down next to him on the couch and eased out of his shoes. As though his feet hurt. Which they probably did. He had been on them all day.

"Sesame chicken. Egg rolls. Shrimp fried rice. It just got here a few minutes ago. I'm not even sure you'll need to heat it up."

"I'll get a plate."

While his father was away in the kitchen, Raymond closed his laptop and took a deep breath. Prepared himself mentally as much as possible.

"I need to talk to you about something," he said, before his father had even sat down again.

"Okay. Talk."

"There's something I really want to do. It's important to me. But it would involve missing some school. But it's educational, so I think it's a reasonable thing to miss school for, and I'd get my work from my teachers and keep up from home in the evening. I wouldn't let my grades slip. But I'd still need a note."

"What does your mother think about it?"

Raymond said nothing. He sat and watched his father tilt the sesame chicken carton and pull food out onto his plate with a fresh pair of disposable chopsticks. He felt he should say something. But there was no safe place to go.

"I see," his father said, sitting back with a sigh. "Why haven't you asked her?"

"Well. You know how she is. She just wants everything to go the way she wants it to go. She's not real flexible when somebody wants to change the plan."

"You know that's not going to work, though, Raymond. Were you really thinking I'd write you a note, and she'd never find out?"

"It was a thought."

Then Raymond laughed. Just a quiet little breath of a laugh. And, to his relief, his father laughed as well.

"What's this thing you want to do?"

"It's a . . . trial."

"Like a criminal trial?"

"Yeah."

"What kind of crime?"

"Voluntary manslaughter."

"Do you know the person on trial?"

"No. But I know the victim's family."

"I see. This is about your friend, right? Your older woman friend?"

"How did you know that?"

"I pay attention when you talk to me, son. When you first told me about her you said she's blind, and needs help, and that the person who was helping her just got killed."

"Oh," Raymond said. "Did I?"

Then he was so surprised that for a time he did not—could not—speak.

"Did you not realize I listen to you?"

"I . . . guess I'm not used to it. Mom and Ed don't. Well. Ed doesn't listen. Mom takes in everything you say, but then it drops right out of her head again."

"But you should have noticed that I do."

"You don't say much," Raymond said, falling unexpectedly into honesty. "So sometimes it's hard to tell."

"Be that as it may, I think your mom will understand about what you're asking. Seeing as this person is so close to you."

Another long silence. This one lasted at least a minute. Maybe two or three. Raymond hoped his father would break down and fill the gap with words. Because Raymond had no intention of doing so himself.

"You haven't even told her about your friend," his father said at last. It was a statement. Not a question.

"No."

"Why not?"

Raymond sighed. "It's kind of hard to explain. But you know how sometimes something is really important to you, and you just know somebody else would never understand it? So it's almost like you want to keep it safe from them. Like they would only get their fingerprints all over it and mess it up. And like this thing about missing school for the trial—that's a perfect example. It's so important to me, and she's the one who's going to mess it up for me, and we both know it."

More silence. Long enough for his father to finish his sesame chicken and dump the last two egg rolls onto his plate. Raymond picked up a fortune cookie and tore off the cellophane. He rolled the cookie around in his fingers for a time without breaking it open.

"And what do the people at your school think about the absence? Have you asked the principal?"

"Not yet. I'm starting with you."

"You need to start with your mom. And then the principal. And then I'll write you the note, but only if your mom is on board. If you think I'm going to take a chance by crossing that woman, you don't know me very well."

Raymond sighed again. He looked down at the fortune cookie in his hand and broke it open. Pulled out the paper fortune.

YOU WILL SOON BEGIN A BIG ADVENTURE

"What does it say?" Raymond's father asked.

Raymond handed him the fortune. His father held the scrap of paper out at arm's length. He didn't have his reading glasses on. Raymond could tell when he had successfully read it, because he cracked a wry smile.

"I wonder who at the fortune cookie factory knows your mother."

They both laughed again, which came as a welcome relief.

———

If this had been a movie, Raymond thought, the assistant principal would have said something crisp and official. Something like "The principal will see you now."

But this was Raymond's real life.

She snapped her fingers to get his attention as he sat staring out the window. Then she tossed her head in the direction of Mr. Landucci's office.

"Got it," Raymond said.

He stood. Breathed deeply. Walked in.

Mr. Landucci was a short, wide man of about fifty who wore his collars too tight, forcing a spill of plump neck skin up and out over the Windsor knot of his tie. He wore half glasses, and he looked at Raymond over the top of them. He narrowed his eyes, as if trying to classify Raymond in some way.

"And you are . . . ?"

"Raymond Jaffe."

"Have I ever had you in my office before?"

"No, sir."

"Good. That's a score in your favor. Have a seat."

Raymond perched uncomfortably on the edge of a hard wooden chair. It had no arms, so Raymond had no clue what to do with his own. *Just like the old days,* he thought.

The principal seemed to be watching him try to settle his body. With some interest, as though he couldn't imagine how it felt to have to tame one's own limbs on a daily basis. Then he stared at his computer monitor for a time, but Raymond had no idea whether his life was any part of what the man was reading.

"Now what can I do for you?" Mr. Landucci asked at last.

"I want to talk to you about an absence."

"All right. How long were you absent and how recently?"

"No. Not a past absence. A future one. I want to do something that will make me miss some school. But I feel like it would be educational. This thing I want to do."

"I'll need a note from your mother."

Raymond sat stunned a moment, feeling his ears tingle.

"My mother?"

"Yes. Your mother."

"Why didn't you say 'my parents'?"

"Because it says here you have a joint custody arrangement. That you live with your mother and spend every other weekend with your father."

"Oh," Raymond said. "It says all that? Why does it say all that?"

"This is information we need to know. If a student is late on certain days, he might be coming to school from farther away. Or if a student is more distracted or shows signs of abuse . . . well, it's just helpful information. But back to the question at hand. Is your mother in favor of your taking this time off school?"

"My father said he would write me a note."

"I see."

Raymond figured the principal did see. Probably far too much. More than Raymond had meant to reveal.

"So let me tell you about this thing I want to do. Please. It's about me learning more about our criminal justice system. Firsthand. Well, not literally firsthand. I'm not on trial or anything. But hands-on. And I'd get my assignments from my teachers and do the work at home at night. I won't fall behind. I won't let my grades slip. I never let my grades slip. You can probably see that. Since you're looking at my whole life there on your screen."

At first, no reply. Mr. Landucci was not looking at Raymond. He was reading on his computer monitor. It struck Raymond that the principal hadn't looked at him since that moment when Raymond had been trying to sort out his limbs. The man seemed to have lost interest after that.

"Yes," Mr. Landucci said suddenly, startling Raymond. "You're a good student. Wish we had more like you. But I'll need a note from your mother. And after you went and made it ever so clear that you hope to bypass her, I'll probably call her and verify. But beyond that

I have no issues with what you propose, providing you keep up with the work."

Raymond sat a moment. He knew he was supposed to get up and leave now. But for an awkward length of time, he didn't.

"I don't understand," he said.

"What don't you understand? You seem like a smart young man, and none of this is complicated."

"My father is just as much my parent as my mother is."

"But she's your primary caregiver. And he's the secondary."

"Oh," Raymond said, reminding himself briefly of his dad. The man of few words. Oh.

"So I'll see you again when you get that note from her."

It was the principal's polite way of saying the meeting was over now, and Raymond knew it.

—

He walked down the street with Mrs. G, his arm hooked through hers, on their way to the bank to deposit her two monthly checks. They were hurrying slightly, to get there before it closed for the day. Still, their version of hurrying was hard for Raymond because it felt so slow.

"So what did you find out about going?" she asked as they stood waiting for a light to change.

"Not sure yet," he said. "I'm still working on it."

She seemed to pick up on his discouragement. She seemed to pick up on everything, Raymond thought. He waited for her to ask more about it, but she never did. They crossed the street in silence.

"For myself, I think I'm putting too much on it," she said. "Investing too much."

"I don't follow."

He watched her white-and-red cane sweep back and forth in front of them as they walked. He was never sure why she used it in that way, since he would have told her if she was about to trip on—or walk into—something. But maybe that was easy for Raymond to think. He'd never had to walk down a busy Manhattan street wondering what he might be just about to run into.

"I'm trying to think how to put it better," she said. "So it makes sense. You know how sometimes you have pain, so you call the doctor? Well, maybe you don't, because you're healthy and young. But there must be something in your life like this. So you make an appointment, and let's say it's weeks away. You start hanging on the calendar and putting all your hopes in that day. Like if you can just make it to the doctor's appointment, then everything will be okay, but really you know in the back of your head that you might be setting yourself up for a big fall. Maybe he'll know what's causing the pain, or maybe he'll have to run more tests. Or maybe he'll know what it is, but there's no easy cure. You know there's a good chance you'll walk out of that office still in pain. And then you'll be faced with that very difficult task where you reset that internal clock of yours to some *other* time when it might be okay. Ever had something like that in your life?"

"Yeah," he said. "I think so." He looked up to see the bank at the end of the block. He glanced at her watch. They were going to make it with seven minutes to spare. "So you're saying you feel like you're doing that with the trial?"

"Exactly."

They walked in silence down the block. Through the doors of the bank, which an older male customer held open for them. Inside, where Raymond guided her into place at the end of the medium-length line.

"Is there anything you can do to fix that?" he asked as they waited.

"Not that I've discovered so far."

They waited in silence until they reached the head of the line and a teller window opened up. It was Mrs. G's favorite teller, Patty.

"My two favorite customers!" Patty crowed, a bit too loudly, as they stepped slowly up to her window. "Mrs. Gutermann and Raymond!"

Raymond led her up to the window, where she set her purse on the counter and began to plow through its contents.

A moment later he looked up and past her, to the door of the bank. And there Raymond saw . . . his mother.

It had been inevitable, and he'd known it. It was nothing short of a miracle that they hadn't bumped into her in the hall of their building in all these months. Or bumped into one of his sisters. Raymond had assumed some special brand of luck had attached itself to him. But if so, it had just run out.

She looked right into his face, and he had no choice but to return her stare. His heart began to drum and his ears felt hot. She continued to question him with her gaze. She didn't look mad. Just curious.

"Excuse me," he said to Patty and Mrs. G. "I'll be right back."

Heart pounding at a dizzying rate, he walked to her. He felt slightly outside his body, detached from his usual self.

They stood in front of each other for a silent second or two.

"This is not our bank," he said.

"No." Her tone was wry, as was the angle of her eyebrows. And the rest of her face. "It's not."

"So what're you doing here?"

"I could ask much the same question of you."

"No, seriously. What're you doing here?"

She placed her hands on her hips, elbows wide. That was never a good sign.

"Not that it's any of your business, but somebody at work wrote me a check, and I thought I'd cash it at their bank, because then it's just like cash, you know? Not like income, like the IRS'll ask me why I didn't pay taxes on it if I ever get audited. Okay. *Your* turn."

Raymond opened his mouth to speak. But just as he did, Patty called to him.

"Raymond! Raymond, honey, she needs you back now. We're all done."

His mother's eyebrows did that wry thing again. Or maybe still, only more so.

"I'll be right back," he said.

He walked to the teller window to fetch Mrs. G. He reached out for her hand as he always did, and placed it on his upper arm. Then, having located the arm, she slid her own arm through it. And they walked together.

"Where did you go?" she asked. "It's not like you to take off while I'm at the window. Not that I wasn't okay there. I just wondered."

"My mom is here."

A lot came through in those simple words. He heard it in his own voice, and he knew Mrs. G heard it, too.

"I would love to meet her," she said, leaving the subtext alone.

"Good. Because that seems to be where things are headed."

He led her up to his mother and stopped a couple of steps away. It hit Raymond that the bank was only open for a couple of minutes more, and that his mother might not get her banking done at the rate they were going.

"Mom," he said, "this is Mrs. Gutermann. She lives in our building, on the second floor. She needs help getting to the bank, so . . ." But he didn't go on to finish his thought.

"I'm delighted to meet you," Mrs. G said to fill the silence.

She held out her hand. But his mother hadn't said anything yet, or made any noise. So the hand ended up about thirty degrees to the right of its intended target. Raymond took hold of it and steered it closer to his mother, who reached out her own hand to take it.

They didn't shake hands, exactly. It was more a gesture in which Mrs. G squeezed his mother's hand, and his mother allowed it.

"You must be very proud of your wonderful son," Mrs. G said. Her voice was glowing, if such a thing were possible. "He has been such a good friend to me. He helps me to do so many things that I don't know how I would do on my own. And always with such a gracious attitude. I don't know exactly what would go into raising such a caring and thoughtful young man, but you've obviously done your job well."

Raymond's mother turned her eyes to his face. She had caught on now, and realized she could do so without Mrs. G observing. So she questioned him with her eyes. And as she opened her mouth to answer Mrs. G, she never took her eyes off Raymond's face.

"That's all very interesting. How long has he been so helpful to you?"

"Oh, many months now. Since October, I believe. We have become very good friends. Haven't we, Raymond?"

"Definitely," Raymond said, the skin of his face feeling hot under his mother's unwavering stare.

Raymond's mom mouthed the words "many months." Then she reached out and pinged Raymond hard in the middle of his forehead with one snap of her index finger.

"Ow," Raymond said.

"Are you all right, Raymond?" Mrs. G asked. "What happened?"

"Nothing. It was just . . . nothing." Raymond shot his eyes up to the clock. "Mom. The bank closes in, like, two minutes. If you don't get up there and cash that check right now you'll have come down here for nothing."

"Good point. We'll talk at home. Nice meeting you, Mrs. . . . ."

"Gutermann. But Millie is fine. It was lovely meeting you, too."

Then Raymond's mother walked around them and was gone. And Raymond could breathe deeply again. He led Mrs. G to the door, where another customer, this time a young woman, held it open for them.

They stepped out onto the street together. For a time, they didn't talk.

The weather was cool spring, the traffic noisy with the end-of-the-day commute. People pushed past them, sometimes jostling Raymond's shoulder in their hurry to get by.

"So I never told her about helping you," he said after a time.

"I sensed that."

"It's kind of hard to explain why."

"You don't need to. It's all right. I understand."

"I don't think you do."

"It's not a thing a boy brags about, having an old woman as a friend. It's not exactly a point of pride."

"I'm not ashamed of you. Not at all. It's almost the opposite."

They walked another half a block in silence. Another pedestrian nearly slammed into Raymond's shoulder from behind in his hurry to get home.

"That you will have to explain to me, then," she said. "Because I am not managing to imagine it on my own."

"Oh. Wow. Hard. Okay. It's more like I was ashamed of my family. Which I guess I shouldn't be, but . . . I mean, my mother isn't *terrible*. She takes care of us, and I guess she's a good enough mother. But she gets mad real easily, and she never seems to let any new ideas in. Whatever she thinks is just what she thinks, and it's always going to stay that way. And if I tell her it's really important to me to do *this*, she'll tell me she wants me to do *that*, and she won't give an inch about it. I'm not sure what the word is for that."

"Contrary?" Mrs. G offered.

"Yeah. Contrary. And I knew she wouldn't understand our being friends. She doesn't understand things. *You* understand. All kinds of things. You understand people."

"I don't understand people at all. I would even go so far as to say I feel more perplexed by them with every passing day."

"Well, you understand them better than anybody else I know. You understand just about everything compared to everybody I've ever met. And my family . . . doesn't. They just don't. I guess I felt like being friends with you was this really nice thing and my family would only ruin it."

They walked in silence until Raymond saw their building at the end of the block.

"You must try to make your peace with your family, Raymond," she said.

"Why?"

"Because they are your family. You will be eighteen in less than a year, and then you can go away and be on your own and find your own family, in whatever way you care to do. But you still only have one family of origin. One mother. So I advise you to make your peace with them, and with her. If she drives you crazy, you can spend less time with her when you're grown. But if you don't work out these basic differences, if you don't talk out what is going wrong, you will regret it when all is said and done. I have some experience with this in my own past. So when we get home, and I get safely inside, you should go upstairs and talk with her—in a better way than perhaps you have done in the past."

"Okay," Raymond said. "Okay. I will."

It's not like he had any other options now.

"I'm going to be there for you at the trial," he said as they walked slowly up the steps to their building.

"Don't say that yet. You don't know. It might not be possible."

"You need me to be, right?"

"It would be a great help to me, yes. I think Isabel would take me, but she will have so much on her mind. Plus she could go into labor at any moment. It's a terrible time to ask her to attend to the needs of someone else."

"So you need me at the trial."

"I suppose it's fair to say so."

"Then I'll be there. And nobody's going to stop me."

—

In a relatively unprecedented move, Raymond sat on the couch in their apartment and simply waited for her. Waited for his mother to arrive home.

It didn't take long. Less than five minutes.

When she came through the door, she seemed surprised to see him there. She pasted on that same wry expression, as if the whole thing were a big, sarcastic joke to her. Raymond had begun to find it deeply irritating.

"This will be very interesting," she said, locking the door behind her. Then she turned to him and assumed the position—hands on her waist, elbows angled out. "I can't tell you how interesting I think this all is. I can't wait until next time I go out for a drink after work with the other ladies. Imogene will tell me all about her son who's back using crack cocaine, but of course he tries to hide it from her. And Paulette has a daughter who got eleven parking tickets, and she never paid a one of them, and they went to warrant, but Paulette wouldn't even know about it if the notice hadn't come in the mail on a Saturday. Because, you know . . . kids. They don't want you to know about all the bad stuff they get up to. So then I get to say, 'Oh yeah, girls. I know exactly what you mean. My son Raymond helps little old blind ladies cross the street, but of course he keeps it from me, because what kid would want his mother to know *that*?' What the hell, Raymond? What the actual hell?"

Raymond only looked up at her and blinked too much. He could feel himself doing it, but he couldn't stop.

Inside, two very distinct parts of him had declared war on each other. One part wanted to stay quiet and calm, and keep her calm, because he needed her permission to miss school. The madder she got, the less likely she was to help him. The other part of him just wanted to fire back at her in rage.

He waited to see which one would win.

"Why would you not tell me a thing like that, Raymond? I asked you over and over to tell me about your new friends."

"I didn't think you would understand."

"What wouldn't I understand? You thought I'd tell you it's bad to help the elderly and the blind?"

"I thought you'd tell me I need to make friends my own age."

"Well, you *do* need to make friends your own age. That goes without saying."

Raymond spread his arms wide, as if to show her what had just occurred. He thought the situation would speak for itself if he could only jog her into noticing. She did not notice. She seemed to have disappeared into her own head, her own world.

"In fact, when you think about it . . . it's weird. It's just weird, Raymond. A seventeen-year-old boy being friends with a woman who's like . . . a hundred. There's something kind of icky and weird about it. Oh, I'm sorry—that's too harsh. But it's sure not what I expected."

And then you have the nerve to ask me why I didn't tell you.

"And then you have the nerve to ask me why I didn't tell you," Raymond said. Out loud.

He sat frozen and listened to the words, which seemed to vibrate in the air between them. For years he had said things like that in his head while interacting with his parents. This was the first time one had come out of his mouth.

"I'm just expressing my opinion," she said.

"And I didn't want to hear your opinion, but you never, *ever* keep your opinion to yourself. So that's why I didn't tell you."

He stood and walked off toward his bedroom.

"You're being too sensitive," she called after him.

No, you're not being sensitive enough.

"No, you're not being sensitive enough," he called back over his shoulder.

He wondered if this was just the way of things now. If he would never be able to hold his comments inside again.

He closed himself into his room and decided he would not find that magic moment to ask her. She would always be just like this: defensive, quick to anger, slow to understand. So maybe he wouldn't ask her. Maybe he would just skip school and go to the trial.

She could punish him any way she chose to afterward. It would be worth it.

———

He sat at the dinner table, pushing something around on his plate with a fork. He wasn't even entirely clear on what it was. Could have been chicken, or it could have been some cut of pork.

He looked up at his two middle sisters, who looked back. Then they looked at each other and burst into giggles. He looked away from them. At Clarissa, who was shoveling rice into her mouth and paying no attention to anyone. He looked back at the two middle girls, and the scene repeated itself.

"What?" he yelled suddenly.

It came out much louder and angrier than he had intended. It startled Clarissa, who jumped. Her eyes immediately filled with tears.

Rhonda was the one who said it out loud.

"Raymond has a girlfriend. And she's . . . like . . . a *hundred!*"

Raymond jumped up from the table, purposely catching the edge of his plate and flipping it up into the air. It came down hard, a foot nearer the center of the table, pitching the slab of mystery meat off onto the plastic tablecloth.

He turned his eyes on his mother, who threw both hands in the air as if being held at gunpoint.

"I didn't say anything to them," she said. "One of them must have overheard."

"See, this is why I can't stand being part of this family. You treat me like I'm totally weird, like I'm from outer space or something. We have nothing in common. Look at me. I don't look like I belong with you people, and I don't act like it, and I don't feel like it. We don't even have the same last name. And you all drive me crazy, acting like there's something wrong with me—well, I've got news for you. Maybe it's not me. Maybe I'm perfectly okay, and there's something wrong with all of *you*."

He froze there, towering over them, and looked at the horrified faces. He had never spoken to them like this before. He had never spoken to anyone like this before. The middle girls sat with their mouths hanging open. Clarissa was crying openly.

"Not you, Clarissa," he added. "You're okay." He looked down at the tablecloth. Shook his head. Hard. "I'm not hungry. I'm going to my room."

As he walked away down the apartment hall, he heard Ed say, "You gonna let him talk to you like that?"

He couldn't hear what his mother said in reply.

——

She came to his room a minute or two later. She knocked, but didn't wait for a reply. Raymond was lying facedown on his bed. He didn't move as she crossed the room and sat on the edge of the mattress beside him.

She placed a hand between his shoulder blades.

"Please don't," he said, because he wanted to stay angry.

She took the hand back.

"We don't mean to make you feel like you don't belong here."

"The point is not whether you *mean* to make me feel that way. The point is not even whether you make me feel that way. The point is that it's true. I don't belong here. I don't fit with this family. It's just a fact."

A pause fell.

Then Raymond dropped a bomb that had been in the bay of his aircraft for a very long time. He had never paid it any conscious attention. He hadn't thought it through. But it was always there.

"Maybe I should just go live with Dad."

Silence. Deadly, nearly radioactive silence.

Then, with an eerie tightness in her voice, she said, "You honestly think his new wife would put up with that? That she'd treat you better than we do?"

"No. I think she'd treat me like I don't belong. But at least I fit with Dad. That's one person, anyway."

Then he realized that move would put him a subway ride away from Mrs. G. But maybe it wouldn't matter. Luis had moved farther away, and he had continued the friendship just as well.

He felt a slight bounce to the bed and heard the door open and close. He had to look around to confirm what he knew, but he knew it. She had gone away and left him blessedly alone.

—

When Raymond arrived at the breakfast table the following morning, both his mom and stepdad were there. Which was . . . wrong. It never happened that way.

Ed immediately rose from the table and took his coffee into another room. Whether he was angry at Raymond or had agreed to leave them alone to talk, Raymond couldn't tell.

"Why aren't you at work?" he asked his mother, a note of anxiety creeping into his belly. He heard it come through in his voice.

"I made an arrangement to go in late so we could talk. Sit."

Raymond sat. He always wished she would say "sit down," so it sounded less like a command you would give your golden retriever. Still, it did not feel like the time to bring it up.

"What can I do," she began, "to make you feel like I respect the differences between us?"

Raymond felt stunned. He was aware of his own rapid blinking.

Meanwhile she was still talking.

"And I don't just mean the outer differences like height and skin color and last names. Yes, you seem to care about a whole different set of things from the rest of us. Obviously. And when you try to tell me what you care about, I don't understand. I get that. So what can I do to make you feel like I see you, and that what you are is okay with me? Because I really want to do that if I can."

"Whoa." For a moment, Raymond had no idea what else to say. And then, just like that, he did. "There's something I want to do. It's coming up in a couple of weeks, and it's really important." He filled her in quickly on the trial. Four or five sentences, maybe. The least he thought he could get away with saying. "Like you just almost can't imagine how important it is to me. But I'd have to take some time off school, and I'd need a note from you."

"No," she said. Fast and immediate. "No, you know I'm not into any of you kids missing any school. That's out of the question."

Raymond dropped his face into his hands. And left it there for a time. A rush of anger came up, but he let it go again. Let it pass through him. It wouldn't help him now. It would only cement her resistance.

He dropped his hands again, and looked at her face. To gauge where she stood with all of this. It was the usual Mom face. She wasn't treating him any differently yet.

"So what you're saying," he began, "is that you want to see me differently and respect what you see and get along with me in a whole new way . . ."

"Right."

"You just don't want to make any changes at all."

He watched her face as she took in those words. Watched her "Mom resistance" crumble, one brick at a time. He knew he had said the right thing for a change.

"You'll keep up with your schoolwork?"

"I promise."

"Oh, I hate this."

"I know you do. I know it's really hard for you. That's why it would mean so much to me if you did."

She sighed deeply, and Raymond knew she would write him the note. They'd go around a few more times about it. But in the end she couldn't very well refuse him now.

Chapter Twelve

Weight and Labor

Raymond crouched on his knees in his room, digging through the pockets of his backpack. Going over his provisions for court. Making sure he had each item in a series of snacks he'd bought out of his allowance for both himself and Mrs. G. Going over his school assignments, some of which had been written down for him on paper, some of which he'd gathered onto a flash drive in digital format. He figured he could plug that into his notebook computer if he had time to get some work done between court sessions.

He was looking through the side zip pocket for the flash drive when his hand stumbled onto an unfamiliar scrap of paper, which he pulled out into the light. It was crumpled and creased from having been stuffed in there, unnoticed for half a year.

He held it into the glow from his desk lamp.

It said, in neat block printing, "LUIS AND SOFIA VELEZ AND FAMILY," followed by a phone number.

Raymond froze a moment, there on his knees, remembering them. The chocolate cake, and the way they had noticed how he'd seemed dispirited and tired. The way they had wanted to help, even though they didn't know him. The way the teenage girl's hand brushed against his hair as she placed the religious medal around his neck. The way the Spanish-speaking abuela had more or less suggested it would be a good idea for the girl to give the medal up for Raymond.

His hand came up and touched the medallion through his clean white dress shirt. He wondered briefly if his and Mrs. G's cause was still hopeless. All he wanted was for Mrs. G to find some solace in the trial. And maybe some closure for himself. She had already made it clear that she anticipated finding no such thing.

He stuffed the paper deep into the front pocket of his good slacks and trotted downstairs to Mrs. G's apartment.

"It's me," he called, after doing his special Raymond knock. Which was silly, because he had just done his special Raymond knock. Who else could it have been?

Then he let himself in with the key.

She was sitting on the couch, wearing a dark-blue dress and heavy black shoes, a patterned knitted shawl around her shoulders. She was clutching her purse tightly against herself. She did not look up or speak to him. She appeared to be lost in thought. She also looked deeply frightened, but Raymond chose not to say so.

"Would it be okay if I used your phone to make a very fast call?" he asked instead.

She didn't answer in words. Just flipped her head in the direction of the old-fashioned landline telephone.

"If it turns out to be a toll call, I promise I'll pay you back for it."

She turned her face in his direction and sighed deeply.

"Oh, what does it matter, Raymond?"

That just hung in the air for a moment, as if Raymond could continue to listen to the words long after they had been spoken. The longer he listened, the more it sounded as though she were asking "What does anything matter?"

He didn't know what to say or do about it, though. So he just pulled the scrap of paper out of his pocket and walked to the phone.

Dialed the number. Well, punched the buttons for the number. It wasn't literally a rotary dial. It wasn't *that* old.

It rang and rang, then clicked over to voicemail.

Luis's deep, booming voice invited him to leave a message.

"Hi," he said. "It's Raymond. Maybe you don't remember me, but I was at your apartment last fall. Looking for a Luis Velez who turned out not to be you. I said I'd call when I found him, but I forgot. I'm sorry. But it was nice of you to want to know how it turned out. Well, everything about you was nice. So I wanted to let you know what I found out, even though it's not a happy ending. Turns out Luis had . . . passed away. But anyway, I found his family, which is a good thing. And at least this way we know. So . . . you know. Just to tell you that. And to thank you again for being so nice."

Raymond took a deep breath and replaced the receiver.

"We should go," he said to Mrs. G.

"All right," she said.

But she showed no signs of moving.

"Did you eat any breakfast?"

"I couldn't stomach anything, no."

"Would you eat a granola bar on the way if I gave you one?"

"For you, at least I would try."

She shifted her weight forward in preparation for getting up, and Raymond hurried to her and held his arm out, placing one of her hands on it. He bore her weight as she rose to her feet.

It seemed to Raymond that every time he did so there was less of her weight to bear.

———

"Hey!" he said to her. "There's Isabel!"

His voice sounded barely audible over the din of so many other voices.

They were in a hallway of the courthouse. It was three minutes until 9:00 a.m. The hallway was lined with doors to individual courtrooms. Apparently each courtroom had a trial scheduled, and each trial began in three minutes.

Men and women in business suits hurried along, some carrying briefcases, others wheeling cases of records that looked like a series of suitcases on wheels, only more heavy and complex. Uniformed officers and bailiffs herded groups of jurors. Everyone seemed to be talking about everything, and all at once.

Raymond had his right arm around Mrs. G's shoulders for safety, his left hand gripping her elbow.

He raised a hand and caught Isabel's eye. Then he looked back down at Mrs. G, and just in time.

A man wheeling cases behind him was passing far too close to her legs, and he veered suddenly to avoid a woman who almost slammed into him. The cart was headed fast for Mrs. G's feet.

Raymond held her more tightly with his right arm and pulled her sharply out of the path of danger, steadying her on her feet as soon as she was safe.

"Oh dear," she said, clearly not knowing quite what was happening.

"Hey, watch what you're doing!" Raymond shouted at the man. "You almost hit her with that."

The man looked over his shoulder at Raymond but said nothing. His face registered nothing. He seemed to be in a world all his own, and he apparently had no intention of leaving it for Raymond or Mrs. G. He looked forward again and walked on.

Raymond took a deep breath and tried to settle himself. He looked up to find Isabel standing in front of them.

"I know which room it is," she said. "Follow me."

"I thought your parents were coming," Raymond said, not yet moving. "You know. In case you go into labor."

"They have the flu. I can't be around them while they're sick."

"So if you go into labor . . ."

"Then I guess my only hope is you," she said.

They walked through the sea of humanity together. Raymond could tell that Isabel felt a sense of hurry. She was nervous and preoccupied, and it was clearly hard for her to slow down to Mrs. G's speed. Every few steps she had to stop to let them catch up. Raymond could feel the anxiety rolling off her in waves, and he was catching it like the flu that Isabel had so recently evaded. But there was nothing he could do. Mrs. G could only walk as fast as she could walk. It was neither realistic nor fair to ask more of her.

Meanwhile the same thought was spinning around in Raymond's head again and again.

Please don't go into labor. Please don't go into labor. Please don't go into labor.

A young woman in uniform—Raymond wasn't sure if she was a police officer or some kind of officer of the court—stood in front of Isabel, blocking her way. She was staring at Isabel's huge belly with her face lit up as though she had seen some kind of religious miracle. Isabel had no choice but to stop. The woman reached her hands out and placed them on Isabel's belly.

Raymond winced, because he knew Isabel hated that. And who wouldn't, really? Nobody wants to be touched by a total stranger, and pregnancy is hardly an excuse. Or so it seemed to him, anyway.

"Oh, when is your due date?" the woman asked, her voice breathy and high.

Raymond knew Isabel was tired of answering that question, so he answered for her. "Five days ago," he said.

"We're going *there*," Isabel said, pointing to a room number: 559.

"Yeah, so am I," the woman said.

They all walked inside together.

Raymond had expected to see the courtroom filled to overflowing, like the hallways. Standing room only. He expected to have to stand in the corner, or sit on the floor. Or take a seat all the way in the back. Instead, he saw the room populated almost entirely by people on the other side of the low gates. The nonpublic side. The bench side. In the seats provided for a public audience, Raymond saw only a blond-haired thirtysomething man and woman, sitting behind the defendant and her attorneys. Raymond tried to get a good look at her, the defendant. Some sense of her. But there wasn't much to be gathered by the back of somebody's dark hair.

Isabel led them up the aisle to the front row of seats, and they chose a bench right behind the prosecuting attorney—the district attorney, or an attorney from his office, Raymond guessed. He realized he'd better find out who was prosecuting this case, and keep those details straight. And make careful notes. Because a report was due at the end of the trial. The principal had hit him with that requirement last-minute.

They sat in silence, waiting for . . . well, Raymond wasn't sure. Waiting for whatever would happen next to begin.

"Where is everybody?" he whispered to Isabel.

She turned her eyes to him, and in them Raymond saw utter confusion. As if he'd spoken to her in an ancient, dead language. The Latin he'd grown to despise, maybe.

"Everybody?"

"Yeah."

"What everybody?"

"Well . . . I thought there would be other people here. You know. Wanting to see the trial."

Isabel laughed one bitter little bark of a laugh. "Welcome to the world," she said. "Luis is dead, and the world can live with that. It's fine just going on without him. Nobody really cares what happened to Luis except us."

—

Raymond made careful notes on his laptop during the almost two hours of jury selection. He made observations beyond what was actually said, noting his thoughts as well as the procedures themselves. He nervously eyed his battery readout, worrying he'd be using pen and paper before the end of the day. Unless he could find someplace to plug in over lunch.

Both lead attorneys asked questions of the prospective jurors. Raymond could feel what the questions were getting at.

Have you ever been mugged or otherwise robbed? Ever been a victim of violence? Are you a gun owner? Are you for or against gun control laws? Ever heard of Stand Your Ground laws, like the ones they have in Florida and several other states—though not this one? What are your thoughts about them?

Each lead attorney could dismiss potential jurors. For obvious cause, or without stating a reason. But if they did so without stating a reason, they had only a limited number of those wild cards.

"Peremptory challenges," he typed. "Three for each side."

But that much he could have learned by reading a book.

What Raymond observed on his own was this, though he might not have gathered it into these words: The idea, on the surface of the thing, was to weed out prejudice. But underneath the surface, Raymond saw that both attorneys were quite aware of prejudice, even in the jurors they let stay. Their whole job seemed to rely on prejudice. Prejudices in a courtroom felt to Raymond like a deck of cards to be strategically played in some kind of cynical game. Everyone had some prejudice, and that seemed to be part of the process. And the attorneys seemed to want that.

Just not against *their* client.

The tricky part appeared to be that people rarely stated their prejudices out loud. You had to read between their lines and hope you were reading them correctly.

———

"I want to start by making one thing very clear," the attorney said. The one Raymond had been calling "their" attorney in his head. "I am *not* against carrying a licensed handgun for the purpose of self-protection."

Raymond typed the words "Opening Statement: Prosecution" on his keyboard.

The man paced back and forth as he spoke, briefly turning his back on the jury, then facing them to drive a point home.

"And of course we all want to have the right to protect ourselves. And we should have that right. It's a funny thing about our rights, though. There's a fact about them that we don't want to see, but we have to see it. We simply have to, if we're expected to live together in any kind of peace. We're all living right on top of each other in this city, and there will be times when our rights will be in conflict.

"What's the first thing you ever learned about rights in school? I know the first thing I ever learned about them, and it was in kindergarten. My kindergarten teacher taught us that the right to swing our fist ends where the other guy's nose begins. Remember that?

"So maybe you're sitting here thinking, I have a right to fire my gun if I think I'm in danger. But does your neighbor have a right to fire his gun *at you* if he thinks you're a danger *to him*? You might notice how the question looks very different from the two different ends of the firearm.

"Now for the really important question."

He turned quickly to face the jury. Swept his gaze from one face to another. Met as many eyes as he could.

Raymond was still wishing there was even one Latino or Latina face on that jury. But there had been only three in the jury pool, and all three had been excused by the defense attorney, ostensibly over unrelated concerns.

"What if your neighbor is wrong? What if you're only trying to help, but he—or she—mistakenly thinks you mean him some kind of harm, and he fires on you? Ends your life? Takes you away from your spouse and your children? Does he have that right? What about your right to walk down the street in safety?

"Look, I have a handgun in the drawer of my bedside table. If someone breaks in and tries to do any kind of harm to my wife or me . . . well, all I can say is, God help that person. But with the license to carry and use a gun comes an enormous responsibility. And it's pretty simple, ladies and gentlemen: You have to be right. You owe it to the guy who's trying to give you back your wallet to be sure you know the difference between a robber and a good Samaritan. You have to be willing to hold your fire for just a moment—even a split second—until you know for a fact what kind of situation you've got on your hands. Sure, it's a temptation to think there's some risk involved in waiting that split second. And maybe there is. But to fail to take that risk is to put too much weight on your own rights and not enough on the other guy's. It's thinking only of yourself. We all put ourselves first. That's just human, and maybe it's not even a bad thing. But we at least have to make the other guy a very close second. Because, you know what? Luis Velez had a right to go home that night. He had a right to raise his children. He had a right to be there when his wife gave birth to their third child."

He stopped—stopped talking, stopped pacing. Turned his eyes to Isabel. The jury's eyes followed his gaze.

Raymond looked over at Isabel and watched her squirm under their gazes. Watched her face flush red.

"Mr. Velez had those rights violently ripped away from him. Did the defendant, Ms. Hatfield, wake up that morning with thoughts of murder?" He paused. Looked in the direction of the defendant. So far Raymond had still only seen the back of her head. "Did she bear ill will toward Mr. Velez and premeditate his demise? Of course not. She was just afraid. But afraid or not, we still have to use reasonable judgment before we use lethal force. And if we don't, there has to be a price. A fair price, but a price nonetheless for taking an innocent life first and asking questions later. Over the course of this trial, I will be trusting you to make a fair and reasoned judgment regarding what that price will be.

"Thank you, ladies and gentlemen. Thank you, Your Honor."

As the prosecutor moved to take his seat again, Raymond realized he had been so caught up in listening that he'd forgotten to take notes. He typed as fast as he possibly could while the defense attorney rose to begin his opening statement.

"Ladies and gentlemen of the jury, I ask you to use your imagination. What would you do if you were walking down the street at dusk and a stranger came up behind you and grabbed you by the shoulder?"

"He didn't grab her by the shoulder!"

Raymond jumped at the sound of Isabel's voice, coming from right beside him. She had pushed to her feet with surprising speed, considering her condition.

"He *tapped* her on the shoulder!" Isabel shouted. "Both witnesses said so!"

The judge rapped his gavel hard against the bench.

"Silence!" he bellowed at her. "One more outburst like that and you'll be looking at a contempt charge. Now be seated."

Isabel did not move. She stood frozen like a statue, teetering slightly, staring off into space as if listening to voices no one else could hear.

"I said be seated!" the judge roared again.

Isabel turned her gaze to the judge and spoke four words that nearly stopped Raymond's heart. They actually did stop it, but only for the space of about one and a half beats.

"My water just broke," she said.

———

The uniformed woman who had touched Isabel's belly ushered them out of the courtroom and down to the lobby.

She was New York City police, he saw as they trotted along together. He could see her badge. The nameplate on the pocket flap of her uniform shirt read "J. Truesdale."

Raymond looked behind him for the tenth time at least, uneasy with leaving Mrs. G behind in the courtroom. She had told them to. She had promised to remain seated until Raymond returned. But it still made him deeply uncomfortable to leave her out in the world without his help.

Officer Truesdale left them standing in the lobby of the courthouse.

"My patrol car is parked around the corner," she said. "Wait here and I'll bring it around."

Raymond held on to Isabel's elbow. He felt, briefly, dizzyingly, as though he were the only thing holding her up. Her face looked bloodless and pale, tight with fear and pain.

"Contraction," she hissed.

Her face contorted with the agony of it, and Raymond felt a sickening pain run down through his gut and then the insides of his thighs. A visceral reaction to what he was able to imagine.

"Okay," Isabel said a minute or two later. "Okay."

But it was only okay until the next inevitable contraction, and Raymond knew it.

———

He sat beside her gurney in the hospital labor room, feeding her ice chips from a tiny paper cup.

"You should go back," Isabel said.

"You sure you'll be okay?"

"Look around you, Raymond. I'm on a maternity ward. Everything that can be done to help a woman in labor is right here. I have a whole hospital staff to help me. But it was really sweet of you to make sure I got here okay. Thank you for that. I was scared, and I really needed somebody."

Raymond felt around in his gut for what he wanted to do. He immediately felt himself torn in two directions at once. It felt like being ripped apart down the middle.

"Maybe I should wait until the baby comes."

"It could be hours. It could be a day."

"*A day?*"

"Maybe. We don't know."

"I guess I should get back to her, then."

"When court shuts down for today, you can bring her back here. If I haven't had the baby yet, you can wait with me. If I have, you can see him."

Raymond rose to his feet as she spoke. He was just about to move to the door, but one word stopped his motion.

Him.

"You already know it's a boy?"

"Yes. Don't go for just a minute. There's something I want to say."

Reluctantly, Raymond sank back into the white plastic chair beside her gurney. He had set his internal clock for getting back to Mrs. G and the trial, and it hurt to delay that aim. But Isabel had something to say to him. So he worked to breathe more deeply, and he listened.

"Okay," he said. "Go."

"Almost the whole time I've been pregnant, I thought I knew what I was going to name the baby. I was going to name him Luis Jr."

"That works."

"I thought so, too. But it turns out I was wrong. Night before last I had this dream. I dreamed I was talking to Luis. For a long time. It felt like an hour, but I don't know how long I was really dreaming it. You know how dreams are weird that way. They play tricks on you."

"Right," Raymond said, even though he wasn't sure he did know.

"We talked about all different kinds of things. Just the way we used to in real life. And then at the very end, right before he got up and walked away, he said, 'Don't name the baby Luis.'"

"Why not? Did you ask why not?"

"Sure I did. He said it wouldn't be fair to the boy. He said it would be asking him to be something—or maybe he said 'someone'—that he could never be. Like asking him to fill that hole left by Luis's . . . passing. And he said the kid would grow up sad because he could never be what everybody wanted him to be."

"Oh. I guess that makes sense. Is that the kind of thing Luis would say in real life?"

"Just exactly. It was a very realistic dream."

"So what are you going to name him?"

"Contraction," Isabel said.

Raymond watched beads of sweat break out on her forehead. He wiped them away with a tissue from a box on a nearby tray table. A terrible sound burst out of her and chilled every inch of Raymond's gut. Then she pushed panicky breaths in and out between gritted teeth for a painful length of time. Painful even to Raymond.

They were lasting longer now, the contractions.

How could anybody go through a thing like that for *a day*?

"Okay," she said as the pain subsided. "Okay. No, I'm not going to name the baby Contraction, in case that's what you're wondering. I asked Luis. In the dream, I mean. The dream Luis. I said, 'So what do I name him, then?' He said, 'Name him after that nice kid. Millie's new friend.'"

"Me?" Raymond asked, his voice full of disbelief.

"That's what he said."

"Whoa. That's really nice. But . . . Raymond is kind of a geeky name, though. Don't you think? I always thought so."

"Ray could be kind of cool, though."

"Right," Raymond said. "No wonder nobody ever calls me that."

She laughed a little. As he had hoped she would.

Then a silence fell. Raymond braced himself against the announcement of another contraction. But it was probably too soon. He felt the pull of Mrs. G waiting for his return. He felt the burn and swell of the honor being bestowed on him.

"Just one thing, though," he added. "Your other two kids have Spanish names."

"This one can be different."

"Kind of hard to be different from your own family. Take it from somebody who knows. Is there a Spanish version of the name Raymond?"

"Well. There's Ramon."

"That's so much better. You should definitely name him Ramon."

"You think so?"

"I'm sure of it. I'll always know you named him after me. Which is incredibly nice, by the way. And he'll feel like he fits in with the rest of the family. And that's a big deal. Take my word for it."

———

When Raymond arrived back at the courtroom, out of breath from running, he was startled to find the door to the room locked. He rattled the knob several times. Pushed against the door with increasing distress.

He looked back and forth in the hallway and saw no one but a uniformed officer strolling as if on patrol.

"Excuse me!" he called, surprised by the panic in his own voice. "Where is everybody?"

"Lunch break," the man called back.

"But I left my friend in this room, and she was supposed to sit right there until I got back, so we couldn't lose each other. Neither one of us has a phone. They wouldn't have locked her in, would they?"

"Oh, I doubt that," the officer said, moving closer to Raymond. "I'm sure they cleared the room."

"So *where is she?*"

It came out as nearly a full-throated shout. Raymond stood back from himself and realized he was officially losing it. It was an unfamiliar feeling. Normally he did not allow himself to become so outwardly, overwhelmingly emotional.

"Well, I don't know. But take a deep breath. Most people go to one of four or five restaurants in walking distance of here. But I'd start by looking in the cafeteria. It's on the first floor, at the back of the building. Straight back down the hall from the lobby."

"Thank you," Raymond said, and took off running again.

He hadn't even managed to get his breath back from the last marathon sprint.

———

He stuck his head into the cafeteria and saw her immediately.

She was sitting at a table with that thirtysomething man and woman. The ones who had been watching the trial with them, but from the other side of the aisle. From the defense side.

He leaned his shoulder against the doorway and gasped air for a long time. Until he could breathe normally again and the bulk of his panic had drained away.

Then he walked to her.

"Oh, Raymond," she said, turning her face in his direction. "Thank goodness. You're back. Is Isabel all right?"

He almost asked how she did that. But then he remembered. It was the sound of his left shoe.

"Yeah. She's okay. She's at the hospital. Scared me to death when I didn't know where you were."

He pulled the fourth chair out from the table and sat.

"Oh dear. Didn't that officer give you the message?"

"No. I talked to him, but he didn't know anything."

"That must have been a different officer. The one I left my message with was a she. What a shame. She said she'd be there, and then she went and let me down. I'm so sorry to throw a scare into you like that, Raymond, but I really had no choice. They cleared the room for lunch, and I didn't see that coming. But I'm being very rude. Forgive me. This is Peter Hatfield and Mary Jane Hatfield Swensen. Peter and Mary Jane, this is my good friend Raymond. Peter and Mary Jane helped me to come down here for lunch, and we've been having a nice talk."

Raymond stared at the couple and said nothing. They shifted their eyes away, maybe in slight discomfort. Maybe even in shame.

Hatfield. Relatives of the defendant.

"Oh," Raymond said. "Pleased to meet you."

But he wasn't.

The Hatfields only nodded in silence. Raymond remembered something he'd read about a famous generations-long feud between a family called the Hatfields and . . . he couldn't remember what the other family had been called. But it struck him as ironic.

"So, how is Isabel? Did she have the baby?"

"Not yet. I mean, she hadn't yet when I left her. She said it could be a long time. She said I should come back here and be with you, and when court lets out we can go back there and see the baby. Or wait with her. You know. Depending."

Peter and Mary Jane made a show of wiping their mouths with their napkins and dropping them on their empty plates, as if underlining the fact that they were done eating. Which was already clear.

They rose to their feet.

"We'll go back up now," Peter said. "You have your friend here to help you when you're ready. Right?"

"I think the room is still locked," Mrs. G said. She lifted the hinged crystal of her watch and felt its hands. "It's not two o'clock yet."

"We'll take a little walk before the afternoon session," Mary Jane said.

They hurried away.

Raymond watched them go, then turned his face to Mrs. G. He noticed for the first time that she appeared to have eaten something. An empty plate sat in front of her with a small scrap of sandwich left uneaten.

"That was weird," he said.

"Which part of everything was weird?"

"Those two people. Their names are Hatfield. Are they related to the lady who shot Luis?"

"Yes. They are. They're her son and daughter."

"And you were sitting here having lunch with them."

"Yes. They were nice enough to see I was in trouble as the room was being cleared. They helped me down here."

"And you had a nice chat, you said."

"We did."

"What did you chat about?"

"Oh, this and that. Not the shooting. We left that subject alone. But pretty much everything else."

"Didn't you feel weird having lunch with that lady's son and daughter?"

"Yes. In many ways I did. But then I thought, they are not their mother. How would you feel if somebody blamed you for something your mother did?"

"Oh," Raymond said. "I guess I hadn't thought to look at it that way."

Chapter Thirteen

Just the Facts

"Mr. Adler," the prosecuting attorney said, "please tell the court what you witnessed on the evening in question."

"Okay," Ralph Adler said.

He was a heavy, fiftyish man with thinning dark hair. He seemed to wear a look on his face as though smelling fish that had gone bad. *But maybe that's only the stress of the courtroom,* Raymond thought. *And it must have been hard to witness such a terrible act of violence and then be asked to relive it.*

"I was walking down Third Avenue. I was behind them. The victim, you know, and the lady. The defendant, I guess I should call her. I was behind them both. We were all walking in the same direction. So the victim, Luis—Mr. Velez—he was closer behind her than I was. And he was a faster walker, so he was gaining on her. But he wasn't paying any attention to her—just walking down the street, you know? But I guess I noticed that he was gaining on her because she started glancing over her shoulder, kind of nervous-like. And I was watching her, because I could see she was nervous, but I was trying to see if she had any reason to be, but it didn't seem like she did, because Mr. Velez wasn't paying any attention to her, like I said."

The defense attorney rose to his feet. "Objection, Your Honor. Conjecture. The witness is not qualified to judge what Mr. Velez was paying attention to or whether my client had reason to feel concern."

"Sounds to me like Mr. Adler is sharing his observations," the judge said. "So I'm going to overrule your objection, but let the jury be advised that this is only one witness's assessment of the situation."

The defense attorney shook his head and sat.

Raymond typed with nearly blinding speed, trying to get all this down. He hadn't had a chance to charge his laptop battery over lunch, and it was down to thirty-nine percent.

"Go on, Mr. Adler," the prosecutor said.

"So, okay. So after a time she's looking over her shoulder like every second, and then she starts digging around in her purse. You could kind of tell there was a lot in there. Not that I could really see the inside of her purse, but you could tell by the way she was digging around. It looked like it was hard to find anything in there. So then she pulled something out. I know now it was the gun. At the time I figured she had some mace or pepper spray or something. It must not have been a very big gun, because I couldn't really see it there in her hand. But it was a big *enough* gun, I guess, because the guy is dead."

"Objection, Your Honor," the defense attorney said again. He rose to his feet more slowly this time, as if tired from all the exertion.

"Sustained. Mr. Adler, please tell us the facts of what you saw and refrain from any kind of editorializing."

"Sorry, Your Honor. Anyway, just as she was pulling the . . . well, object, I'll say, because I didn't know it was a gun at the time . . . just as she pulled it out of her purse, she dropped something. Like she pulled up on this object, and it upended something else that was in there, and it fell out onto the street. It didn't seem like she noticed. But the victim—Mr. Velez—he saw that right away. I don't think he paid attention to her before that. Not that I could tell. But he saw that wallet drop, and it woke him up, sort of. It was kind of a wallet and kind of a change purse. It had a change purse attached to one side of it. I only mention that because later she kept calling it her purse, and that was kind of confusing, because her purse was on her shoulder, but she was talking about this wallet-and-change-purse-combo thingy.

"Anyway. Mr. Velez, he picked it up. He picked up what she dropped. And he tried to call to her. He didn't go up to her right away. He didn't just run right up and tap her on the shoulder. He tried calling her, over and over. 'Ma'am,' he said. And then he said it louder. And then even louder than that. 'Ma'am, you dropped this! You dropped something!' He must have said it ten times. Maybe twelve times. There were a few people on the street. One of them was the lady who testi-fied earlier, but then there were also a couple others who never came forward. But I remember one of them, and the way we kind of looked at each other, like, What, is this lady deaf or something?" Then, turn-ing his eyes to the defendant, he added, "Sorry, ma'am. Turns out you really were hard of hearing, and I didn't mean any offense by that. Just telling you what we were thinking. Or what I was thinking, anyway."

"That's fine, Mr. Adler," the prosecutor said. "Go on."

"Well, he just kept getting louder and louder, but it wasn't doing a damn bit of good. Sorry. A darn bit of good. So that's when he went up and tapped her on the shoulder. But I swear he never even really tapped. He reached out to tap, but by then she was already spinning around. And it was dusk, nearly dark, so the next thing I remember was the muzzle flashes. You could see the muzzle flashes from the gun real good in that light. I know there was sound. I know the shots were loud, but somehow that's not what I remember. I just remember how that gun spit out this fire. It scared the bejesus out of me, because I was right behind him. Right behind Mr. Velez. I felt like she was shooting right at me, so I jumped out of the way. Lost my balance and slammed into this building and bruised my shoulder. And then I looked again, and she just kept firing. And firing. And firing. And I was thinking, like,

What the hell? Even if a guy really was trying to steal your purse . . . I mean, why would anybody put that many bullets into anybody?"

The defense attorney struggled to his feet again, but he never got the chance to open his mouth.

"Sorry," the witness said. "Right. I get it. Stick to the facts. Sorry. I get a little emotional talking about this, because it was a very bad experience witnessing it. I mean, I know not as bad as it was for Mr. Velez, but . . . Oops. I guess I just did it again. Okay, I get it. I'll go back to just the facts."

The defense attorney sighed and lowered himself heavily into his chair.

Raymond glanced over at Mrs. G. She had her eyes squeezed tightly shut.

"You okay?" he whispered.

"Tired," she mouthed back.

But she looked more than just tired.

"Go on, Mr. Adler," the prosecutor said.

"So, I guess she didn't stop firing until there was nothing left to fire. I say that because I remember hearing a few dry clicks. Like there were no bullets left, but she was still pulling the trigger. And Mr. Velez was on the ground, and there was a lot of blood, more and more the longer he lay there, but she was still aiming the gun down at him and pulling the trigger. Click, click, click. And I thought . . . Oh, right. I'm not supposed to tell you what I thought."

"Just tell us what happened next, Mr. Adler. After the shooting was over."

"Well, there were all these people standing around. Just kind of staring. I think we were all in shock. I know I was. So this lady, the defendant, she starts looking around at all of us and saying, 'You saw, right? He tried to steal my purse. See, it's right there in his hand, my purse. You saw him try to take it, right? You're my witnesses.'"

"Did you speak to her? Did you tell her you had seen things differently?"

"No, sir. Like I said, I was kind of in shock. So then all of a sudden there was a cop there. Like a beat cop, I think. I guess he heard the shots and came running. But I don't think he saw the shooting with his own eyes, because he was asking what happened. And the woman, the defendant, she starts telling him the same stuff she was trying to tell us. 'Oh, he took my purse. Look, you can see, it's right there in his hand.' I kept thinking this cop was going to tell her you can't shoot a guy dead for that even if it's true. But he didn't say anything to her. He was calling on his radio. Calling for some sort of backup. And then . . . well . . . I feel kind of bad about this, but I was upset by what I'd seen, and I didn't want to get involved, so I just slipped away."

"You left the scene."

"Yeah."

"When did you decide you were willing to be a witness?"

"Couple days later. I was dreaming about it at night. It was giving me nightmares. It was just a terrible thing to see. And I started worrying that maybe nobody else stayed around and tried to be witnesses, either. I started worrying about the guy's family. Like, maybe he had kids, which it turned out he did, but even if he didn't have kids, he had parents, and what if this woman said he was a robber and nobody else said anything otherwise? That's a terrible thing to be left with after your loved one is gone. So I walked into a police station and admitted what I saw."

The prosecutor simply stood a moment, allowing silence to echo through the courtroom. He seemed not to want to cut the witness off if there was anything more the man cared to say.

"I thank you for coming here today to do your civic duty, Mr. Adler." The witness only nodded, so he added, "No more questions, Your Honor."

The judge raised his eyes to the defense table. "Does the defense care to cross-examine the witness?"

"Yes, Your Honor."

The defense attorney rose again, with even more effort. Maybe he really was tired or sick, Raymond thought. But it felt like an act to Raymond, and made him feel resentful. Like the defense attorney was putting on a show of how much trouble this all was to him.

Sorry if Luis's violent death is too much of an imposition for you, Raymond thought as the man ambled over to the witness stand.

"So. Mr. Adler." He paused, as if for effect. Too long, by Raymond's internal clock. "You said several times that Ms. Hatfield told everyone Mr. Velez had tried to steal her purse. Meaning not the purse on her shoulder, but the wallet and change purse combination he had in his hand."

"Yes, sir. That's correct."

"And I'm afraid the jury may have inferred that you felt she was lying."

"I did feel she was lying."

This time Adler's words came out definite and strong. He did not glance at the judge. He did not hedge or apologize.

Raymond looked at the back of the defendant's head, but of course it told him nothing.

"That's a strong statement, Mr. Adler. My client is fighting for her freedom here, and I'd like you to think about the prejudice in that statement and reconsider."

"There's no prejudice. I know what I saw."

"But why do you not consider the idea that maybe she really thought that was true? She didn't know she had dropped the wallet. She looks down at Mr. Velez, and she sees her wallet in his hand. How is she to think it got there? And by the way, are you sure he literally had it in his hand? I should think he would have dropped it after being shot six times."

"No, sir. He didn't drop it. You would think so, yeah. But it was kind of the opposite. Like I guess it just caused him to grip on even tighter. But it was in his hand even after he was down on the street."

"Okay, fine. Whatever. But back to my original question. Did you not even consider the idea that Ms. Hatfield thought what she was saying was true?"

"No, sir."

"You didn't even consider it."

"No, sir."

"Will you please tell the court what made you so sure?"

"Because there was no time. He was just reaching out for her shoulder when she spun on him. And she had her darn purse clenched under her arm. She stuck it under there real tight after she got the gun out of it. Or anyway, what I found out later was a gun. There was no way he could have gotten into that purse before she shot him dead."

This is going badly for the defense, Raymond thought, typing wildly. Making dozens of typographical mistakes he had no time to correct. *Good.*

"With all due respect, Mr. Adler, the question was not whether Mr. Velez had time to take the wallet out of Ms. Hatfield's purse. My question was why you're so sure she was telling a premeditated lie. That's quite an accusation to level against my client, to suggest she knowingly lied. You said yourself that you were in shock. Shock creates confusion. It warps a person's sense of time. It all happened very fast. Ms. Hatfield looked down, and there was her wallet in the hands of a man she thought was trying to steal it. Doesn't it make sense that she thought he had?"

"Maybe if she hadn't been so damn sure he was about to steal from her, we wouldn't all of us be in this mess!"

Raymond heard an audible pull of breath. A hushed gasp. Both from Mrs. G and one woman juror.

"Your Honor," the defense attorney said.

"I'm warning you again, Mr. Adler," the judge said. "Tread lightly."

Mr. Adler did not apologize. He only sat in silence.

"So I'll ask you again, Mr. Adler," the attorney said. "How can you look me in the eye and claim to know for a fact that the defendant didn't think, in the heat of the moment, that her version of events was the truth?"

The witness continued to sit in silence. Long enough that a couple members of the jury began to shift uneasily in their seats.

"Well . . . ," Adler said at last, ". . . I guess I can't know what was going on inside her head."

"My point exactly. No further questions, Your Honor."

—

They sat on the subway car together, Raymond feeling the familiar rocking of the car's movement along the tracks.

When he glanced over at Mrs. G, she seemed to be slumping over on her seat, as if passing out and falling. He reached over and grabbed her around her shoulders and brought her upright again, and she roused herself suddenly.

"Oh," she said. "Oh."

"Are you okay?"

"I guess I dozed off for a minute there. I'm just very tired, Raymond. It's just been a very long day. It's been years since I've tried to do this much in one day."

"Yeah. That's true, all right. But other than being tired, are you okay?"

"No."

They rode in silence for a few seconds.

"We could just go home if you need to," he said.

"Oh no. We can't abandon Isabel. She's having her baby. We said we would be there after court. And we're going to be there, even if it's the last thing I ever do."

"Don't say things like that."

"It's just an expression."

Silence. He did not attempt to reply. Raymond was tired and upset, too. Maybe not as much as Mrs. G. But enough.

"I'm sorry, though," she said. "It's a hard time for both of us. I will try to speak in lighter terms. Besides . . . maybe I will get a second wind when I experience this beautiful little new life. What could be better for the spirit than a new life in the world?"

—

Halfway up the stairs from the subway to the street, Raymond knew they had a problem on their hands.

He stopped and waited with her. Let her catch her breath. He knew she would make it up the stairs if he gave her enough time. But she was clearly digging down into her last energy reserves.

It was a seven-block walk from the subway station to the hospital, as best Raymond could figure.

And then they had to get home.

He placed a hand behind her back and tried to give her something of a push. A lift. It seemed to work fairly well.

In time they stood on the street together, Mrs. G panting for breath, her head down. Raymond looked around and thought about hailing a cab. But he didn't have much money on him, and he wasn't sure if she did, either. It didn't seem right to ask her for money, even at a time like this.

"It's seven blocks to the hospital," he said, finally gearing himself up to break the bad news.

"Oh, I don't know, Raymond. That might be too much. I will try, but I don't know if I can."

"I don't think I have enough money on me for a cab. Do you?"

"I might. I would have to look in my purse. But I really don't know what cabs charge anymore. Do you?"

"Not exactly. My dad always pays."

Raymond allowed himself to realize, for the first time, that he had led them into trouble. That this was a serious situation. They were far from home, and he had asked her to do more than she could do. It rose up over his head like a tsunami and swept him away. He had no idea how to fix what he had broken.

He looked up to see a cab pull over to the curb for a sharply dressed businessman carrying an expensive leather briefcase. Raymond looked into the man's face, and the man looked back at him, and Raymond wasn't sure why. He wasn't sure what they had done to draw this man's attention. But he was standing only a few steps away, and it struck Raymond that he might have overheard their conversation.

"Take this one," the man said, opening the back door of the cab and pointing into its back seat.

"But we might not have—"

Before he could even say the word "money," the man reached out his right hand as if to shake hands with Raymond. Raymond thought it was an odd gesture—an odd moment to conduct a meeting ritual. But he reached in return and shook the man's hand.

As soon as he did, he felt the folded bill. Felt it silently, invisibly pressed into his palm.

"Thank you," Raymond said.

But he wasn't sure if the man had heard. He was already gone, trotting into the street with his hand up to hail another cab.

"Good news," he told Mrs. G, steering her toward the back seat of the taxi. "We can take a cab."

"Oh, thank goodness. Turns out you have enough money after all?"

"Yeah. Turns out I do."

"I can pay you back some of it."

"Don't worry about it. I just came into a little more money, that's all. It's taken care of."

———

Raymond stuck his head into the hospital room and saw Isabel looking back at him, exhausted—nearly wounded, as if she had just survived a war—but beaming. In her arms was a tiny newborn, mostly wrapped in a blanket.

"Oh, he's here!" Raymond said.

He noticed Mrs. G quicken her step at the news.

They walked into the hospital room together.

"I'm so glad you both came," Isabel said. "There's someone you need to meet. This is Ramon."

Raymond stepped closer, leading Mrs. G along. He looked down into the face of the child at close range. He was . . . unbelievable. Unbelievably tiny. Unbelievably perfect. It was hard to take at face value that such a perfect little being could be real.

"Oh, he's beautiful!"

"Describe him to me," Mrs. G said.

"Okay. I'll try. But I don't think words will do him justice. But he has this little tuft of soft-looking dark hair, but only right on top of his head. And his little lips and ears are so perfectly shaped, I swear it hurts to look at them. And his skin is almost . . . like you could see through it, it's so new and perfect. You can see the little veins under his cheeks, but just in a nice way. I mean, it's good skin. It's enough. It's just so new."

"Here," Isabel said to Mrs. G. "Give me your hand."

Mrs. G reached out carefully, and Isabel took the hand, and guided it to the top of Ramon's soft hair. Mrs. G stroked the baby's head slowly, her eyes closed, head cocked as if listening to faraway music. Then she very gently touched his cheeks and nose.

Raymond was watching her face, so he noticed the moment when everything changed. When the rapture fell away, and was replaced by . . . well, he wasn't sure what. And he wasn't sure why. But it wasn't good. Somehow she had fallen into some kind of emotional pit in that moment.

Maybe she's just really tired, he thought.

He helped her sit in one of the plastic chairs.

"So tell me what I missed at the trial," Isabel said.

Raymond pulled himself up another chair, still staring at that tiny brand-new face. Realizing it was the closest he had come to seeing Luis Velez.

"Well, I missed a big part of the morning, too, of course," he said, because Mrs. G seemed to be lost in another world. "But in the afternoon, they examined one of the witnesses. It was good, what he said. He made it really clear that he thought the defendant was lying about parts of the thing. He was very direct about that, even when it got him in a little trouble with the judge. He wasn't supposed to give his opinion, but he did anyway. So at that point I was thinking it was going really well for the prosecution, but then at the very end of the cross-examination, the defense attorney just sort of turned it all around again."

Isabel's smile dropped away. "Yeah, they'll do that," she said. She turned her face to Mrs. G, who was staring in the direction of the wall. "And what did Raymond and I miss in the morning, Millie?"

Mrs. G turned her face back toward them as if waking from a deep sleep. "I'm sorry. What again?"

"What did I make Raymond miss in the morning?"

"Oh, not very much, I'd say. The first of the two witnesses. But she didn't say anything very different from the second one. She was more shy about her observations. That was the main difference. If she had opinions about the whole thing, she kept them to herself."

They sat quietly for a brief moment. Then Raymond heard a knock at the room's open door. He turned around to see the young police-woman who had driven them to the hospital that morning. Though, looking back, Raymond thought that ride felt like a thing that had taken place weeks ago.

"May I come in?" she asked.

Raymond looked to Isabel to see if she still felt bristly about the officer's presence. But her face looked open and soft.

"Yes, of course you may," she said. "I'm glad to get a chance to thank you for getting me here safely this morning."

The officer moved close to the bed, slowly and reverently, as if in church.

"I hope it's okay that I'm here. I know I came on a little strong when I first saw you this morning, but I'm two months pregnant, and I'm just so excited about it I can hardly contain myself. I didn't know who you were at the time—just that you were ready to go into labor any minute. But after I found out you were the widow, I wanted to . . . you know . . . do something helpful."

"Getting me here in time was helpful," Isabel said. "This is Ramon."

The officer gently stroked Ramon's head. "He's gorgeous," she said. "Are you staying tonight?"

"No, I can't. My insurance doesn't cover much. My sister is coming by to get me after work."

"Oh dear. You'd think one night in the hospital would be good."

"Hard to pay for, though."

"You're not going to try to come to court tomorrow, are you?"

"Probably not. I'll ask Raymond and Millie to fill me in on what I missed. But the day after, most likely. Oh, the judge will just love that. Won't he? First I shoot off my big mouth when I'm not supposed to. Then I come back with a newborn who cries . . ."

"Well, just don't do both at once," the officer said.

"No, I won't. I'll be quiet. I'm embarrassed about that." She looked down at the baby in her arms for a beat or two. "It's hard not to say the truth, though."

"Yeah. That's the problem with trials. Somehow they have it in their heads, the judge and jury, that they'll decide what's the truth. But the truth already happened. They can't decide what happened. They can only be right or wrong about it. Seems like too many times they're wrong."

The officer fell silent, as if regretting the direction in which she'd taken the conversation.

No one else cared to speak after that.

"Well," the woman said. "I'll leave you be."

She turned and walked out of the room with no more words spoken.

Raymond jumped up and followed her out into the hall.

"Excuse me," he called after her, because he had forgotten her name.

She stopped. Turned around.

"I need to ask a favor of you," he said.

"Okay."

"It's kind of a big favor. You might say no."

"Try me."

"My friend who I brought to the courthouse today. The elderly woman. She's really tired. I mean, it's a little scary how much this day was too hard for her. I was wondering if you could give us a ride back to the subway station."

He watched her face soften, and a deep fear in his gut softened with it. And he knew they—both he and Mrs. G—would be okay.

"I'll go you one better than that," she said. "I'll give you a ride home. Wherever you live, I'll get you home safely."

—

Mrs. G fell asleep on the ride in the back of the patrol car, then woke with a start for no reason Raymond could see or hear.

"Ramon," she said.

"What about him?"

"Isn't that something like Raymond, only in Spanish?"

"It is, yeah."

"Is that a coincidence?"

"Nope. No coincidence."

She fell silent again for long enough that Raymond thought she might have fallen back asleep.

He looked past her slack face and watched buildings and pedestrians flashing by. It was dusk, almost dark. The time of day when Luis had been shot. Raymond wondered what a muzzle flash from a gun would look like in that light. Also, he hoped he would never find out.

"See?" she said suddenly, surprising him. "You're making your mark on the world."

"Think so?"

"I know so," she said.

Then she definitely fell back asleep. Raymond knew because there was snoring involved.

Chapter Fourteen

What Kind of Person?

Raymond knocked on her door at 8:00 sharp the following morning.

"Come in, Raymond," she called. But her voice sounded oddly distant and small.

He let himself in with the keys.

"Where are you?" he called, looking around the empty living room.

He hoped she was in the bathroom putting the finishing touches on her preparations for the morning.

"I'm in the bedroom," she said. "You may come in."

He walked to the doorway and stopped dead, looking inside.

She was still in bed.

Her hair was down, long and unbraided. She wore a high-collared nightgown. She lay holding the blankets up to her chest with both arthritic hands. Louise lay curled against her right hip, looking over her own shoulder blades at Raymond.

In the middle of his wave of disappointment, he found one bright little moment. He was happy that she had arrived home the night before with enough energy to put herself properly to bed.

"You're not ready," he said.

"I'm not going."

"Oh."

"I'm sorry. But I can't. I just can't. It's too hard."

"Physically hard?"

"Well, yes," she said. "That, too. You don't have to go, of course, if it's hard for you, too. But if you do, will you please take notes and tell me more or less what I missed? Just the generals, though. The big developments. The details are too much to bear. You will be the only one there representing us today. If you go."

"Will you go tomorrow?"

"I think I will go when the jury is ready to decide. I want to hear what they decide. Do you think that will be tomorrow or the next day? Or later?"

"I don't have any idea."

"Well, you let me know. Please. If you can. I'm sorry, Raymond. I know you wanted me to go. But I have a long, sordid history with death and dying. When something brings it back up, it just knocks the legs right out from under me. Not that Luis's death in the present is not enough, but the combination of past and present is more than I can bear."

He stood a moment, his shoulder leaning against the doorjamb, hoping she would volunteer more about her past. Failing that, he hoped he would discover that he had grown into someone who was brave enough to ask.

Neither wish came true.

"One thing I want to ask you before I go," he said, but it was a milder, easier thing. At least, he hoped it was. "Last night when you met the baby. You were so thrilled. And then all of a sudden . . . you . . . weren't."

"True."

He leaned in silence for a few additional seconds, wondering if it would be right to ask more. As it turned out, he didn't need to.

"At first I was just so taken by him," she said, "and how perfect and innocent and vulnerable he is. And for a while that seemed only like a wonderful thing. And then I started to worry about the world into which he's just been born. What will it do to him? How much will it take from him? Look how much it's taken from him already, and before he could even so much as come out of his mother and look around to see what he's gotten himself into."

He waited, but she did not seem inclined to say more. He glanced at her clock radio and saw he didn't have a lot of time to spare. Besides, nothing he could say would be any more optimistic than her assessment.

"Okay," he said. "You just rest. I'll come by later and tell you how it went."

———

"Ms. Hatfield," the defense attorney said to his client, "will you please explain to the jury why you turn off your hearing aids when you're walking on the street?"

It was nearly three hours into the morning court session. Almost the whole session so far had consisted of the defendant testifying, questioned by her own attorney.

Raymond looked down at his notes and realized he hadn't typed much. Because she hadn't said much. Granted, she had spoken many, many words. But in Raymond's mind they didn't seem to add up to anything.

Raymond felt he could sum up the whole morning session in just a sentence or two.

Look at me; I'm a nice person. I'm just like you.

But it would have felt weird to type that in his notes. Besides, he didn't think their campaign was working. She was nothing like him, and he didn't think she was a nice person. She was defensive. That was all he could see or feel. Defensiveness.

He looked up at her face in that split second before she spoke again. She had big, round cheeks. Plump. They seemed a strange contrast to her nose and chin, which were sharp. Her brown eyes were small and set strangely close together.

"Believe me, if you wore hearing aids, you'd understand. They amplify background noises. It's very irritating. It's grating, you know?"

"Okay," her attorney said. "I think we understand. No more questions."

Raymond thought it was a weird place to end the testimony. He wasn't sure what the defense attorney felt he had just accomplished.

He typed a few quick notes, then looked up to see the prosecutor approach the witness stand and the defendant.

"I'm not at all sure I *do* understand," he said. "So I'd like to clarify this, in case the jury is confused as well."

"What don't you understand?" she asked.

Defensive.

"Why don't you just turn the hearing aid down until the background noise is bearable?"

"You can't understand unless you wear them."

"That really doesn't answer my question. Help us understand."

"It's a very grating noise, even on low volume. The traffic and all. It's artificial sounding, like static. It irritates me."

"I should think it would be an important safety issue to have it on."

"In what respect?" She sounded suspicious. As if he were trying to sell her something. Something she knew better than to buy.

"What if you were crossing the street and there was a car coming?"

"I look both ways."

"I'm sure you do. But what if a driver was honking his horn and you didn't hear it?"

"I would hear a blaring horn if it was right on top of me."

"But you didn't hear Mr. Velez."

"No."

"Do you regret that now? I mean, a man lost his life because you turned off your hearing aids. If it were me, I'd lose quite a bit of sleep over that decision."

"I'm not sure what you're getting at," she said, seeming to draw more deeply into her own skin for safety.

"You've made several statements about the inconvenience of the hearing aids when there's traffic around. I think that's fallen on my ears in a particular way, and it's made me want to ask more about it. Mrs. Velez, the widow of the victim, is not here in the courtroom this morning because she gave birth yesterday. But what if she were? What if she were sitting right there beside that gentleman?"

All eyes of the jury, as well as those of the defendant and her two grown children, turned to Raymond. He looked briefly behind himself, but there was no one back there. *He* was the gentleman in question.

"Don't you think she might wince inwardly, hearing you talk about your inconvenience? I mean, you keep saying the hearing aids are very irritating. But they would have saved that man's life. I certainly don't think you want the jury to get the impression that you're still thinking of your own convenience after a man lost his life."

"Objection, Your Honor," the defense attorney said. He did not struggle to his feet. He did not go on to classify what sort of objection he was raising.

"Counselor," the judge said, frowning at the prosecuting attorney, "wherever you're going with this, hurry up and get there."

"All right, Your Honor. I'll be extremely direct. Ms. Hatfield. You've been out on the street many times since this unfortunate incident occurred, correct?"

"I have."

"Were your hearing aids on or off?"

"Off."

"Even after a man lost his life."

"I had no way of knowing that would happen."

"But now it *has* happened. And you know it."

"It was a freak accident. A once-in-a-lifetime occurrence. It's not going to happen again."

"If you could, would you still carry a handgun when you go out?"

"Of course I would. It's dangerous out there, and this 'unfortunate incident,' as you called it, only proves it."

Raymond looked up from his typing. Looked at the prosecutor's face. Silence fell over the room. And hovered for a strange length of time.

Then the attorney seemed to pull his thoughts together.

"Are you honestly saying, Ms. Hatfield, that this shooting proves that you are the one in danger on the street? Because I thought it proved that you *are* the danger."

"Objection, Your Honor."

"Withdrawn. One more question for now, Ms. Hatfield, and then I think we'll be recessing for lunch. It's a very important question, so I hope you'll take a moment before answering. Do you feel remorse?"

"Excuse me?"

"It's a pretty straightforward question. Do you feel remorse over what happened?"

"Well, of course I do. What kind of person do you think I am? Do you think I'm a monster? Well, I'm not a monster! Of course I'm sorry that man is dead, but I made the best decision I could in the heat of the moment."

"So you still think it was a good decision."

"I think I did my best."

"So you don't regret what you did."

A pause. Raymond watched the back of the defense attorney's head. Waited for him to pop up and object. He never did.

"You've got a lot of nerve saying that to me. You don't know what I think or how I feel. How could you even say such a thing to me?"

"Well, if you really want to know, Ms. Hatfield, I'll tell you. I'll tell you how I arrived at that conjecture. The one time you referred to the victim and said you're sorry he's dead, you immediately followed it with the word 'but.' Even more to the point, when a person does something she deeply regrets, it tends to bring changes in her behavior. She sees how certain actions on her part led to a certain outcome, and . . . well, it seems it's human nature to want to make some changes if you really want to be sure you never create that outcome again."

The defendant sat back with a thump, eyes narrowing. "I resent the implication," she said.

"I'll just ask again. Very point-blank, if that's not a bad choice of phrasing. It probably is, though. Do you feel remorse over what happened to Mr. Velez?"

"I made the best decision I could at the time."

"Right. Got it. This might be a good time to break for lunch, Your Honor."

———

Raymond stood in line at the cafeteria, where he ordered a turkey sandwich. He placed it on his plastic tray, keeping his eyes down. He picked up a stainless steel fork, spoon, and knife, but then he wasn't sure why. He wouldn't need them to eat a sandwich. But he felt too embarrassed to put them back.

He paid at the cash register, then stepped away from the line and looked around. There was no place to sit. Not one free table.

He headed for the door, thinking he would find a place to sit outside the cafeteria. In a stairwell, maybe. But a uniformed guard at the door turned him back inside again.

"You can't take that out of here."

"I paid for the sandwich."

"But you didn't pay for the plate, and the tray. And the silverware. Sorry. You have to sit in here."

"*Sit?*" he asked, his voice making a point about the likelihood of that. "Where do you see a place to sit?"

"You can ask to share somebody's table if it's not full."

"But they all are."

"No. That one's not."

He pointed to a table for four, currently only occupied by two people. Unfortunately the two people were Peter and Mary Jane, the son and daughter of the woman who had just nearly obliterated his appetite.

Raymond sighed, and walked to their table.

If Mrs. G can do this, so can I.

They looked up. Nodded. Looked quickly away.

If Raymond had been called upon to write thought bubbles above their heads, as in a cartoon, he would have had them saying, "Oh. Hi. It's you. Good to see you. Go away now."

Raymond did not go away.

"I'm sorry," he said. "But there's literally no place else to sit. Not one other place."

Peter made his neck long like a giraffe and peered around the room, as if hoping to prove Raymond wrong.

"Well," he said. "Then . . . sit here, I guess."

"Okay. Thanks."

Raymond sat down and focused every ounce of energy he had onto that turkey sandwich. He never took his eyes off it. The silence was onerous. It seemed to vibrate on the table between them.

Raymond did not break it.

They ate for a good five minutes in that awkward silence.

"There are a lot of good things about my mother," Peter said suddenly.

"I'm sure there are," Raymond said without taking his eyes off the sandwich. Though he wasn't sure at all.

"She just has trouble with that one thing. Well, I don't mean that. I don't mean everything else about her is perfect. I guess I mean everything else about her is reasonable. But she's just not one of those people who says she's wrong. I think it's a generational thing. But otherwise she's a good woman."

"Why are you saying that about her?" Mary Jane asked. She was clearly upset. It made Raymond want to abandon his food and run. "It's not just Mom. It's her attorney. He told her not to say she was wrong."

"Who told you that?" Peter asked his sister. "Do you know that for a fact? Did she tell you that?"

"No. She didn't have to. It's just common sense. You don't get up on the stand and admit you did the wrong thing. She's looking at jail time."

"It's a risky strategy," Peter said.

Another silence reigned. Even more awkward than the first.

Raymond thought maybe he should say something. Then a moment later he figured he shouldn't. He went back and forth about it several times. When he finally spoke, it was mostly because the back and forth was making him crazy.

"I've heard the court goes easier on you if you show remorse."

Mary Jane pushed away from the table and stomped off. Straight out of the cafeteria without pausing. Or looking back.

Raymond pulled a deep breath and tried to sigh out his tension. It didn't sigh out.

"Well, say what you want about strategy," Peter said. "I've known that woman for thirty-four years. She's my mother and I love her. But I've never heard her say the three words 'I was wrong.' And I'm worried about the way that's characterizing her now, especially for people who don't know her at all."

Raymond chewed a mouthful of turkey sandwich and tried to swallow it. It had been dry to begin with. Now it felt like swallowing a mouthful of cotton. And he hadn't even gotten a beverage he could use to wash it down.

"What did you and Mrs. Gutermann talk about yesterday?" Raymond asked when he was able.

"Oh, a little bit of everything. She's an amazing lady. Why?"

"I was just wondering how she managed to make a thing like this work. And I so . . . couldn't."

"Not your fault. It was my sister's and my fault. We brought it up. We shouldn't have. It was just hard to sit there all morning and listen to her testimony and wonder what the people who heard it were thinking about her. It's hard not to want to tell people to please try to have a higher opinion of her. But we don't get to talk to the jury, so . . ."

"Right. Doesn't matter what *I* think."

"I should go find my sister."

He rose from the table and walked away, leaving half of his spaghetti lunch uneaten. Raymond leaned back in his chair and sighed deeply. Squeezed his eyes closed.

I'll have to ask her how she does a thing like that. Like yesterday's lunch with the Hatfields. There must be a secret to it.

Then he decided the secret was probably ninety-two years of experience, and that it probably wouldn't help to ask.

———

The prosecutor dug into the defendant again after lunch.

"I'd like to go a little deeper into the nuts and bolts of the shooting," he said.

The Hatfield woman flopped against the back of her chair in obvious disgust. "I can't imagine what there is to say about it that hasn't been said a hundred times already."

"Bear with me. Please. I want to ask about something Mr. Adler said yesterday. He said you couldn't possibly have turned around and seen Mr. Velez holding your wallet and decided he stole it, because there was no time. There was no time for him to steal it. You had your purse clenched under your arm. He said you put it under there tightly after you got the gun out."

"That's right."

"And Mr. Velez had just barely caught up to you enough to reach out."

"Look, I know what you're getting at. But I wasn't lying. I turned around. I saw the wallet in his hand. I call it a purse, but I don't want to be confusing. I concluded it was a robbery, and I acted accordingly."

"I think you have the chronology wrong."

"No," she said. "I have it exactly right."

"Turns out, though, there's evidence to the contrary. Before you turned to face him you had already fired off a shot."

The woman's face went slack with surprise.

"That's a perfectly ridiculous thing to say. How could I have fired a shot before I even turned around?"

"I don't know," the prosecutor said. "You tell me." He walked to the table where his notes and files lay stacked. "Your Honor, I'd like to enter into evidence Exhibits D, E1, and E2."

He handed two photos and some kind of document to the judge, who scanned them with his gaze, nodded, and handed them back.

He approached the witness with them, and she sat back, away from him and them, as though they might be poisonous.

"The newspaper report of the incident said you fired six bullets into Mr. Velez's torso, emptying the gun. But that's not quite right. I have a crime scene photo here of the body that clearly shows five entry wounds. And I also have the medical examiner's report, which says the same."

"Well, I don't know where the other one went. I guess I just missed."

"Yes. You did. You missed by nearly forty-five degrees. I also have a photo of the spot that took the first bullet. Or what police concluded was the first. It's in the building that you were passing at the time of the shooting. The building that was on your right before you turned around."

"So? So, I missed. Like I said. I was upset."

"But you don't stand and face a man at point-blank range and then fire a shot forty-five degrees off to your left."

"So what are you saying happened, then?"

"I'm saying you fired off one shot while you were spinning around."

"Okay. Fine. I was afraid. So what if I did?"

"If you hadn't turned around, then you hadn't seen the wallet in his hand."

He waited, in case she wanted to say something. She did not. Her face seemed to be growing whiter.

The prosecutor continued, filling the silence.

"A few moments ago you said you turned around, saw your wallet in his hand, concluded it was a robbery, and acted accordingly. But apparently you had your finger so tightly on the trigger of that gun that you fired before you had even turned to face Mr. Velez. Now, I know it was not your intention to try to hurt the building you were walking past. So I can only figure you were quite fearful and all too ready to defend yourself."

"Yes," she said. Tentatively. As if it could be a trap. "I was."

"Why?"

"*Why?*"

"Yes, why. Why were you so afraid? Why had you already concluded it was time to fire the gun in your own defense?"

"I told you. I thought it was a robbery."

"But we've just concluded that you had no reason to think that yet."

"Of course I did. He was coming closer to me. He was reaching out a hand. He was about to touch me."

"How did you know?"

"That he was reaching out?"

"Yes."

"I turned my head partway and saw it out of the corner of my eye. Anyway, what difference does it make what exactly I thought he was going to do in the way of a crime against me? I just knew I didn't want it, whatever it was."

She stopped as if out of breath. She had clearly put a great deal of energy and tension into those words. Raymond was aware of himself sitting half off the wooden bench. He could feel the edge of it pressing into his buttocks.

"I see," the attorney said. "So let's back up a little. Back when you first took the gun out of your purse . . . what was Mr. Velez doing wrong then?"

A freighted pause.

"Wrong?" she asked. "I don't understand the question."

"You said you fired the gun because he was reaching out."

"Yes."

"So when you took the gun out of your purse . . . what was he doing?"

"Just . . . walking."

"So why did you take out your gun?"

"He was getting closer."

"You mean he walked faster than you did."

"Yes, but . . . something felt threatening about it."

"What?"

"I don't know if I can explain it."

"Well, I hope you can, Ms. Hatfield. Because I don't think we live in a society where you get to shoot a man dead without being able to explain what he did to make you feel threatened. At least, I hope we don't."

"Objection, Your Honor," the defense attorney said, struggling to his feet. "Badgering the witness."

"Overruled. It's a fair question, and the witness needs to answer it."

Silence in the court. For maybe the count of five.

"I'm a good judge of character. I can feel in my gut when something's wrong."

"If that's true, Ms. Hatfield, then this incident is a terrible example. I mean, you couldn't use this case to prove it. Mr. Velez was trying to return a dropped item. You just about couldn't have been more wrong about him. Your judgment of his character couldn't have fallen further from the truth. But let's just go with this for a minute. Someone is behind you in the street. You judge their motive. Based on what?"

A stunned silence.

"The defendant will answer the question," the judge said.

"I don't know, really. It's just a feeling."

"Okay. A feeling. I want to go a little deeper into these feelings. If I was walking behind you on the street, would you judge me a threat?"

"I don't know. No. Maybe."

"That's a lot of answers, Ms. Hatfield. You told the court you were good at this."

"On the one hand, you're a man. But you obviously have plenty of money."

"Interesting. So a richer person is less of a threat?"

"Don't twist my words."

"I think I was paraphrasing you accurately."

"I only meant . . . why would you need to rob me? You have money."

"So poor people steal and rich people don't?"

"I didn't say that. I just said you'd have no need to steal."

"So if people who have plenty of money aren't interested in stealing any *more* money, then I'm curious as to what's in all those offshore accounts in the Cayman Islands."

"Objection, Your Honor."

"Overruled," the judge said. "The defendant opened this line of questioning herself when she claimed she could correctly assess a threat."

The defense attorney sighed and slumped into his chair again.

"What about this young gentleman?" Raymond looked up from his notes to see everyone staring at him. "If he was walking on the street behind you, what would your judgment say?"

"I don't know. I don't know anything about him."

"You didn't know anything about Luis Velez, either. What about the elderly woman who was in court with this young man yesterday? Do you remember her?"

"I do."

"What if she was walking behind you?"

"That's a preposterous question."

"Why?"

"Because she couldn't outrun a two-year-old on a wobbly tricycle. Why, she can't even see. What possible harm could she do me?"

"So it's about the physical ability to do harm."

"Well, yes. He was a big man. A big man can hurt me."

"How did you know?"

"How did I know what?"

"How did you know he was a big man? You hadn't turned around yet."

"I saw reflections in the windows as we passed them."

"I see. I can't imagine that would provide much detail. Especially since it was nearly dark."

"It did, though. Plenty of detail. I could see him very well. Everything about him. He was big. He probably outweighed me by a hundred pounds."

"And I outweigh you by sixty or seventy, but you say you don't find me threatening. And whether it's seventy or a hundred, you're still outmatched."

"I know what you're getting at," Hatfield spat. "And I don't appreciate it."

"What am I getting at?"

"You're suggesting prejudice."

"Am I?"

"You know you are, now don't play games with me. Look, all I knew is that he was a man and he was big. I didn't even know anything about his . . . you know. Race or nationality. How could I? I hadn't even looked around."

"But you said you saw him in reflections in the windows. You said the images were very detailed. You said you saw everything about him."

"You're a very frustrating man," she said, blowing out an audible breath of disgust.

"All I'm doing is going over what you could possibly have known about Luis Velez so we can figure out what part of it felt threatening to you. You knew he was a man, that he was big, and that he was Latino."

"That's not why. There are other things you're not taking into account. Feelings you get. Sometimes a person just feels menacing, and you can't point to why. You just know it."

"But he wasn't menacing, Ms. Hatfield. We've well established that you were wrong about that. He was just about the least menacing person you could have had walking behind you. He was a good Samaritan. He was trying to make you see that you had dropped an important item. He was a loving husband and father. Three times a week he rode more than half an hour round-trip on the subway to help an elderly blind woman do her errands."

"But I had no way of knowing that!"

The defendant was shouting now. Raymond was typing as fast as he could.

"But you said you're a very good judge of character. You said sometimes a person just feels menacing and you know it. Something threw your sense of judgment way off, and I'm trying to get to the bottom of what it was."

"You're just trying to trip me up!" She was standing now, as if ready to walk off the stand without permission. "I need a break from this. Do I get to take a break?"

"No need, Your Honor," the prosecutor said. "I have no more questions."

———

"Oh my," Mrs. G said. "The man is very good at his job!"

Raymond had just finished reading her the notes he'd taken during the afternoon session.

She was still in bed. He was sitting on one of the dining room chairs that he'd pulled into her bedroom.

He looked up. Closed the cover of his laptop.

"So that was all for the day?" she asked.

"No. It dragged on. But I didn't take too many notes after that because it wasn't as interesting. It didn't seem to change much. Her attorney questioned her again, but just to sort of try to repair the damage. He just kept asking questions that went to how normal it is to make a mistake. How perfectly good people make mistakes. And then the officer who was first on the scene testified, but he didn't have all that much to add. He didn't see it happen. It was just a lot of repetition with him."

"So what is left to the trial? Do you know?"

"Well, the defense and the prosecution both rested at the end of the day."

"So jury deliberations tomorrow? That was fast."

"I think closing statements and then jury deliberation."

"Oh. Closing statements, yes. But the jury will go out tomorrow."

"Looks that way," he said, thinking she didn't seem rested enough to attend.

"I will have to be there, then."

"You sure you're up to going?"

"I will be there because I have to be there."

"I could call you from the courthouse and tell you how it went."

"No," she said. With surprising firmness. It was a "no" he knew it would be pointless to question. "I need to be there when the verdict is announced. Oh. By the way. That nice woman called."

"What nice woman?"

"The one whose husband is also Luis Velez. She got this number from the caller ID."

"Oh. Yeah. She *is* a nice woman."

"Very much, yes. We talked for a long time. She had already seen the story about Luis in the paper, so she knew what had happened, but she was very happy to hear from you again. She invited us to come to a Sunday supper with them. Anytime we want. We are just to call and let them know which Sunday we would like to come, so they know to make extra. She said she will make again that chocolate cake you liked so much."

"Would you want to do that?"

"I don't see why not," she said. "In my very long life so far I have never met a Luis Velez I didn't like."

Chapter Fifteen

Objective Reality, or Lack of Same

"In conclusion," the prosecuting attorney said, "I realize the defense has gone to great lengths to paint the defendant as a law-abiding citizen. Above reproach. But nobody does anything wrong until the moment they do. Everybody has a clean record the first time they break the law."

Raymond thought the man looked tired. He wondered briefly if the attorney took on the stress of these cases as if the victim were one of his own. Or whether it simply mattered to his career whether the outcome of this trial fell into the win or loss category. Or maybe it was unrelated. Maybe he'd stayed up partying too late the night before.

He glanced over at Isabel, who was bouncing the baby gently in her arms. Ramon was fussy. Everyone could hear him fussing, and Raymond could see everyone try to focus away from it. Whatever the prosecutor said next, Raymond missed it, thinking about the baby.

Ramon let out one scorching cry before Isabel managed to swing him back and forth to settle him.

Isabel rose as if to offer to step out of the room. But the prosecutor directed her to sit. Guided her with a motion of his hand.

"No," he said. "You have a right to be here. That baby has a right to be here. He's an important reminder for the jury. He's growing up without a father. The defense will ask you to imagine what it would be like to be Ms. Hatfield," he said, turning back to face the jury. "To be looking at jail time when you'd left the house that fateful morning not planning to do anything wrong. I'm going to ask you to imagine how it would feel to be Mrs. Velez, or her baby. Or one of her two other young children. You're going along living your life, planning to grow old together. And then along comes a woman who thinks she knows who should be feared. She's wrong about your loved one, but she comes to trial still claiming that she knows a threat when she sees one. But you know your loved one was not a threat. Everyone knows it by now, but it's too late. One bad decision from her, and your life is blown apart. And it never goes back together again. She shot a man to death who meant her no harm, and she will tell you it was an accident. But it was an accident with life-changing consequences for this woman and child. Shouldn't there be some consequences for the shooter?

"I mean, ladies and gentlemen, there are accidents, and then there are accidents. If she had dropped the gun and it had gone off, that would be a pure accident. But she pulled that trigger. Six times. A voluntary act every time. And she was wrong. I'm sorry, but when you fire six bullets at a fellow New Yorker, you can't be wrong. He has to have meant you harm. Or you at least have to be able to point to some very real evidence that made you *think* he meant you harm. Otherwise it's voluntary manslaughter.

"Sure, we all want to live in a safer city. We all want to live in a safer world. But Luis Velez was not the one making us less safe. A woman with a handgun she was far too quick to use, she was the one who made our streets even more dangerous. She's the one who brought this instance of gunfire onto our streets, and she killed an innocent man. And there has to be a price to pay for that. What is a life worth? You tell me."

He walked back to his table.

Raymond waited. Everybody waited. The attorney never said, "Thank you, ladies and gentlemen of the jury." He never said the equivalent of "That is all."

He just sat down.

"Well, all right," the defense attorney said, and struggled to his feet. "My turn, I guess. Ladies and gentlemen of the jury, you're reasonable people. You look at my client, and you know in your heart she's not a killer."

Raymond typed a few notes about that. Because it seemed like an odd thing to say. How can you kill someone and not be a killer?

"She's a mother of two grown children. She plays bridge every Thursday. She goes to church. Now I ask you, what justice is served by putting this good woman in jail? Even for thirty or sixty or ninety days? Look at her. Does she look like the kind of person who belongs in a jail cell to you?"

In the space of silence that followed, Raymond's fingers flew over his keyboard, noting personal observations.

"Defense seems to be suggesting there is a 'kind' of person who belongs in jail and another 'kind' who doesn't," he typed. "Based on what? It's supposed to be based on their criminal actions, but you can't see those. What are we supposed to be seeing here?"

"Of course not," the defense attorney bellowed, his voice too loud. "You put a person in jail because they're a danger to society. My client is no danger to society, and you know it as well as I do. She's never going to hurt anyone again. This was an accident, my friends. A terrible accident. Why would you choose to punish her for that? Isn't she being punished enough already? She's been put on trial like a common criminal. Forced to fear for her freedom. She has to wake up every morning regretting that terrible mistake. Why would you want to make it even harder for her?

"She could so easily be you. Think about that. How would you want somebody to treat you if you were in her shoes? You stick with that little bit of the Golden Rule in the jury room, and I just know we'll be okay. I'm trusting you to do the right thing."

And, with that, the trial they had waited so long to attend, pinned so many hopes on, was over.

Just that quickly, Raymond was thrust into a post-trial world for which he did not feel properly prepared.

———

"You folks should get up and walk around," the prosecuting attorney said. He was leaning over the railing, addressing them directly. "It could be hours."

"The only thing is," Raymond said, "my friend here. Mrs. Gutermann. She can't walk around for hours."

"And I just gave birth day before yesterday," Isabel added.

"They could be out for a long time, though. I mean, we don't even know that they'll come back with a verdict today. At least maybe go down to the cafeteria and get a cup of coffee. I promise I'll come down and get you if the jury is about to come back."

———

"Doesn't it seem weird to you?" Raymond asked. "I mean, that it's over?"

He and Mrs. G were drinking tea with milk and sugar at a table in the empty cafeteria. Isabel was sipping distractedly at a bottle of mineral water. The baby lay fast asleep against her shoulder.

"I feel like . . . ," he continued. Then he had to stop and assess what he felt like. Or at least find a way to frame it in words. "Like I spent all this time getting ready for the trial, but I forgot to get ready for what my life would be on the other side of it."

Mrs. G nodded with surprising vigor. "That's very well put, Raymond, and I know just exactly what you mean."

"I think it went well, though," he said. "Don't you?"

It was the first time any of them had dared to go there. It was clear they were all three eaten up with thoughts of the verdict. But Raymond hadn't been sure if it was a good idea to speculate about it.

"I think so," Isabel said. "I think the prosecutor did a good job. Nobody could listen to what he said and then let that woman off." A long pause fell. Several seconds. Then she added, with less confidence and less volume, "Could they?"

"I don't know," Raymond and Mrs. G said, more or less at the same time.

Isabel stared at them both, first one and then the other.

"You don't feel good about it?" Isabel asked.

"No, I do," Mrs. G said. "The prosecutor was very good. If life is fair, we'll get a good, satisfying verdict."

Another very long silence.

"Is it?" Raymond asked when he could bear the stillness no longer.

"Sometimes it is and sometimes it isn't," she said.

They sipped their drinks in silence for a time. Maybe a minute. Maybe three.

Then Raymond looked up to see the prosecuting attorney standing in the doorway of the cafeteria.

"They're back," the man said.

He spun away.

"Wait," Raymond called. "Wait. What does this mean?"

"It means they're back," he called over his shoulder as he strode away down the hall.

"Wait! I have to ask you something."

"I have to get back," he called. And kept walking.

Raymond turned his face to Isabel. "I have to ask him something. Can I meet you upstairs? Will you help Mrs. G get back up there?"

"Of course."

Before she had even finished the second word, Raymond was running. He flew down the hall in a breathless sprint.

"Wait," he called as he caught up to the attorney.

Raymond slowed to a walk, panting, and more or less dropped in beside the prosecutor. They walked quickly, the way Raymond had used to walk all the time before meeting Mrs. G.

"Why are they back so soon?"

"I have no idea. But we're about to find out."

"It was only . . ."

"Thirty-eight minutes."

"What does that usually mean? When they only deliberate for thirty-eight minutes?"

"It means they pretty much already knew what they were going to decide. So it's either very good or very bad."

"Right," Raymond said. "Thanks. I better go back for my friends."

The prosecutor walked on without him.

Without comment.

—

"Have you reached a verdict?"

"We have, Your Honor," the jury foreman said.

In a ritual that played out at a maddeningly slow pace, a bailiff walked to the jury foreman and took a paper out of his hand. He carried it to the judge and handed it over. The judge stared at it for what felt like forever to Raymond. Then he nodded and handed it back to the bailiff, who carried it back to the jury foreman.

Raymond felt anxiety pouring off Isabel and Mrs. G—one on either side of him—in waves. Felt it mixing dangerously with his own.

For a minute it struck him that he wasn't breathing. At all. He gasped oxygen to compensate.

"What say you?" someone asked the jury foreman.

Raymond was watching Mrs. G's face, so he never knew who had said it.

"In the matter of the People versus Vivian Elaine Hatfield . . . on the charge of voluntary manslaughter . . . we find the defendant . . ."

Then came the pause that Raymond thought might kill him. Stop his heart for good. He leaned forward and tried to suck in air, but no in breath happened.

"Not guilty."

——

They sat for several minutes after most everyone else had left the court-room, Raymond, Mrs. G. Isabel and Ramon. They said nothing to each other. What could they possibly have said, Raymond wondered?

The silence took on a life of its own and became an entity, a physical thing. Like a fourth adult sitting on the bench with them, overpowering them with its presence.

"We should go home," Mrs. G said after a time.

They stood. Walked out of the empty courtroom together. Slowly.

Raymond spotted the prosecutor standing in the hallway. He was leaning his back against the wall, legs crossed at the ankle, talking on his cell phone.

"Can you guys please wait for me for just a minute?" Raymond asked his two friends.

They did not speak in reply. But it was clear that they would wait.

Raymond walked closer to the man. Close enough to indicate that he wanted to speak with him. Not close enough to be rude or to appear to be eavesdropping on his conversation.

"Let me call you back," the prosecutor said into his phone, and clicked off the call. Slipped the phone into his breast pocket and looked up at Raymond. Scorched him with his eyes. "You wanted to talk to me about something?"

"Yes, sir."

"If you came to tell me I let you down, there's no need. I'm thinking worse things about myself than you could ever say about me. Believe me."

"I don't think you let us down. I thought you did a good job."

The man laughed a bitter laugh. "If I'd done a good job that woman would be staring down the barrel of six months in prison."

"I think you laid it out well, but the jury just decided to ignore it. Or that's how it looked to me, anyway. But I just wanted to ask you . . . I have to write a report about this for school. And I guess that means I have to come to some kind of conclusion about the whole thing. But I've got nothing."

It was true and it wasn't true. Yes, he had to write a report. Yes, he wanted it to be a good report. He wanted a high grade to help justify the three-day absence. But he wanted to understand this moment not for his teachers and classmates. He wanted to understand for himself and his own sense of peace.

"I mean, I'm just completely . . . ," he added. Because the man wasn't talking. "I don't get it at all."

"Welcome to the club."

"You have no idea why juries do that?"

"Oh, I have my theories." He paused. Sighed, as if resigning himself to a longer conversation than he had wanted. "Okay. Here's what I think, but don't quote me on it. If you agree with it, make it your own observation. Tribalism."

"Tribalism?"

"It's how our brains evolved. Caveman thinking. Well . . . no. Not thinking. More like . . . reactivity. The whole problem is that there's not a lot of thinking involved. It's knee-jerk emotional. It goes like this, but purely subconsciously: Is this person I'm supposed to be judging our tribe, or another tribe? If she's us, mistakes can be forgiven. Hell, everybody makes mistakes. The mistake becomes an anomaly, because it's us, and we're good people. If she's them, mistakes need to be punished, because that's just how *they* are. The mistake only proves the point that that's always how they are. So I tried to appeal to the jury as the tribe of the law abiding. We don't shoot people, and that's the us in question. Didn't work, though. And I'm sorry it didn't work. I hope you'll tell your friends I'm sorry I let you down. Now if you'll excuse me."

He walked away down the hall.

Raymond almost pulled his backpack off his shoulder and took out his laptop again. He wanted to type out everything the attorney had just said to him in his notes. But he glanced back at Isabel and Mrs. G, and saw how exhausted and dispirited they looked, and knew they needed to go home.

Besides, he thought, what the attorney had just told him felt burned into the synapses of his brain. It was not going anywhere. He should be so lucky, he thought, to forget those words anytime soon.

Raymond looked up and saw that the attorney had stopped and was staring back at him. As if there were more on his mind. The man walked closer.

"And another related thing, but don't quote me on this either. They could imagine being *afraid* of Mr. Velez better than they could imagine *being* him. I shouldn't have pushed the prejudice angle. Because the whole time the defendant was pushing back, the jury was pushing back, too. And I knew it. I knew it was a mistake at the time I was doing it. But it was just so . . . *there*. It was all just so there, in front of everybody's face, and I couldn't bring myself to coddle the jury by pretending I didn't see it. But now you and your friends have to pay for that lack of self-control on my part. Wherever you are tonight, know that I'll be getting very, very drunk over that decision."

Raymond opened his mouth, but no words came out.

It was too late, anyway. The man had already walked away.

—

"So, is there anything else I can get you before I go back to my dad's?"

She was sitting on the couch, petting the cat. Listlessly. Everything about her seemed listless. Raymond thought even her breathing looked indecisive, as though she were deciding between every breath whether it was worth it to her to take another.

"No, Raymond," she said. "Thank you, my valued friend. I trust you to hear this in the spirit I intend it. I really think some time alone to think my thoughts will do me good."

"Will you eat something if I go now?"

A long silence, followed by a sigh. Hers.

"You are too good a friend for me to lie to you," she said at last.

"What if I just warmed you up some chicken broth? I could put it in a cup. It would be more like drinking something than eating."

"If it's important to you, then yes. I will drink it."

He walked into her kitchen and got out a saucepan. And a can of broth. And the can opener.

"What did you talk about with Mr. Newman?" she asked, calling in.

"Who?"

"The lawyer from the district attorney's office."

"Oh, is that his name? Well, it was interesting. In fact, I have to get back to my laptop and get it all down before I forget. He had some theories as to why juries do things like this."

He lit the flame under the pot. Poured a medium serving of broth into it. Then he moved to the kitchen doorway and leaned his shoulder on the jamb so he could talk to her more easily.

"He said it was a kind of tribalism. The defendant was a person from their tribe, so whatever mistakes she made, she's still a good person to them. Luis was from another tribe, so it will always be his fault somehow, because that's just how those other people are. And the more I think about it, the more I remember your saying something like that to me."

"Did I?" she asked dreamily. As if far away. "I don't recall."

"Back when I first met you. I stopped to talk to you. You said most people don't stop, because you're a 'them' and not an 'us.' I don't think you were talking about race, though. Just the way people stick with those they know."

"There are many kinds of tribes, Raymond. But I don't claim to remember having said it. It sounds like something I would say, though."

He leaned in silence for a minute or two, staring through the filmy curtain at nothing. Just a muted view of the building across the street. Then he checked the broth and found it was ready. She liked her drinks warm rather than hot.

"If I just hand this to you and go . . . do you promise to drink it?"

"I promise."

He set it on the coffee table in front of her.

"You sure there's nothing else I can do?"

"Oh, Raymond. You have done so much. Do for others, but don't do *only* for others. Take care of yourself as well. You must be upset by this outcome, too. So tell me. What do you think about it?"

"I told you," he said.

"Let me start again. You haven't told me how you *feel* about it."

"I don't have a right to feel anything about it. How can I? I didn't know him. You and Isabel have a right to those feelings." He started to say more on the subject, but the words didn't come. "I'm just going to go back to my dad's and work on that report. I want to have it done by Monday morning. I have some more homework to get done over the weekend, too. I got behind, you know . . . with Isabel having her baby and all."

"Okay, good. You go work."

"I'll come visit you over the weekend," he said.

"All the way from your father's? You don't need to."

"But you know I will."

"Raymond," she said, before he could hurry out the door. "You have a right. You always have a right to feel."

———

Raymond handed in the report to his social studies teacher, as he'd been instructed, first thing Monday morning before homeroom. He was proud of it, and anxious to hear what she thought.

"Oh," Miss Evans said. "You're back. That was fast."

She flipped the pages on the report faster than she could read or even skim them. She was a sixtysomething woman with porcelain skin, a fiercely fair complexion. Aging had left her skin papery and nearly translucent. She wore big floppy hats from the front door of school to her car, even on overcast days.

"Seven single-spaced pages," she said, sounding impressed. "Quite ambitious."

"I guess I had a lot to say."

"I'll try to get it read at lunch," she said. "So that when you come into class this afternoon, I can have a grade for you."

———

He sat down at his regular desk in her class and waited. It was early. Six minutes to 1:00. There were no other students in the room.

"I'm just finishing it," she said without looking up.

"Okay. I'll wait."

Less than a minute later she flipped back to its cover page and scribbled something on it with her red pen. She stood, walked down the aisle to him. Dropped it on the desk in front of him.

He looked down at his grade.

C-.

"*C minus?*"

"Did you think it deserved more?"

"Yeah. Much more."

"Well, I'm sorry, but that's my honest opinion. You took very good notes, and I gave you credit for that. But I didn't like the conclusions you came to. I thought you went way off the beam with that. First of all, I'm not even sure why you thought you were supposed to draw your own conclusions about why the jury decided the way it did. Those people were there to do their civic duty. They listened to the facts in front of them and did what they thought best. You're seventeen years old, and you weren't in the jury room, and here you are going on about how people see facts differently based on a theory of *us* and *them*. It just sounded like a teenager thinking he knows better than our tried-and-true system of justice."

Raymond sat stunned for a moment. Then his brain seized on one aspect of her little speech.

"Wait. So, the whole thing about tribalism . . . that sounded to you like something a seventeen-year-old would come up with?"

"Very much so. And it was a little bit New Agey, too, if you ask me. Like you have this theory that reality is completely subjective. But there's such a thing as objective reality, you know, and those jurors were trying to find it."

He opened his mouth to argue with her. To tell her she hadn't been there. That if reality wasn't subjective, she wouldn't be assigning perfect civic honesty to a bunch of people she hadn't met, or even seen. Maybe even to tell her that his seventeen-year-old's theory of tribalism had been borrowed from a forty-year-old district attorney.

He closed his mouth again. Because he realized, clearly in that moment, that she had made up her mind. Nothing he said would change it.

—

He stuck his head into Mr. Bernstein's English class at the end of the day.

Mr. Bernstein stood at the blackboard, erasing. Cleaning the board before leaving for the day. He was a young man, probably less than ten years Raymond's senior, with a full, dark beard and a quick smile.

"Raymond," he said. "What can I do for you?"

"Not sure if it's okay to ask this."

"Well." The teacher dropped the hand with the eraser to his side. Offered Raymond his full attention. "You can always ask."

"I wrote a report. You know, about the trial."

"Right, right. How did that go?"

"Not so well."

"Oh. I'm sorry. Were you supposed to hand it in to *me*? If so, nobody told me."

"No. I was supposed to give it to Miss Evans for social studies class. But I was just . . . I'd really like to hear more than one opinion on it. I was wondering if you'd read it and tell me what you think. You know. As a piece of nonfiction writing. Maybe even give it a grade. It doesn't actually have to count for my English grade if you don't want it to. I'm just interested to hear what somebody else thinks."

"Not a problem, Raymond. Not a problem at all. Leave it here and I'll take it home tonight. You can come in first thing before homeroom tomorrow, and I'll give you my honest opinion."

"Oh," Raymond said. "I just thought of something." He felt foolish for not having thought of it sooner. "I need to be able to print out"—he almost said "a clean copy," but he changed it quickly before he spoke—"another copy."

He didn't want Mr. Bernstein to see his social studies teacher's grade, or the notes she had scribbled throughout. He wanted a fresh take, with nobody else's opinion in the back of the man's head.

"I'll walk with you down to the office," the teacher said. "I think they'll let us use their printer."

———

"Are you sure I can't talk you into going to the store with me?" Raymond asked.

Mrs. G sat slumped at her dining room table, across from Raymond. Not drinking her tea. Not eating her cookie.

"I need more time to rest," she said. "I would be very grateful if you would go and shop for me."

"Okay. But sooner or later I'd like to see you get out in the fresh air again."

"Yes. Later. In the meantime we should speak of something else. Did you hand in your report today? How long will it be before you get your grade on it?"

"I already did."

"You don't sound happy."

"She gave me a terrible grade."

"Like an F?"

"No! Not *that* terrible. I'd kill myself. C minus. That's terrible for *me*. It's for credit. It's going to pull my average down."

"What didn't she like about it?"

"She wants to think the jury was fine and upstanding, and that they listened to the facts and did their civic duty. And that reality is not subjective."

"Oh. I see. She is a believer in the idea that there is such a thing as objective reality."

Raymond stopped chewing and just sat a moment with a mouth full of cookie. But he couldn't answer around it, so he chewed and swallowed quickly.

"You don't think there is?"

"It's hard to know. A very debatable point. But science now makes a good case that perhaps not."

"What science? I never learned any science like that in school."

"No, this would likely not be what they would teach you in school. Newer science. Quantum mechanics—that sort of science. Luis brought me a couple of audiobooks about it. It's very fascinating, but then it stretches your mind until you think you might be a little bit crazy. The core idea is that a thing is not a thing until it has an observer. And the observer seems to play a role in what kind of thing it will snap into being. But beyond that—no need to be so esoteric. Let's say I witness an accident, and I have one view, and you witness it, and you have a wholly differing opinion. And let's say we argue and argue and argue, but in the end the truth is simply that we were standing in two different places. And that from my angle I saw things that from your angle could not be seen. Well . . . not all angles are physical or logistical. That's all I'm saying."

He chewed in silence for a moment longer, buoyed by the idea that the conversation was bringing life back into her demeanor. He reached inside himself and took a chance.

"Come to the market with me," he said. "It'll be fun. Just like the old days. We'll talk more about this on the way."

"Oh, Raymond. No. Please go for me. I am not feeling good, and I am just so very tired."

———

Raymond was in his room, more or less minding his own business, when it all came up. And out.

It started over nothing. He placed his math textbook on the desk next to his laptop, but he had several books and stacks of notes lying around—he hadn't been as good about organizing his desk as he normally would be—so it slid to the floor again. He sighed. Picked it up. Slammed it down on the desk again. It slid off again.

Next thing he knew, Raymond was scraping everything off his desk with one arm. The notebook computer landed on the carpet with a painful thump. Papers fluttered down.

But even that wasn't enough. It only stoked the fire he felt inside. He lurched over to his bookshelves and scraped them clean, knocking all his books to the floor. He picked up a big handful, as if to put them back, but ended up bouncing them hard off the wall instead.

He looked up to see his mom standing in his open bedroom doorway, one hand on the knob. She had the toddler, Clarissa, on her hip. The little girl's eyes had gone wide with fear.

Raymond stopped hurling and let the rest of his armful of books fall to the floor.

"Well," his mother said. "I've been meaning to ask you how the trial went. Now I guess there's no need."

—

Raymond arrived at school more than fifteen minutes early and ran straight to Mr. Bernstein's classroom. Literally ran.

The teacher stood by the window, leaning on the cold radiator and talking on his cell phone. He held up one finger to ask Raymond to wait.

Raymond's report was sitting on Mr. Bernstein's desk. He moved closer to it, then looked up at the teacher for permission. Bernstein met his eyes and nodded, then turned away to finish his phone conversation in private.

Raymond approached his paper, his heart thumping.

On the cover sheet, he saw a large red A+. "Excellent work," the teacher had written underneath.

He flipped through the pages to see if there were additional notes.

"Good observations," it said beside the conclusion.

Everything else he had written remained whole and not dissected.

He looked up to see the teacher standing in front of him. No longer on his phone.

"I thought it was an impressive piece of work," Bernstein said. "Your thoughts about tribalism as it affects the justice system seemed very advanced to me. I was surprised to hear those observations from a teenager."

"Oh. Well. I'll be real honest. I based that on some stuff I heard from one of the attorneys."

Raymond figured that, by not saying which one, he was staying true to his agreement not to quote the man.

"Okay. That makes sense. But it doesn't change my thoughts about your grade. You understood what you heard, clearly, and you pulled it all together well. You made a compelling case."

Raymond stood silent for a moment, not sure what he could—or should—say.

"What?" Bernstein asked. "You look . . ."

"It's just that . . . Miss Evans didn't like it much. She said my conclusion sounded like something a seventeen-year-old would think up. And she didn't mean that as a compliment, believe me."

"I guess different people will see it different ways. But I stand by my assessment. And I'm calling it an extra-credit assignment for English, so that A plus will count toward your final grade."

"Good. Thank you! That'll help balance off her C minus."

"She gave you a C minus? Seriously?"

"I would never joke about a thing like that."

"And she said the conclusion sounded juvenile," Bernstein repeated, paraphrasing. "And I said it sounded too advanced for your age. And it turned out to be based on thoughts you got from an adult attorney. That's funny."

"Yeah," Raymond said. "I thought that part was funny, too. She seems to think there's just one objective reality, and good people will all see it if they're willing to."

"Hmm," Mr. Bernstein said. "That's a nice, predictable world she's living in. It must be very pleasant there. I almost envy her that kind of thinking."

———

Raymond stepped into the school library after last period. He almost skipped last period to go, but he had done that once before, and the librarian hadn't reported him. He hated to press his luck with that.

"Well, look who it is," she said, barely looking up from her book. "How's the self-taught Spanish coming along?"

"Oh," he said. "Well, I hate to even tell you. But it was kind of . . . for a specific purpose. That I don't need anymore. So I haven't done a very good job of keeping up with it."

In fact, after he had returned the Spanish-English dictionary to the library, he hadn't gone on to buy a phrasebook of his own. Because there had been no more Luis Velezes to find.

"Well, I just knew that was too good to be true. A student wanting to learn something just for the sake of learning it."

"Don't be too sure," he said. "I came here to ask if you have any books about quantum mechanics. Not for any special situation this time. Just for the sake of learning it."

"Interesting," she said. "You almost renew my faith in students, Raymond. It just so happens I have a fair amount on the subject. Follow me."

Chapter Sixteen

Despair

"I'm starting to get worried about you," Raymond said. "You haven't been outside for almost eight days."

"Has it only been eight days?"

She looked up at him from her bed. Turned her face in the general direction of where he stood in her bedroom doorway. It was after ten o'clock on a Saturday morning. She was awake. But she still hadn't gotten up and dressed.

"Time has been going so slowly," she added. A bit wistfully, Raymond thought.

"I want my old friend Mrs. G back," he said, surprising himself. He had thought it many times, but hadn't expected to hear himself say it out loud. "I miss her."

"She is here," Mrs. G said in a thin and unenthusiastic voice.

"No. Not really, she isn't. I haven't seen her since the trial. And I'm getting worried about you. I think I should call that nice Velez family who invited us to supper. We could go tomorrow."

"No, not tomorrow. Please, Raymond. Next Sunday. Or the Sunday after that."

"Tomorrow is better. You've had plenty of time to rest, right?"

"Physically, yes, but . . ."

"I'm going to call her right now and tell her we're coming tomorrow."

"Wait!"

He was halfway out of the room, but he stopped. Because she sounded too serious to ignore. Almost approaching the border of desperate.

"Don't go," she said. "Don't call. All right, if you want me to get outdoors, fine. Let's go outdoors. But only you and me for now. Please. To meet new people, to be around a lot of people right now . . . I need more time. Tomorrow we will go somewhere, just the two of us. In a couple of weeks maybe we will go to supper with your friends."

"Okay. That's okay, I guess. Just . . . where do you want to go?"

"Give me until the morning to think. Come and get me in the morning, and I will tell you where we should go and what we should see. Only, you will have to see it for us both."

———

At 9:00 the following morning he knocked on her door, then opened it with the key.

"You're ready!" he said.

She was sitting up on the edge of the couch, wearing her red dress and white shoes, and the shawl she had worn to court. Her hair was neatly braided, the white braid falling forward over one shoulder. Her red-and-white cane was propped next to her against the couch. She held her purse tightly on her lap.

"Of course I'm ready. I told you we would go, so we will go."

Raymond felt something dark and heavy drop away from his mood. Drop physically away from his body, from the feel of it. He had been carrying it for longer than he realized. He felt buoyant without it, almost as though he were in danger of floating away.

She'll be okay, he thought. *She'll be okay after all.*

"So where do you want to go?"

"New York Harbor," she said.

"What part of it?"

"Doesn't matter."

"We could ride the subway to Battery Park. Take the ferry over to Ellis Island."

"No! Definitely not to Ellis Island. I just want to visit that shore."

"Which shore, though?"

"The Battery is fine. That is all well and good. But no ferry ride. No Ellis Island."

———

"So, you must have been here before," Raymond said, spotting a bench that had just been vacated.

He hurried to it and placed her cane across it to save it for them. Then he slowly walked her over to sit down.

The morning was brisk for spring, with a strong wind. It was a little cold, Raymond thought. He thought the cold was perhaps why that couple, who had not been wearing jackets, had moved along and left the bench to them. It was one in a line of benches closest to the iron railing at the water's edge.

The benches had no backs, so Raymond and Mrs. G sat forward, huddled over themselves in the damp cold.

"I have been here before, yes," she said. "The first time I was here was in 1938. I was eleven years old. My family and I came into New York Harbor on a ship to Ellis Island. That was the first I saw it."

Raymond fell silent and waited to see if she cared to say more.

"You are being awfully quiet," she said after a time.

"It's just that . . . you never told me anything about your past. You didn't seem to want to talk about it."

"Today I will talk about it," she said.

But for a few moments, nobody talked about anything.

"It was very different back then," she said. "In many ways. But in some ways the same. The statue of course is the same. Can you see the statue from where we sit, Raymond?"

"Oh yeah. Good view of it from here."

"And the sound of the boat horns. That is much the same, though I am sure the boats look more modern. The sea air and the wind, that never changes. I remember that so well from the whole voyage. I do think the harbor smelled better back then, though. Not so much pollution."

"You really remember all the details from when you were eleven?"

"Oh yes. I have very detailed memories. Only . . . sometimes I wonder. You have the memories, and you go over and over them in your mind. And after a time I wonder if I am remembering the actual event or just remembering the memories."

They fell silent for a moment. Seabirds wheeled over their heads, calling out strange sounds. Raymond thought they were strange, anyway.

"You saw things back then you would not see today," she said. "Masted schooners were still docked, and the skyline was different. Many tall buildings, yes, but I remember they all had smoke or steam pouring up from them. They heated the buildings differently back then. All brick, they were. Not steel and glass. Oh, they had windows, yes. But they were not made entirely of windows as they are these days."

"You lived in New York almost your whole life," he said after a time. He did some quick math in his head. "Eighty-one years. Didn't you ever come back here?"

"Oh yes. A handful of times. But I have not for a long time. Maybe twenty years. And it's funny, but I don't remember much from the later visits. I remember mostly that first time."

Another moment of silence, but it felt peaceful to Raymond. She was going to tell him something that would help him make sense of her world and her reactions. He could feel it. But there was nothing he needed to do. It would come in its own time, and that time would be soon.

As if hearing his thoughts, she said, "What I am about to tell you I have told to no one except Rolf, my late husband. My family of course knew, because they were there, but they are all gone now. I am the only one left. I never even told Luis, though now I very much wish I had."

He waited. He did not dare speak.

"You know your world history well," she said. "Don't you?"

"Pretty well, I think. Yeah."

"Good. So . . . I was born in Germany in 1927. And I have already told you I came to America by boat in 1938."

She didn't speak for a moment. She seemed to be wanting something from him. Some reaction.

So he said, "Good thing you got out when you did. Because things got bad there after you left."

"Yes, my young friend. That is the understatement of a lifetime. Things got very bad after we left."

"Especially if your family was Jewish."

He had been afraid to say it. So he watched her face to see how it would land. She only smiled sadly.

"It's a funny thing about that. We were and we were not. My father was not Jewish. My mother was. In the Jewish religion, it is the mother who confers Judaism on the children, so in that sense, yes. We were. But from a more secular viewpoint . . . in the eyes of the society we grew up in . . . my brothers and sister and I, we were half of this thing that it was so dangerous to be. And now I feel bad because I did not tell you this sooner, because it's a thing we have in common. We both know a strange truth about the world: that people judge you by your most controversial half. If you meet a person, Raymond, who is prejudiced, this person will not think to himself, 'This Raymond has a white half, and I will respect that half of him.' People judge you only by the half they don't like. If my family had stayed in Germany, they would not have put half of me in a camp or sent half of me to the gas chamber. No. I would have been completely killed."

A seagull landed on the pavement in front of Raymond and stared at him, wiggling closer. As if fascinated by their words, it seemed to him, but he knew it wasn't that. Hoping for food, most likely.

He waved his hand and the bird flapped away.

"How did your family get out?" he asked after a time. "Wasn't it hard to get out?"

"Ah," she said. "Now we move closer to my shame."

A sudden memory flooded into Raymond's head. A time when she had told him that guilt can tear a person apart—told him as though she knew from personal experience. She had done something to bring herself guilt, and a shame that still had not left her alone all these decades later. He could only wait, frozen, to hear what it had been.

"My father was not a rich man, but he was a businessman, and the family did well enough. He owned a haberdashery, and business had been fairly good until the neighbors began to whisper that his wife was a Jewess. Then things fell apart, and he had to shutter the shop because of serial vandalism. But he had a little money put aside. Really it was our whole life savings for our whole family. I won't tell you how much it was in German marks, because that will not help you picture the sum. The exchange rate is constantly changing, and of course inflation. If it were in American dollars, and if it were today, I would have to say it was a sum in the neighborhood of maybe fifteen or twenty thousand dollars. He used the vast majority of it to bribe an official. Simple as that. He had this money in cash, and he put it in the pocket of a corrupt official, and the next thing you know, we were steaming across the ocean to start all over again from nothing."

"Okay . . . ," Raymond said. He was waiting for the part that caused her guilt and shame. But he had no intention of hurrying her there. "So you came all the way across the Atlantic on a boat. I thought maybe you were afraid of boats."

"Why would you think that?"

"I asked you if you wanted to take the ferry over to Ellis Island, and you had a very strong 'no' reaction."

"Oh, but not because of the ferry. It's the island itself. It was so frightening to me. Even my parents were frightened. I could see it and feel it. The officials herded us through that immigration building like cattle. And they had so much power over us. We were so helpless. No, that was bad. Earlier, when we came into the harbor, we all came to the railing of the ship to see the statue, and that was a very good and heady feeling. We were experiencing the country itself, and the promise of what it might have in store for us. But it's different when you have to deal with the officials of the government of that country. I never want to set foot on that island again."

"So . . . ," Raymond said.

"So?"

"There's something in all this that you think is shameful, and that you never even told Luis. But I'm not hearing it."

"Well. It may be hard for you to understand, Raymond. But I need you to understand it, so try very hard to put yourself in my shoes. We paid off a corrupt official and left everybody else behind. All my friends from school. All my friends from school were Jewish, because we weren't allowed to mix with the non-Jewish population as time went on. My grandparents. All my extended family. We just left them there. We ran away and left them all behind."

"You were eleven."

"Yes. I was eleven."

"You had no control over any of this."

"No."

"This is what you feel shame about? You couldn't have done anything! What could you have done?"

Mrs. G sighed deeply. She looked out across the harbor as though there were something out there for her to see. But maybe she was only hearing and smelling.

"Seven years go by, and of course you know the war ended in '45. My parents had been following the news, but trying to keep it from me and my siblings as much as was possible. But you hear things. After the war, my father, I think he would have been satisfied leaving the past alone. He did not care to know too much. But not my mother. My mother wrote letters to everyone. Every single person we knew in Germany whose address she had noted in her book. Jews and non-Jews alike. She wrote to every one. Guess how many letters she got back?"

"I . . . I don't know. I can't guess."

"Zero. Not one letter. Not even from the neighbors who were not Jewish. Surely some of them still lived in their homes and had survived the war. But they did not write back and answer my mother's questions. So she traveled there. By herself. We were in school, and besides, they would not have subjected us to that avalanche of horror. My father had to work, but I don't think he would have gone either way. My mother traveled there to see who was left of all the people we knew. All the people we called family or friends."

Raymond pulled the collar of his jacket more tightly around his neck and waited for her to say more. He glanced over at her to see if she looked cold. But she seemed comfortable wrapped in her knitted shawl.

A gaggle of young tourists ran to the railing, laughing and talking in a language indecipherable to Raymond, taking pictures of each other with the statue far in the distance.

Mrs. G did not say more.

"So . . . ," he began. Tentatively, in case she wanted to stop him from asking. "Did she find any family or friends alive?"

"She did not."

"Every single one of them had died?"

"Well, we don't know, Raymond. It is hard to know. There was research involved to learn the fate of each person who had gone into a camp during the war. Maybe someone else was able to slip away as we did. Maybe someone survived the camp and staggered out with the Allied troops and went somewhere that felt less like hell to them. But that is all optimistic thinking. My mother, who was a realistic woman, called them 'missing and presumed dead.' If anyone survived, we never found out about it."

"That must have been . . ." But he could not think of a way to say more.

"I wonder if you can imagine it, Raymond. If you can possibly think of everyone you know, all your friends, the teachers and students in your school, all your cousins and grandparents and aunts and uncles, and then imagine that they are all gone, leaving you and your immediate family alone standing."

For a moment, he tried. And it might not have been that he couldn't have imagined. It might have been that he wanted badly not to.

"So . . . ," he began. "The part of this with the shame. I'm still not sure if I'm clear on that or not. You feel guilty because you . . ."

"Survived."

Silence. For maybe the count of ten.

"If you had stayed and died with them," he said, "I don't see how that would have helped their situation."

"All right. You look at it that way. I look at it this way: Who was I to survive? What was so special about my life that I was allowed to keep it? It weighs on you, Raymond. Millions of people had their lives taken, but I was allowed to keep mine. At first I felt I had to live on their behalf. I thought I would have to live the most remarkable life anyone had ever lived in the history of the world. I felt as though I had to live life *for* all of them. But then after a couple of years that idea grew utterly overwhelming, and I fell to the other side, and I lived the least remarkable life one can imagine. I worked as a seamstress all my life and never had children. But I was always determined that I would live a very long life. To one hundred or better. Because it was my duty to make the most of what I was given. But still I was haunted by why I was given it. You know why, don't you?"

"Because . . . your father had money."

"Yes. Because my father had the equivalent of a few thousand dollars, and their fathers had nothing. Money, my friend. Money bought us our lives. And that is called privilege. We bought our lives, while those who couldn't afford to were slaughtered like animals. Does that make our lives worth more? Of course not. No life is worth more, except by virtue of one's character. But I was eleven. My character was no better than that of my peers."

She sniffled slightly in the cold. Took a cloth hankie out of her purse and dabbed at her nose.

"I do not want this privilege," she added. Firmly.

"I don't know that growing up half-Jewish in Nazi Germany was a lesson in privilege."

"No. It was not. So now I know this story from both sides. And now I am on the wrong side, and I do not want to be here. How many times do you think I could tap a person on the shoulder and return a dropped wallet? How many wallets will I hand back before someone shoots me?"

"I . . . don't know."

"Yes you do, Raymond. Yes you do. Nobody will ever shoot me, and you know it. They will shoot my friend Luis, but they will never shoot me. And the people on the other side, they don't even see it. I see my privilege because I have lived both with it and without it. The jury did not even see. *They did not even see*, Raymond. What can you do with a world where people do not even see?"

They continued to sit by the water for a time. Another ten or fifteen minutes at least.

Raymond never managed to come up with an answer to her question. He had no idea what you do with a world where people do not even see.

———

Raymond arrived at his father's door at a little after three o'clock in the afternoon. He knocked, more tentatively than he had intended.

Please let Dad answer. Please let Dad answer. Please let Dad answer.

Neesha answered.

He watched her eyes narrow as she took in his face.

"This is not your weekend," she said.

Duh. If I didn't know that I would have been here on Friday.

"I just need to talk to Dad."

"Right. That's why you're here every other weekend. To give you plenty of time to talk to Malcolm."

"It'll only take a minute," he said.

For several seconds, nothing happened. No words were spoken. It was beginning to dawn on Raymond that she might not let him in.

Then he heard his father's booming voice.

"Who is that, honey?"

A second awkward pause fell, and seemed to amount to a tug-of-war without words or motion.

Raymond looked up to see his father's face appear behind her.

"Raymond. What are you doing here?"

"I just wanted to ask your advice about something."

"Is this some kind of emergency?"

"Not really, I guess. It's just important to me."

Malcolm sighed. Not as though disgusted with Raymond, Raymond thought. More as though he was gearing up to fight about it with his wife.

"Give me a minute to get a jacket," he said. "I'll take you out for an ice cream soda like we used to do in the old days."

While he was waiting, no one invited Raymond in.

He stood out in the hall, one ear near the narrow opening of the door, and listened to them going back and forth about it.

"He's my son."

"I'm your wife."

"He's just a boy. He needs a strong adult in his life."

"I'm making us a special dinner, and you knew it."

"I'll still eat it. That's hours away."

"He could have called."

"I'll talk to him about that."

"No, you won't."

"I said I will, and I will."

"You always say that, but then you never want to ruffle anybody's feathers."

"I'll be back in less than an hour. Love you."

No reply.

Raymond's father popped out into the hall with him, and Raymond jumped back to give him room.

"I suppose you heard all of that," his father said.

Raymond didn't offer any reply.

They walked toward the elevator side by side.

"So why *didn't* you call?"

"I figured Neesha would answer and not let me talk to you and tell me not to come."

"That's honest enough. And I'm not going to stand here and tell you that couldn't have happened."

—

Raymond ordered a root beer float, his father a single scoop of vanilla. Raymond knew his father was being careful not to spoil his appetite.

They sat at a round stainless steel table by one of the front windows, where they could watch what looked like the entirety of the human population of Earth as it teemed by. The table had sparkly stars on its surface. Slightly raised. Raymond traced them with his finger as he spoke.

"So, what would you do if you had a friend who was just . . . completely . . . I'm not sure what the word is I'm looking for. I want to say *depressed*, but I feel like it's more than that. Like she's just given up on the world. Like the way the world is, she just can't face it."

"Sounds like the word you're looking for is *despair*."

"Yeah," Raymond said, looking up directly into his father's face. "Despair."

Malcolm sighed deeply. "It's probably not what you want to hear, but there's a limited amount you *can* do. You can listen."

"Listen? That doesn't sound like much help."

"Well, here's the problem, son. I think you're asking me how you fix a thing like that for somebody else. And unfortunately the answer is . . . you can't. In fact, sometimes that gets in the way, when we try to fix what somebody else is feeling. Ever had somebody telling you what you ought to do to get out of what you're feeling when you wish they would just hear you out?"

"Yeah. More times than I could count."

"When we care about somebody, we don't want to see them in pain, and that's normal. But when a person is in despair about the world, I mean . . . what can you do? You can't change the whole world into something they'll like better."

"No," Raymond said.

A waiter in a red-and-white striped apron appeared with the ice cream and the root beer float. He seemed to catch the mood at their table, and he quickly left their order and retreated.

"This is about the trial?" his father asked. "And that woman shooter getting acquitted?"

"I thought so. At first. But it turns out it's partly about that and partly about some other bad things from her past that I think she never really got over."

"I see."

"*Listen?* You really think that'll be enough?"

"I couldn't say."

Raymond took a big gulp of his root beer float. Or tried to, anyway. The straw was full of ice cream, and it was hard to pull much in. But it was good, the little bit he got.

"You know anything about the law?" Raymond asked his father.

"Not too much. Probably just what your average person who's not a lawyer would know."

"Is there anything we can do about that woman now?"

"Like what?"

"An appeal or something?"

"I don't think you can appeal an acquittal. I think you appeal a conviction. Otherwise you'd run into that double jeopardy thing."

"Oh. Right."

"I think you'd need to talk to an attorney about whether there are any options left in a case like this."

Right. Like I can afford to talk to an attorney.

Then it hit him. He *knew* an attorney. Luis Javier Velez, Esquire. The man who had given Raymond his business card in case there was anything he could do to help. Now Raymond just had to figure out where he had put the card. Then again, he'd already found the man without a card once.

They spooned and sipped in silence for a minute or two.

"It's nice to see you caring about the world," his father said, "and having people you care about. But you have to let people go through whatever it is they have to go through. Just be there for your friends. That's all we can really do for each other sometimes."

Raymond nodded, though it was far less than he had hoped to hear.

"You know what I think is nice? That we talk to each other more than we used to."

"Absolutely," his father said. "I think that's nice, too."

"I have two more little favors to ask you," Raymond said. "Can I borrow your cell phone? And, next Sunday, would it be okay if I left early? Like right in the middle of the day?"

His father reached into his jacket pocket and frowned. "I think . . . I forgot it."

"Then can I come in and use your phone when we get back?"

"Seems a shame to come all the way back to the apartment just to make a phone call. You need to go the exact opposite direction to get home."

Raymond turned his face away. Looked out the window and watched people hurry by, so his father wouldn't see the disappointment in his eyes. He was not welcome back at his dad's apartment after they were done with their ice cream, because his dad wasn't willing to fight it out with his wife.

"Tell you what I'll do, though," Malcolm said, digging in his wallet. *Money won't help this.*

"You can take my phone card. It has a PIN number, and you can use a pay phone, and the charges will go directly to my phone bill. And yes, of course, if there's someplace you need to be on Sunday, then go ahead and be there. We'll work around it."

———

"Mrs. G told me about your nice invitation," Raymond said. "Thank you for that. I can still close my eyes and taste that chocolate cake. I was thinking maybe next Sunday."

He stood at a fully exposed pay phone on a busy sidewalk, halfway to the subway station. When Sofia Velez answered him, the din of traffic nearly drowned out her voice.

"Next Sunday would be fine. It'll be good to see you again. Come around and bring your friend about twelve thirty or one."

"Okay, good. That'll be good for her. I hope. She's been very . . ."

But he couldn't find the right way to fit the word *despair* into the sentence.

"Oh, I can imagine it's hard for her. We heard about the trial. Luisa followed it on the internet. It's really too bad when a thing like that happens and it's not even in the news more. You would think people would care more about it."

"Yeah," Raymond said. "You would think. Can I ask you a question? What would you do to help a friend of yours if she was just completely in despair?"

A long silence. At least, on the line. In Raymond's left ear. The rest of the world, in his right ear, nearly overpowered him with its noise.

"That's a hard question," she said. "Can I think about it?"

"Sure."

"Maybe when you come on Sunday I'll know more what to say."

—

Raymond stuck his head into the library the following afternoon. Last period, when he should have been in study hall.

Every time he did, he expected to find other students using the facility. But once again there was nobody there but the librarian.

"Raymond," she said. Wryly, as if his name were a nice bit of irony. "Where are you supposed to be?"

"Study hall." He moved closer to her desk as he spoke. "But, seriously . . . can't I study here? I mean . . . it's a *library*."

"Sure," she said. "I'll write you a note."

Raymond breathed more fully. He grabbed a chair by its wooden back, pulled it up close to her desk, and sat facing her. He dug in his backpack and took out the book he'd borrowed. The beginner's book on quantum physics.

"Are you returning this?"

Raymond only nodded.

"Did you read the whole thing? It's not exactly light reading."

"No. It's really not. But I read every word."

"Do you feel like you understood it? Because I know people two or three times your age who can't grasp this stuff at all."

Raymond sat back and thought a minute. He wanted to give her an honest answer. Not fire something off the top of his head. She seemed to be offering him a real conversation. He wanted to take her up on that.

"Kind of yes and no. A few things I had to read four or five times. Sometimes I could just sort of turn off my imagination, my reactions to things, and take it at face value. But some of the stuff . . . like the part about how when you're not looking it's a wave, and then when you are looking it's a particle. Like it's not actual matter till you look at it. And the thing about quantum superpositioning? How one thing can be in more than one place at the same time but still have the same reaction to some kind of stimulus even if the two things are miles apart, because it's not two things, it's one thing in two places? If I try to think about that too hard, it feels like it wants to break my brain."

"Good," she said. "Then you understand it."

"It almost sounds . . . like it's saying reality is only real when we make it real."

"Something like that, yeah."

"So, this is the truth? This is, like, actual science?"

"Hard to say. It's new science. It's controversial science. Then again, new science is usually controversial. I mean it's not *new* new, but . . . compared to Galileo . . ."

They sat quietly for what might only have been a second or two. Raymond was looking at the book, which he had placed on her desk—at its cover illustration that looked like a flexible surface of light waves bending.

"Can I ask you a question that has nothing to do with books?"

"Sure," she said. "Why not?" She swept her arms wide to indicate the empty room. "I can fit you into my busy schedule."

"What would you do if you had a friend who had just fallen into total despair about the world?"

"Hmm," she said. And sat back. "Interesting question. So, this friend. Does the despair have to do with the world being a place where people do terrible things?"

"Right. That."

"I figured. That's usually what it is. Well, then I'd say you have to do wonderful things."

Raymond felt his eyes go wide. "Me?"

"Somebody has to. And you're the one asking the question."

"So if I do wonderful things . . ." He stalled there.

"The world will still be a place where people do terrible things. But here's the thing about despair. We fall into despair when the terrible gangs up on us and we forget the world can also be wonderful. We just see terrible everywhere we look. So what you do for your friend is you bring up the wonderful, so both are side by side. The world is terrible and wonderful at the same time. One doesn't negate the other, but the wonderful keeps us in the game. It keeps us moving forward. And, I'm sorry to have to tell you this, Raymond, but that's as good as the world is going to get."

Raymond didn't answer. He just sat thinking.

"Is that a bad answer?" she asked after a time.

"No. Actually, I've asked a couple of people, and that's the best one I've gotten so far."

Chapter Seventeen

Flames in the Darkness

Raymond opened the door and stepped into the upscale outer office of Luis Javier Velez, Esquire. The receptionist was a pretty, middle-aged black-haired woman with flashing eyes. Not in a good way. She turned those eyes on Raymond, and he froze.

There was no one else in the outer office. But someone was in with Mr. Velez. Raymond could hear the dull murmur of voices and make out vague shapes through a tinted glass window.

"Can I help you?" she asked. It was clear by her tone that she did not want to help him, and assumed she could not.

"I was hoping to get just a minute to talk to Mr. Velez."

"But you don't have an appointment?"

"Well. No."

"He doesn't see anyone without an appointment."

"Okay. I get that. I almost called. But I know him. I've met him. I've been to his apartment, actually, and I know his wife. But it was a while ago now, and I thought if I called on the phone, he might not remember me. I wanted him to see my face."

"Regardless—" she began.

But Raymond simply kept talking.

"See, he gave me his card." He held the card out for her to see, but her eyes just bounced across it and came up to his. He kept his gaze averted as he spoke. "He told me if there was ever anything he could do to help . . ."

The receptionist sighed. Raymond braved a glance at her face as she lifted the receiver of her telephone. She was disappointed, he thought. Because she had to deal with him now. She couldn't just turn him away.

"Mr. Velez," she said. "Sorry to disturb you while you're with a client, but you didn't tell me to hold calls. There's a young man here to see you, but he doesn't have an appointment. But he says you gave him your business card and told him to get in touch if there was anything you could do to help him."

A pause as she listened.

"Right," she said, and hung up the phone.

Raymond's heart raced, waiting to hear what she would do.

"He says that doesn't narrow it down much. But if you want to sit and wait, if he has a couple of minutes between clients, he'll talk to you."

—

Mr. Velez did not turn his eyes to Raymond until he had walked his client to the outer door, said his goodbyes, then closed the door behind the man.

Then he gave Raymond his full attention.

"Oh," he said. "Uh-huh. I do remember you, yes. I came home one day to find you in my kitchen having breakfast with my wife."

"Yes, sir."

"I don't remember your name, though."

"Raymond."

"Well, Raymond, I've got exactly three minutes until my next client, unless she shows up late. So come on in and tell me what you hope I can do. And talk fast."

Raymond followed him into his expensively decorated office. It was modern and sleek, all black leather and gleaming stainless steel. He sat in an uncomfortable chair facing Mr. Velez. The attorney sat behind his massive desk, leaning his chair back, steepling his fingers in front of his chin and staring at Raymond. Waiting for him to speak.

When Raymond didn't open his mouth immediately, Velez jumped in.

"I know what happened," he said. "It's hard to escape the details of a case when the victim shares your name. Legal colleagues kept coming up to me and telling me they were so happy to hear I was still alive. I knew that must've been the guy you were looking for. I mean, Luis Velez. Disappeared suddenly. It just all fit."

"Yes, sir," he said, still lost and scared and overwhelmed for reasons he couldn't entirely sort out.

"And the trial was a crap show."

"Oh. So you know."

"Yeah. Ended in acquittal. So now you're wondering if this trigger-happy citizen just wins and gets off scot-free, or if there's anything the law can still do."

"Yes, sir."

"And you'll tell me it's to help your friend, or to help the widow, because you're a helpful sort of guy, but at this point you're trying to figure out what to think about this world for your own self. Am I right?"

"Yes, sir," he said, wishing he could say something better for a change. But Luis was right.

"There *is* more the law can do. Definitely. Two things right off the top of my head. There could be a federal trial in which she's charged with depriving the victim of his civil rights. But it's not really within our control to get somebody to charge her."

"That seems weird," Raymond said. "To call killing somebody depriving them of their civil rights."

"First and most fundamental right we all have is life. But there's a better option, in my opinion. Civil trial. The widow takes the shooter to civil court. The burden of proof is different, so it's easier to win. It's her money at stake, not her freedom, so that tends to make the jury less squeamish. It's the way to go, if you're asking my opinion. That trigger-happy woman should be putting all three of those Velez kids through a four-year university. What right does she have to sit home and spend her money while the widow struggles to raise three kids all on her own?"

"What if she doesn't have that much money?"

"Then she can put all three kids through community college. You know the widow, right?"

"Yes, sir."

"Send her in to talk to me."

His phone buzzed, and he pressed a button, apparently for speakerphone. "Tell her I'll be out in less than a minute, Marjorie."

"There's just one problem," Raymond said, already on his feet. "I just worry about her . . ."

"Which her?"

"The widow. I'm not sure how she would . . ."

"Well, she's obviously just flowing over with money," Velez said, moving with Raymond toward the office door.

"No. She's not."

"You're very bad at sarcasm, Raymond. I know a lady with three kids and suddenly no husband is not flowing over with money. If she was, it wouldn't be so important to get some from Trigger Lady."

They stood a moment at the door to the outer office. Velez had his hand on the knob.

"Are you saying you'll help her for no money?"

"No. I'm saying I'd consider taking the case on contingency. If I lose, I get nothing. But I won't lose. When I win, I take a percentage of what the jury awards. Have her call and make an appointment."

Velez swung the door wide. Nodded to his next client, who sat in the outer office.

Raymond moved through the receptionist's area. Toward the outer door.

"Hey," he heard Luis Velez say. "Raymond."

He stopped. Turned.

"Isn't this Tuesday?" the attorney asked him.

"Yes. Tuesday."

"You skipping school?"

"No, sir. It's spring break."

"Oh. Spring break. Late this year."

"Yes, sir. It's late this year."

Raymond stepped out into the plushly carpeted hallway.

He rode down twenty-one floors alone on the elevator, still processing what had just happened to him. He had won a major victory, but he would be halfway to the subway station before he fully realized it.

It had just all happened so fast.

———

"Get out of those jeans," his mother said. "I'm doing a load of colored laundry, and I need all your jeans."

"I'm wearing them," Raymond said.

It was a bit of an obvious comment. But he had just walked in the door. His head was still spinning from his morning. He wasn't quite ready to deal with his mother's strident style of communication.

"So just put on sweatpants or something. And if there's anything on the floor of your room, bring it out. Chop-chop. I only have one day off this week, and I've got, like, six loads of laundry to get done."

Raymond sighed. "There's nothing on the floor of my room. There's never anything on the floor of my room."

Have you ever actually met me?

"Fine," she said. "Then just the jeans."

———

Raymond was pressing "Send" on his email to Isabel, telling her the big news, when his mother threw open the door to his room. Without knocking.

"And what exactly is *this*?" she asked.

She sounded angry.

She was holding up what was obviously a bill of paper money. But she was not close enough for Raymond to make out the denomination.

"I can't see," he said.

She marched up to where he sat at his desk and pushed it so close to his face that he had to jerk his head back to keep it from hitting him in the nose.

It was a crisp new one-hundred-dollar bill.

"It was in your jeans. You weren't smart enough to go through the pockets before you gave them to me."

At first he just stared at it. She was holding it so close to his face that his eyes crossed in the process. A few seconds later it came together in his head.

"Huh. He's getting better at that. I never felt a thing."

He glanced up at his mother, who looked as though her head were about to explode, letting out a burst of scalding steam.

"Do I even want to know what that means?" she shouted.

"No, it's . . . It's nothing. It's not . . . it's just this guy who drops money anonymously on people when he thinks they deserve it."

"And what exactly did you do to deserve it?"

"Nothing. Just trying to help a friend. I was just trying to get a referral for a friend for something she needs. I didn't do anything wrong."

"You're not selling drugs?"

"Of course not."

"Or yourself?"

"Jeez, Mom. Have you ever met me? I mean, do you actually know me at all?"

"I know you're gone an awful lot these days."

"Just hanging out with my friends."

"All of whom are adults. Which is weird."

It was actually weird to hear her use the word "whom," but he didn't say so.

"None of whom are into any of the things you're accusing me of."

She stood over him in silence for several beats. Then she let out a long and audible breath, and Raymond knew she would let it go.

"Okay, good," she said, and headed for his bedroom door.

"Um. Mom?"

"What?"

He didn't ask. Just held out his hand. She sighed deeply, walked back to his desk, and handed him the hundred-dollar bill.

Nice try, he thought as she walked away without comment. This time he was smart enough to keep his thought to himself.

———

He knocked on Mrs. G's door an hour later, using his special "It's Raymond" knock. In one hand he held a bouquet of flowers—irises and a few roses, with baby's breath in between the blooms. In the other he held a small box from a shop that called itself a chocolatier. In it were four finely handcrafted and very expensive chocolate truffles.

There had been a great deal of walking involved in getting them. His neighborhood did not have florist shops and chocolatiers on every corner.

"You may come in, Raymond," she called through the door.

He let himself in with the key.

She was sitting on the couch, slumped forward, chin nearly on her breastbone—as though holding her own head up required more effort than she was willing to expend. She was still in her nightgown, with a blue terry-cloth robe tied on over it.

"I smell flowers," she said. Listlessly, Raymond thought.

"That's because I brought you some."

He stood in the middle of her living room for a moment, hoping she would say more—wake up in some internal sense.

When she didn't, he said, "Do you have a vase or something I can put these in?"

"In the cupboard over the refrigerator. It's a very high cupboard. You might have to stand on a chair. I put them up high after Rolf died because I couldn't think who else would bring me flowers."

"I'm tall," he said.

"That's true. You are. Well, see how you do."

He moved into the kitchen and pulled down one of her three vases easily. Meanwhile he nursed a gnawing sensation in the back of his mind having to do with her mental and emotional state. He would not have put it so clearly in words if he had been asked. It was just a sense of everything being wrong.

He poured water into the vase at her sink. Unwrapped the flowers and threw away the paper. Arranged the blooms carefully in the vase for display.

He carried them out to her dining table.

"Will you do me a favor?" she asked, her voice small.

"Of course. Anything."

"Bring them here for just a moment?"

He carried them to where she sat and perched on the edge of the couch, holding them out for her. She lifted her chin, which seemed encouraging. He watched her pull in a deep breath through her nose. Then she raised one ancient hand and began to explore the blooms by feel.

"Roses," she said. "And irises. I especially love irises. And is that baby's breath? Thank you for bringing them. They're beautiful."

Raymond sat a moment longer than necessary and realized he had expected her to say "they *must be* beautiful." Not "they *are* beautiful." It was the first time he had stopped to consider that something could be beautiful in the absence of sight. He was glad to know it. Glad for her.

"I brought you these, too."

He handed her the little box from the chocolatier, and she lifted the cover carefully, as if its contents might be as fragile as a blown egg. She inhaled deeply.

"Oh, it smells wonderful. I haven't had good chocolate in ages. But tell me, Raymond, why are you spending so much money on me? I feel bad about that. Don't you have to use your money for your own needs?"

"I just came into some money unexpectedly," he said.

He sat quietly and watched as she took a tiny bite of chocolate truffle.

Then he said, "I say that a lot, don't I?"

"I was just about to point that out. What is your secret? Billions of people will want to know."

"I'm not sure."

But he did have a thought about it. He simply did not feel ready, or even able, to form it into words. But it was something that had started happening after Raymond began helping. The more people saw him trying to help someone else, the more help they seemed to want to drop on him.

"I hope this is okay," he said. "I told the Velez family—the other Velez family—that we'd come to supper this Sunday."

He waited, but she only sighed. She did not refuse, which felt like progress.

"I just want to help you get on your feet again," he added.

"Yes, I know you do. And I am so sorry, Raymond. I know you want me to put this all behind me, but parts of it I have never managed to put behind me, not in decade after decade of living. I feel as though my spirit has been shattered, and into so many pieces that I just can't imagine picking them all up and trying to reassemble myself. And I feel guilty, because I wish I could do better for you. You are so sweet to spend your found money bringing me flowers and candy. And I'm not saying it doesn't help at all. Of course it does. It's like a light in the nighttime. A little candle flame in an otherwise endless night. It's a comfort to have you and your thoughtfulness. But it's still a long night."

He sat for several seconds in silence. They both did.

"But you'll go with me to that Sunday supper?"

"Yes," she said. More resigned than motivated. "I will go because it means a lot to you that I go, and you mean a lot to me."

He almost told her about Luis Javier Velez, Esquire, and the civil case. The acquitted shooter maybe having to put all three of Luis's kids through college. He opened his mouth to tell her. But then he closed it again, and decided to wait until he was sure it would genuinely happen. He didn't figure she could bear even one more disappointment.

—

"I hope you like chicken and dumplings," Sofia Velez said.

They had just been called to the table. Raymond and Mrs. G were standing in the dining room doorway, arm in arm, waiting to be told where to sit.

"Oh, wonderful!" Mrs. G said. Raymond couldn't tell if she felt genuine enthusiasm or was faking it to be polite. If the latter, it was a good fake. "It's one of my favorite meals. I used to make it for my husband all the time, but I haven't had it for years."

"It sounds good," Raymond said, because it also didn't sound like anything he had eaten, ever.

Luis Senior showed them to places in the center of the table, carefully pulling out a chair for Mrs. G and holding it and guiding it as she sat. They waited while every member of the family came to his or her place and took a seat. It was a big family, so it was a big production.

"Abuela will say grace," Luis Senior said.

Raymond felt first alarmed, then relieved. He wasn't sure how Mrs. G would feel about a Christian prayer, being Jewish herself. Then again, she didn't have to say it. Just listen to it. But Abuela would say grace in Spanish, which seemed better to Raymond somehow. Safer.

Luisa, the teen girl who had given him the medal, was sitting to his left. She slipped her hand into his. At first it startled him. But he looked up and around and saw that everyone was joining hands with everyone else. He took Mrs. G's hand with his right.

Their abuela spoke four or five sentences in Spanish, then said, "Amen." Raymond didn't know if she had ended the prayer in English or if the word was the same in both languages.

"Amen," Raymond said, because he couldn't imagine how or why not to.

"Amen," Mrs. G said.

They unclasped hands, and Luis Senior began to spoon chicken and dumplings onto plates, which were passed down the long sides of the table.

"Oh, it smells heavenly," Mrs. G said.

"Well, I hope you'll enjoy my cooking," Sofia said. "We're so happy you came. We're so glad to see Raymond again. He made quite an impression on us. He was so sad because he was worried he wouldn't be able to give you the help you need. You know. Finding this other Luis Velez. And then when we heard what had happened . . ."

The room fell silent save for the sound of plates being picked up, passed, set down.

"All I really meant to say," Sofia said, stumbling on, "is that you're very lucky to have such a thoughtful young man for a friend."

"And don't think I fail to appreciate it," Mrs. G said. She picked up a tiny forkful of chicken and dumplings. "Not a day goes by that I'm not thankful."

She tasted the food, and everyone watched and waited to see what she would think. Everyone. Even the toddler. Maybe because she had made her love of chicken and dumplings so clear.

"So, is it as good as what you used to make?" Sofia asked.

"No. It's better. I never made a batch this good in all my days as a cook. And I was a fair cook, if I do say so myself."

"Well, I'm glad you like it."

They all ate in silence for a minute or two. Raymond was feeling transfixed by the food. It felt satisfying in a way he was not accustomed to feeling. Each bite he shoveled into his mouth grew larger than the last.

Sofia spoke again. "I've been thinking about the question Raymond asked me." She directed the remark more or less to Mrs. G.

"I don't think I know the question," Mrs. G said.

"Oh. Sorry. He asked me what you can do for a person who's going through a bad time." Raymond felt his face flush hot as she spoke. "And I don't know, really. The only thing I can come up with is that you need to know people care. Not only about you, although that's nice, too. But about what happened. About your friend, the one you lost. I thought about it, and I thought that trial would have been very upsetting to me because it would feel like the jury was saying my friend didn't matter. So I just wanted to let you know that he matters to every single person at this table."

Raymond watched Mrs. G carefully as she chewed and swallowed.

"Thank you," she said. "That does help a little."

"I hope you believe us," Luis Senior added.

"I do. I absolutely do. Because you understand what it meant to be Luis. I'm afraid that's where things fell down with the jury."

They ate in silence for an awkward second or two.

Then Abuela began to speak in rapid Spanish. Raymond waited patiently, both for her to be done, and for someone to translate. He vaguely, distantly wished he had gone on studying the language.

When she wound down and finished, Mrs. G surprised Raymond by answering her directly. "Recuerdo también," she said.

Raymond stared at Mrs. G for a moment. Everyone at the table did.

"You speak Spanish?" he asked.

"A little. Yes. I asked Luis to teach me some. First I asked him to teach me to say 'Lo siento, no hablo muy bien español.' I wanted to be able to apologize to Spanish speakers for not knowing their language well. Because I noticed that everyone else in this city seems to do the opposite. You know, make them feel bad for not speaking English. But then I decided that wasn't good enough, because why apologize for not being able to do something that you can just as easily learn to do?"

"No wonder Luis liked you so much," Luisa said.

"Oh, and the feeling was mutual, my dear. I just adored him. He was like a son to me, except he was young enough to be my grandson. But he was more than just family to me. He was . . . I'm not sure of quite the right word. He was a hero in my life. Yes. That's not too strong. He was my hero. Here the world is full of all these men trying to model what it means to be a man, but they don't truly know. They think it means be tough, feel nothing, betray nothing. And then Luis comes along and decides that his definition of a man is someone who is not afraid to be kind. That takes courage. Don't you think?"

"It does take courage," Luis Senior said. A bit wistfully, Raymond thought. As if he had a way to go to reach that mountaintop.

"So what did Abuela say?" Raymond asked, hoping to lead the conversation in a less grave direction.

"Well, if I'm not mistaken," Mrs. G said, "she was telling us that when she was a little girl, a neighborhood would hold a block party for someone who was down. If the world would not care for a person, the neighborhood would turn out and care. I told her I remember that as well. When I first moved to the neighborhood we live in now, Raymond, we would do that. I remember a man was fired from his job. His wife had just had a baby, their first baby, and they were about to be evicted for nonpayment of rent. So the neighbors threw a block party and took up a collection for them, and it was enough to tide them over until he was working again. But I shouldn't make assumptions, because my Spanish is far from perfect, and maybe that's not what Abuela meant at all."

"No, that's right," Abuela said in heavily accented English. "That's what I meant."

"You speak English," Raymond said without thinking. Then he felt embarrassed for assuming otherwise.

"Yes," Abuela said. "I do. But in my own home I like to speak in my own tongue, the one that's familiar to me."

"Sure," Raymond said. "I can understand that."

And he could. It was important to feel at home while at home.

———

"I don't believe this!" Sofia shouted from the kitchen. "Who left the ice cream out on the counter?" She stuck her head into the dining room. "Who did this?"

Raymond already knew that Luis Junior had done it. Because the boy was growing smaller before his eyes, his head shrinking down toward his collar like a turtle retreating into its shell.

Sofia noticed it, too, and fixed him with a withering gaze.

"Sorry, Mom," the boy said, barely audibly.

"What were you doing even taking it out of the freezer?"

"I just had one spoon of it."

"Well, that's bad enough!" she shouted. "But then you just leave it out on the counter? How can you be so careless? How can you not notice that you didn't put it away again?"

"I forgot," Luis Junior said, his face flaming red.

"Go to your room," his father said.

The boy slunk away from the table.

"Can any be salvaged?" Luis Senior asked his wife.

"No, it's completely ruined."

"So we have cake but no ice cream," Luis said. "We'll manage."

"But it's a special day with special company, and I wanted to serve the chocolate cake with vanilla ice cream!"

"I could run down to the store and get some," Luisa said.

A pause.

Then Sofia asked, "All by yourself, m'ija?"

"It's the middle of the afternoon, Mom. But Raymond could walk with me. If that makes you feel better."

"Me?" Raymond asked. Then he immediately regretted it. He leaned to his right and spoke quietly to Mrs. G. "Are you okay here without me if I go?"

"Of course," she said. "I will be fine talking to this lovely family."

"Okay," Raymond said to Luisa. "Fine. Let's go."

———

On the way to the store they had barely spoken. Just walked. But on the way back with the ice cream, Raymond could feel her staring at him. He could see it in his peripheral vision. It made him uncomfortable. He couldn't bring himself to look over.

"So," she began. Tentatively. "I just have to ask. Did you put it back on because you knew you'd be seeing me? Or did you have it on this whole time?"

"The medal? I had it on the whole time."

"Good. You know, I worried about you after you left last time. If I'd had your number, I'd have called."

"No, I didn't know that. But you shouldn't have worried about me. You should've worried about Mrs. G. I wasn't in trouble. I was just afraid for *her*."

"But I didn't know her. And I knew you."

Raymond didn't answer, because it sounded too much like something a jury might say if they could be as honest and unguarded as a teen.

"So, is she going to be okay?" she asked.

"I have no idea. She's sure not okay right now."

"You're so sweet to take such good care of her."

"She's my friend."

She stopped him suddenly. And literally. Grabbed a handful of his sleeve and just stopped him in his tracks on the sidewalk. He almost dropped the ice cream. They stood facing each other for an awkward second or two. He could tell she was staring up into his face, but he kept his eyes trained down to the pavement.

"What?" he asked, feeling defensive.

She reached up on tiptoes and kissed him briefly on the lips. Then she dropped back down to her heels again, still staring at his face.

"Uh-oh," she said. "You didn't want me to do that. I'm sorry. I thought you were just shy but you liked me."

"I do like you," he said.

"But not like that."

"No."

Silence. She let go of his sleeve, and Raymond walked again. Quickly. She ran to catch up.

"You like somebody else? Is that it?"

"No," Raymond said, wishing they could talk about something else.

"You like girls more your own age?"

"No."

"You don't like anybody like that?"

"No."

"But you did, right? You have. I mean, you're . . . what? Sixteen?"

"Seventeen."

"Oh. Okay. We don't have to talk about it if you don't want."

"Thank you," Raymond said, and hurried along, looking down at the sidewalk.

He almost plowed into a beefy, short man, who said, "Hey! Look where you're goin', kid!"

"Sorry," Raymond mumbled, and hurried on.

"Hey, wait!" Luisa called from behind him. "I can't walk that fast."

He slowed for her, but it was hard to do. He wanted to get back to the apartment and not be alone with Luisa.

"So, seriously," she said, as if she had never promised to stop talking about it. "You just don't like anybody like that, and you never did?"

"Right," he said, feeling the ice cream cooling the side of his ribs. He might have been holding it too tightly.

"Is that, like . . . a . . . thing? That people are like?"

"Yeah."

"So, you'll just never . . ." She trailed off, as though she might not continue. Raymond certainly hoped she wouldn't. ". . . have a family?"

"I can have a family. Mrs. G says I can have any kind of family I want. I can have . . . I don't know. A group of friends, or somebody who feels the same way I do."

"But don't you want kids?"

"I never really thought much about it. I mean, I never pictured myself having kids, no."

"Oh," she said. "Well. I didn't mean to make you feel like it's not okay to be whatever you are." But she had. "We can talk about something else if you want to."

"Yes, please," Raymond said. Then he added, "But thank you for liking me. Anyway."

They walked the rest of the way in silence.

———

They sat on the living room couch together, post-dessert, Raymond and Mrs. G. Waiting for cups of tea to arrive. All the kids except the toddler had been sent to their rooms to do homework, including Luisa. That felt like a relief to Raymond.

Mrs. G leaned over and whispered to him at close range.

"So what's wrong?"

"Nothing," he said.

"Fine. All right. Tell me later."

Sofia hurried into the room with milk and sugar, which she set on the coffee table in front of them.

"I'm just so embarrassed," Sofia said.

"About what?" Mrs. G asked.

"Oh, all that trouble. I wanted you to see us as a happy family. Well, we are. I don't mean we were trying to fool you into thinking we are. But then there was all that trouble."

"Where was I during all the trouble?" Mrs. G asked.

She was getting weary. Raymond could hear it in her voice.

"The trouble. You know. With the ice cream. And Luis Junior being asked to leave the table."

"*That?* Oh my goodness, that's nothing. I never would have given it another thought. He's a child. Children do things like that. Their brains aren't fully developed. It's just who they are."

"See, Sofia?" Luis Senior said. He was just walking into the living room to sit down. The sound of those words let Raymond know, for the first time, that the man was even within earshot. "I told you it seemed worse to you than to them."

He settled his bulk into a wing chair and sighed, both hands on his belly.

"Oh my goodness, yes," Mrs. G said. "There's no such thing as a family who doesn't have those little bits of trouble. Who was it who said . . . I can't remember now who the quote was from, but somebody said when you decide to be alone or have a family, you're pretty much choosing between feeling lonely or feeling aggravated."

Sofia laughed, and seemed to feel a little better.

"Well, anyway, it gave the young people a chance to talk. Luisa has been talking about Raymond ever since he was here last."

"Ah," Mrs. G said. "I see. That does explain a lot."

Raymond, who felt revealed, was careful to say nothing more.

———

"I hope you all understand," Mrs. G said about ten minutes later. "I'm just so tired. I get tired when I go out. And then I ate so much. I haven't been eating all that much lately, but everything was so good, and I just stuffed myself, and now I feel as though I'll just fall right to sleep."

"Why, you hardly ate at all!" Sofia said.

Raymond wished she hadn't said it. If she had known Mrs. G, she would know the older woman had put away a remarkable quantity of food—for her.

"But we understand," Luis said. "Of course. You have to promise to come back again, though, and that's nonnegotiable."

He rose, walked to the couch. Helped Mrs. G to her feet.

"I promise," she said. "Thank you so much for your hospitality. I would stay longer, but I'm just so tired."

Raymond hooked his arm through hers, in case she became unsteady on her feet. Which happened when she was very tired. Luis tapped him on the shoulder, and when Raymond turned, he saw a twenty-dollar bill in the man's hand, with possibly another bill underneath.

"I insist you take a cab," he said.

"Thank you," Raymond said, and took the money.

On his own, for himself, he would have refused. He could have ridden the subway. But Mrs. G was tired, so he took it.

———

They rode together in the back seat of a taxi, Raymond keeping one eye on the meter.

It had begun to spatter rain, and the streets slid by behind patterns of droplets on the cab windows. Raymond could hear the distinctive sound of the *shoosh* of tires on wet asphalt.

Couples walked down the street hand in hand under umbrellas, or ran because they had none. On one corner Raymond saw a couple standing on the curb, facing each other, caught up in a shouting match and ignoring the weather.

"Do you think I'll ever have a family?" he asked her.

"Oh, so that's what's troubling you. Yes, of course you will, if you want one."

"But what kind of family?"

"That's the last question you should be asking, Raymond, because it's the part that matters the least. Any kind you want. If you want more emotional intimacy, you'll have a companion who understands the way you are. If you want to raise children, you will. Your own, or adopted or fostered ones. Or you'll just be the world's best uncle to your friends' children. The thing about a family is the love. The 'what kind?' and 'how will it work?' is nothing. That's just a thing you worry about before you learn that those details aren't what matter at all."

Chapter Eighteen

The Cellist

Raymond was walking from his father's apartment to the subway when he first heard it. It was an extended musical note, played live on some string instrument. It had a resonance that he could feel in his gut, as though the string lived in his large intestine, just under his stomach, and some unseen bow was making it tremble. It was a beautiful bass note, but also almost unbearably sad. It made tears spring to his eyes immediately, which surprised him.

He stood in the middle of the sidewalk and looked around until he saw the musician. He was a middle-aged man sitting on a three-legged stool on the corner, close to the subway stairs, playing the cello. His hair was wild and gray, missing on top but full around the sides. In front of him on the street was an upturned hat in which Raymond could see a small handful of dollar bills.

He moved closer.

The man looked up at him and smiled briefly, then returned his attention to the instrument.

Raymond squatted down on his haunches to listen. It was a slow, heartfelt classical piece. The more he listened, the more impossible it felt to hold back his tears. The notes just seemed to find Raymond's sorrow in its hiding places and pull it out into the light. He swiped at his eyes with one sleeve.

He pulled a five-dollar bill out of his pocket and dropped it into the man's hat. It was the only bill the musician had been given that was bigger than a single.

Meanwhile the cellist drew out the last note, and the street fell silent. Well, silent in terms of music. There were still city noises, which Raymond did not find the least bit welcome in comparison.

"Thank you," the man said, looking deeply into Raymond's face. Raymond was careful not to meet the cellist's eyes. "That's a gift right there. I can actually get lunch with that."

A silence. Raymond did not fill it. He was hoping the musician would play again. But he just kept looking into Raymond's face, as if he had lost something important there.

"Seem like the music made you sad," the man said.

"I guess," Raymond replied, still wishing the man would play.

"But you already had this sadness in you before you heard my cello."

"How do you know that?"

"The cello is an amazing instrument. It can slice right through a person's walls and pull things to the surface. Why do you think I play it? But it can't pull out something that wasn't in there to begin with."

Then he began to play again. Raymond sat down cross-legged on the concrete and listened. The tears came back, and he didn't feel able to stop them. So after a while he didn't try.

It seemed to produce an actual physical feeling in his gut, a sort of ache that rose and fell with the music—that ricocheted around in there as each note faded and died.

When the piece was over, and the man's bow had gone still and his strings silent, Raymond asked a question.

"If it slices through walls and pulls stuff out of me, stuff that hurts, why am I sitting here listening to it? Why didn't I walk the other way?"

"Because it's better to feel it."

"Not if it hurts."

"Especially if it hurts. Remember, it was in there to begin with. And as an old friend of mine used to say, better out than in."

Then he played another piece.

When the bow had gone still again and the last note had faded to no note at all, Raymond asked another question.

"Are you going to be here for an hour or so?"

"Son, I'm going to be here all day."

"Okay," he said. "Thanks. I'll be back."

———

"You need to get ready to go out," he said to Mrs. G. "Please. I want to take you someplace."

She was slumped on the couch, still in her nightgown and robe, her hair undone and unkempt, the cat purring on her lap.

"Oh, Raymond," she said, followed by a deep sigh. "Couldn't you go do the shopping without me?"

"That's not where I'm taking you."

"Where, then?"

"I don't want to say. I want you to trust me."

"It's already afternoon. I get tired in the afternoon."

"I really think it will be worth it," he said. "Please just trust me on this."

He knew as he said it that she would not refuse him. Their unspoken deal was that he did as much as he could for her and asked as little as possible in return. When he asked her to do something—if it was a reasonable thing, and within her power to do it—at least she would try.

Another deep sigh. Then she shifted the cat off onto the couch and rose with great effort. Raymond extended a hand to help her, but she didn't seem to notice.

"Fine," she said, shuffling slowly toward her bedroom. "Give me ten minutes. Maybe feed the cat while you are waiting, please."

———

"I had a dream last night," she said to him on the subway ride to Midtown.

He waited, thinking she would say more. But she seemed to be waiting as well, as if to be sure that he genuinely wanted to hear about it.

"What was it?" he asked after a time.

"I dreamt about my friend Anna. Annaliese Schmidt. She was my best friend in school in Germany. She was the same age in the dream— the age she was when I last saw her. And here I was over ninety and Anna still just a young girl, and yet she spoke to me as if we were peers. She said some fairly harsh things."

A pause. Raymond almost thought he would have to ask. But then she cleared her throat and continued.

"She said it was very selfish of me to base my participation in the world on whether the world was pleasing me at the moment. She said of course the world can be cruel; this is a given. She asked if I knew what she would have sacrificed to be ninety-two."

"Whoa," Raymond said.

She seemed done speaking. He watched the side of her face to see if she was upset by what she was reporting, but her face looked slack and calm.

He sat with his question for a few minutes as the subway car rocked its way through the tunnel. Then the question overwhelmed and overpowered him, and came up and out.

"Do you think it was just a dream?"

"As opposed to what?"

"I don't know. I don't know how to say it. As opposed to the actual dead Anna actually wanting to say that to you."

A pause fell while she thought it over.

"Here is what I think," she said. "I think it makes not one bit of difference if those words came from the soul of Annaliese Schmidt or from the inside of my own brain. I think it only matters if the words are right."

"Oh," Raymond said. Then, after a time, "Are they right?"

"I think they are right," she said. "Yes."

———

She stepped up out of the subway, into the air of Midtown, with Raymond's hand in the small of her back. Helping. She stopped on the top stair, almost level with the street, and lifted her chin high. As if there were some magical scent on the wind.

"Listen," she said.

The cellist was still playing.

"I know," he said. "I like it, too. I think it's beautiful. Sad, but beautiful."

"Can we please go closer and listen?"

They approached the cellist and stood quietly. While the man was playing, he did not look up. He seemed entirely lost in the music.

Raymond looked over at his friend to see her crying silently. Big tears, one after the other, dripping off the end of her wrinkled jowls and chin. It made him cry again to see it.

She leaned close to him and reached up on her tiptoes, bracing herself on his forearm. She whispered as close to his ear as possible. She seemed not to want to disturb the musician.

"Am I keeping us from what you wanted to show me? Where did you want to take me?"

"Here," he whispered back. "This is what I wanted to show you."

She sank down to her heels again. Brought her hands together in front of her face as if praying, then lowered them to her heart.

The cellist finished his piece and looked up at Raymond, breaking into a smile of recognition.

"You're back."

"I brought a friend," Raymond said.

"Thank you. I'm honored. Most people pay very little attention. People are funny, don't you think? I used to play for the philharmonic, and people would pay good money for those tickets. Big money. But I sit out here and play the same music, and most people won't even flip me a quarter as they walk by. Same music. Just a different sense of how much they should value it."

"You used to play for the New York Philharmonic?" Mrs. G asked, her voice tinged with awe.

"Oh. No. Not *that* philharmonic. Nothing that good. Smaller city. Now I don't want to say what city, because you thought it was New York, so that would be a total anticlimax."

They fell silent a moment. The cellist sat, and Raymond and Mrs. G stood, and he did not seem inclined to begin a new piece.

"My father played the cello," Mrs. G said. "When I was a child. Then after we moved to New York, he never touched the thing. He brought it with him, but he never took it out of its case again, right up until the day he died. So it's very emotional for me to hear the instrument played. But I don't think I ever told you that. Did I, Raymond?"

"No," Raymond said.

"It was just a coincidence?"

"I just thought it was beautiful," he said. "Sad, but beautiful."

"Yes," the cellist said. "That's what I love about the instrument. It imitates life perfectly. Just the right amount of beautiful. Just the right amount of sad."

Then he raised his bow and began to play again. More tears rolled down Mrs. G's cheeks.

Halfway through the piece a waiter appeared more or less out of nowhere, walking to them from a sidewalk café two buildings down. In his right hand he carried an intricately carved wooden chair with an embroidered fabric seat.

"I thought you might like to sit," he said to Mrs. G. "Just bring it back before you go."

They both thanked him, and Raymond took Mrs. G's arm, carefully settling her into the seat. She sighed as she sat, almost a grunt. It was clearly a relief to get off her feet.

"This is so lovely," she said quietly to Raymond, who squatted at her side. "This is like a concert being played just for me. I haven't been to a concert in decades."

She opened her purse and searched for her wallet. Opened the wallet and pulled up one end of a few bills.

"What denomination are these?" she asked him.

"All fives."

"No tens in there at all?"

"No. Fives."

She pulled two bills free and handed them to Raymond. "Put these in his . . . whatever he's using to collect money."

Raymond dropped the bills in the cellist's hat.

The man stopped playing suddenly. Right in the middle of a note. He raised the hand not holding the bow and offered an expansive gesture of thanks to her, like the tipping of an invisible fedora.

"She can't see that," Raymond said.

It only just then struck Raymond that she had not brought her red-and-white cane. Maybe she had been too tired and dispirited to go fetch it. Or maybe she trusted him now to tell her everything she needed to know about the sidewalk in front of her feet.

"Did I miss something?" she asked.

"It was a gesture of gratitude," the cellist said. He leaned one elbow on his knee a moment, seeming to have lost the will to play, or the thread of the piece he had abandoned. "Your friend here has an emotional reaction to the music," he said to Mrs. G. "A lot of people do. It made him cry. I think he brought you here so you could cry, too. Just a guess. I don't mean that in a bad way."

"I didn't assume you did."

"I think maybe he thought a catharsis would do you good. But I'm only guessing based on my observations."

"He may be onto something there," Mrs. G said. "After all, the only thing that hurts more than tears shed is tears unshed."

"Indeed," the cellist said. "Now I'd better start again at the beginning. I can never pick up the thread of that piece once I've lost it."

For nearly two hours they sat in the street and listened to him play, neither seeming to want to say it was time for the concert to be over.

———

"So, is that true what he guessed?" she asked him on the subway ride home. "Did you think I needed a good cry?"

"I had no idea if you would cry," Raymond said. "I never thought about it. I cried, but I never thought about whether you would. I just thought it was beautiful. I'm always trying to think of beautiful things I can share with you about the world, but usually you can't see them. This one you could enjoy just as much as I could, and so I wanted you to."

She reached up by feel and placed a warm hand on his cheek. Patted it lightly, then just held it there for a moment. Then she patted his cheek again and dropped her hand back into her lap.

"I was hoping it would be another light for you," he added. "You know. In that long night."

"It's getting lighter in here all the time," she said. "I thought it was interesting what the cellist said."

"Which part?"

"The part about his instrument having the same sad-to-beautiful ratio as life. And now I'm sitting here thinking, Who am I to make some big, sweeping pronouncement that the balance of life is wrong? I must have quite an ego to think I know better than God about a thing like that."

"You believe in God?"

Raymond wondered if he had known that already or not. Maybe.

"I believe in something," she said. "Something that I certainly hope knows better than me how the world should be arranged."

Chapter Nineteen

The Block Party and the Sunset

Raymond was on his way to the apartment door when his mother stuck her head out of the kitchen.

"Going out?" she asked. A little too brightly to sound natural.

"Yeah," he said, hoping not to have to say more.

"With your friends?"

"Yeah."

"The older lady? Or that family who lost the father? Or that other family with the same name who still have the father?"

"Yeah."

She fixed him with a curious look. "That last one wasn't really a yes or no question."

"Kind of all of the above. Is there a reason I'm getting the third degree?"

Her look changed then. Wilted. Morphed into something that looked weak and hurt. Raymond wasn't used to that on her, and it made him feel guilty.

"That was so not what I was going for," she said.

He paused a minute, his hand on the knob. Nearly teetered, half there and half gone, at least in his head. Waiting to hear if there would be more.

"I was trying to show some interest in your life," she added.

"Oh. Got it. Sorry."

He opened the door, but she had more to say.

"I know I said I was trying to understand you better. And I *have* been trying. But I think mostly I've been failing."

The conversation hung there in pause mode for a moment. Raymond stepped through the door, nearly desperate for his freedom from this discomfort. But, as he did, he remembered what Mrs. G had told him. About making peace with his family of origin, especially his mother.

He stuck his head back in. "Thanks for trying, though."

"And mostly failing," she said.

"Still, though . . . thanks for trying."

———

They met Isabel and her three children on the corner, Raymond leading Mrs. G slowly by the arm. They walked together, all six of them, toward the apartment of Luis and Sofia Velez and family.

They walked quietly at first.

"So we're just going there to have supper?" Isabel asked after a time.

"I think so," Raymond said. "They wanted to meet you. And the kids. But Sofia was very . . . I don't quite know how to say it. She sounded excited, and she kept insisting that it had to be all of us and it had to be this Sunday, not last Sunday and not next Sunday, so . . . I don't know. Sounded almost like there could be more, but she wouldn't say more about it. So I'm not sure what to tell you. But there might be more."

He heard Mrs. G sigh and knew the older woman hoped there would not be much more. She clearly didn't feel up to much more.

"Hope they have a big dinner table," Isabel said. "That's going to be an awful lot of people eating supper. Okay, I have something to tell you, and I think this feels like the right time, so here goes. It's really good news."

"I can always use some good news," Mrs. G said.

"I met with that attorney this morning, Raymond. That friend of yours. He met me at his office even though it's Sunday. And he's going to take the case. He thinks we have a really, really good case. He gives us a ninety-five percent chance of winning it. And he's taking it on contingency, so I don't have to pay him until we win. Which he's confident we will. So I've just been really excited about that all day."

"Wait," Mrs. G said. "Am I supposed to know something about this? Because I know nothing about it."

"Oh," Isabel said. "I thought Raymond would've told you."

Raymond swallowed hard against a sense of shame—almost as though trying to swallow the shame back down. "I didn't want to tell you until I knew if it would work out or not," he said, his voice small. "I thought maybe it was too soon."

"You have a friend who's an attorney?"

"Yeah. Sort of. He's one of the men named Luis Velez who I went to see, but who turned out not to be the right one."

They walked in silence for a handful of steps. Their heels on the pavement and the roar of traffic provided the only sound.

"But her trial is already over," Mrs. G said.

"But this will be a civil trial," Isabel said.

"Oh. A civil trial. I see."

"We don't know how much money she has," Isabel said. "But in the course of filing the case we'll have a right to find out. He says the court will let her keep enough to live on, but not much more. Rent and food and utilities and such, but no luxuries for her ever again. Everything over what she needs to live will go to me and the kids toward what the jury awards. If we win. Which he's confident we will."

"So she *will* have to pay something for what she did," Mrs. G said, her voice hushed with emotion.

"Looks that way."

"That *is* good news!"

They walked in silence another half a block, each seemingly thinking their own thoughts. Even the children seemed lost in their own heads.

Then Mrs. G said, "There's a band somewhere playing the steel drums. Do you hear that?"

But Raymond didn't. He looked over at Isabel but saw no sign that she heard.

"I hear it!" Esteban shouted.

And then, half a block later, so did Raymond.

———

They turned the corner onto Luis and Sofia's street. There were a good thirty people out in the street. Maybe more. Not on the sidewalk, either. In the street. At both ends of the block someone had placed the wooden barricades police use to cordon off a street from traffic.

The steel drum band was playing in the middle of the block. Smoke rose from a commercial-size barbecue just behind them. People milled about with red paper cups, sipping. Two little girls in fancy dresses danced to the band.

Sofia spotted Raymond and his friends, and hurried to where they stood taking in the unexpected scene.

"Welcome to our block party," she said.

"You put on a block party?" Raymond asked. "For who?"

"Well, for all of you," she said. "Who do you think?"

———

Sofia came by their table and hovered. Someone had set up a folding table for them on the sidewalk in the middle of the block. It even had a bright blue paper tablecloth, taped down so the breeze couldn't take it away, and helium balloons tied to all four corners.

"Right now it's a little lightly attended," Sofia said. "But we have free hot dogs and hamburgers, and when they start cooking, I think the smell will bring more people down." She was clearly stressed by the light turnout, and Raymond couldn't help picking up that stress. "And one of our neighbors contributed two kegs of beer from his work. So that'll bring 'em out, I think. Right now people are looking down from their windows and trying to decide. Everybody wants a crowd to blend into. But I think the more people come, the more people will come."

"You mustn't worry," Mrs. G told her gently. "It's a lovely thing to do no matter how many do or don't attend."

"We're taking up a collection," Sofia said. "All day. For the children. And a lot of people gave when we first invited them, too. A lot of people said they couldn't come, but they kicked in for the collection. So even if we don't get a big crowd, we have a good start on that."

Then she hurried away as though she couldn't bear the pressure a moment longer.

A man in his thirties approached the table. An African American man with a shaved head and a beard but no mustache.

"You're the widow," he said to Isabel. It didn't sound like a question.

"Yes," she said.

"I just wanted to come tell you I'm sorry for your loss. And I'm sorry the jury didn't get it, but I just wanted you to know that a lot of people get it—what a loss it was to you and how wrong it was that it ever happened that way."

He reached out for Isabel's hand, and she reached out in return. The man didn't shake her hand exactly. Just held it and gave it a squeeze.

Isabel opened her mouth, but no words came out.

"It's okay," he said. "You don't have to say anything. I just wanted you to know that. And I put a check in the collection jar. Not a lot, but it's what I can do. You know. For the children."

He let go of her hand and turned to walk away.

Raymond looked up to see an older woman and a young couple standing behind the man. Waiting their turn to talk to the widow.

The older woman stepped up first.

"I just want to say how sorry I am. Your husband might not have mattered as much as he should have to everybody, but he did to me. Even though I never met him. But I have three sons just about your age. His age. So I get it."

"Thank you," Isabel said.

Then the last couple stepped up, but by then they were no longer the last. The line had grown behind them. There were probably closer to fifty people out in the street now, and a good twenty of them had lined up to talk to the widow. To offer their condolences and make it clear that they cared, even if the jury hadn't cared nearly enough.

"Somebody should tell them it was your loss, too," Raymond whispered to Mrs. G.

"Absolutely not," she whispered back. "This is Isabel's moment. You let her have it. This has nothing to do with anyone but Luis's widow and his children. I'm glad to know so many people care, too, but today is not about me."

———

An hour into the party, the band changed. The steel drums were replaced by a four-piece band with a vocalist, who played modern pop songs and asked for requests before each one.

"Something slow!" Isabel called out.

Then she handed the baby to her eleven-year-old daughter, Maria Elena, and reached a hand out to Esteban.

"Esteban likes to slow dance," she said.

Mother and son rose hand in hand and joined three other couples who danced together in the middle of the street.

Esteban's head only came up a little higher than Isabel's waist, but they looked sweet together in spite of that. Or maybe because of it. Raymond noticed that several of the people watching took photos of them with their cell phones.

"Oh," Raymond said suddenly. Seized with a sudden thought. He held a hand out to Mrs. G. "Would you care to dance?"

"I would be delighted," she said.

She had downed two half-full cups of beer on top of her one hot dog and half a hamburger. Somehow the combination of food and drink seemed to have done wonders for her mood.

He rose, and took her hand, and led her out into the street.

"I should warn you," he said, "I'm a terrible dancer."

"I hardly think it matters. You will be the best dancer I've had as a partner in nearly twenty years. You can't lose."

She placed her left arm at his waist, and took his hand with her right. They stood with a good foot of air between them. Raymond tried, pathetically, to lead.

"Sorry," he said in a moment when he had missed the beat badly.

"I thought you were trying to get over being sorry."

"Oh. Right. Yeah."

He almost added the word "sorry," but he caught himself just in time.

—

"I used to know how to cut a rug," Mrs. G said between songs.

"How to what a what?"

"It's an expression. It means I was a pretty good dancer. Or at least an enthusiastic one."

She stood back from Raymond, alone in the middle of the street, and began to dance. She swung her legs back and forth, one leg at a time kicking out behind her, then out front. She held her arms out to the sides, palms out and fingers up. She spun all the way around and began again. People formed a circle around her to watch, some filming her on their cell phones. When she got to the part where her knees knocked together and apart, her hands crossing back and forth in front of them, the crowd applauded.

There were a good eighty people in the street by then.

Mrs. G stopped dancing and stood panting, and the crowd went wild with applause. Her face broke into a grin, the likes of which Raymond had never seen on her before. In time they accepted that they had seen all the dancing she had in her.

"Play the bunny hop song," a stranger yelled in the direction of the band. "Everybody knows the bunny hop."

They knew it. They played it. More than half the partygoers formed a human chain snaking down the street, punctuating their dance with three comical hops each time the music indicated them. Raymond was right behind Mrs. G, his hands on her shoulders, for about three sets of hops. Then he felt her slump and almost fall.

He caught her instinctively and kept her on her feet.

"I need to go sit down," she said.

He led her out of the line and back to the table, which sat empty now. He helped her down into a chair.

"Are you okay?" he asked, feeling desperate. Panicky.

"I'm fine. I just need to breathe a minute."

They sat in silence for several minutes, watching the snaking line of dancers doing their hop, hop, hop. Or Raymond was watching, anyway. He looked back at her to see her eyes wide open, but her body entirely motionless. Just slumping back in her chair, staring at nothing.

Raymond's heart jumped up into his throat.

"Mrs. G!" he shouted, shaking her shoulder.

"What?" she asked. "Why are you shouting at me?"

"Oh." Raymond's breath flew out of him, all at once and involuntarily. "Oh, you're okay. You scared me."

"Did you think I had kicked the bucket?"

"Well, you were just . . . you weren't moving, and your eyes were open, but you weren't looking at anything . . ."

"Raymond," she began. A bit derisively. "I'm blind."

"Oh. Right. Well, now I feel really stupid. You looked different than usual. But I guess just because you were tired."

She reached along the table and felt for his hand, then patted it.

"You're not going to get rid of me that easily, my friend. I'm going to live to be a hundred if I can. Maybe older."

"I'm glad to hear you say that."

"I told you that already."

"Yeah," he said. "I guess you did."

———

Luis Senior came by as dusk fell, and brought the collection jar, which he handed to Isabel with a formal sort of ceremony.

"Every time we count it, we get a slightly different number," he said, looking ashamed. "But it's over seven hundred dollars."

"That's wonderful," Isabel said.

"Listen," Luis said in return, his voice heavy. "I have four kids. I know seven hundred dollars doesn't go very far these days."

"It's wonderful," Isabel said again. "It's a lot. It'll help a lot. And even if you had only raised fifty bucks, I would've been grateful. Because it was just so nice that all these people cared."

"Well, that's the idea behind the block party," Luis said. "That's supposed to be the point of the thing."

———

Raymond and Mrs. G walked slowly toward the subway station together as the sun went down. Isabel and her children stayed behind to party. But Mrs. G had experienced enough for one day, and then some.

The setting sun hovered in front of them, between buildings, causing Raymond to shield his eyes with one arm. He wondered if the light bothered Mrs. G at all. If she was even aware of it.

"I feel like we're in one of those old cowboy movies," she said.

"Not following."

"In the end they would always walk off into the sunset. Or, actually . . . I guess they rode off into the sunset on their horse. But we don't have a horse, so this will have to do."

Raymond smiled.

They walked for a minute without speaking.

"You sure you're okay walking?" he asked.

"Positive. I told you. I just needed to rest for a minute after dancing. Don't treat me like I'm so terribly fragile. If I wasn't a tough old bird, I wouldn't be here. So, had you forgotten that I told you I was going to live to be at least a hundred if I had anything to say about it?"

"No. I remembered. But lately . . . I don't know. You were so down about everything. I guess I thought you changed your mind."

"Well, if I did, I changed it back."

"What changed things for you?"

"Oh, no one thing."

"More like all those little lights?"

"More like having a friend like you who spent so much time igniting all of them, just to try to please me and help me cope. The world is a tough place, my friend. I'm not ready to change my mind about that. And yet we're called upon to be grateful that we're in it. That seems to be our challenge."

"Yeah," Raymond said. "Hard sometimes."

"Well, if we're being honest with ourselves, it's hard most of the time. But we have each other. What else do we have but each other? And what would we do without each other? It would be unbearable."

"I guess it would," Raymond said.

"But at least I have a good friend. And you have me until you're in your twenties somewhere, whether you like it or not."

"I like it fine," Raymond said.

"The world has taken much from me," she said after a pause. A silent space. "Or, anyway, it feels that way most of the time. But it gave me you, and everything you brought to my door with you. Isabel and those three beautiful children, and a Luis Velez who threw us a block party, and another Luis Velez who is an attorney and can get money for the children, and that lovely little cat, who warms me up by sitting on me and purring and who never gets under my feet. And even a personal cello concert! And here you have your own life to be living, but you take the time to do all that for me. That's quite a bundle of good tidings, Raymond, and who am I to say it's not enough? Who am I to say life took too much and gave too little? I just live here. I'm not running the place. And it's a good thing I'm not. I don't know enough."

"You know more than anybody I've ever met."

"Well, it's not enough, my friend. I don't understand the way things are, much less the way they should be. But I'm smart enough to appreciate what I've got, and it's no small blessing."

The sun went down, and they just kept walking together. Slowly. Into the figurative sunset. Into whatever the world had in store for them now.

BOOK CLUB QUESTIONS

1. In the beginning, Raymond uses his small resources and time to help feed and then rescue a cat. In doing so, what is revealed about his character?

2. While Raymond is searching for Luis, many of the people he encounters say things along the lines of "I wish I had more time to help others." Did the book motivate you to question the time you spend helping others in your own life? What other things do you wish you had time for?

3. Despite the ugliness and unfairness of what is going on in the story, many people still step up and show kindness. Do you believe that difficult situations bring out the best or worst in humanity?

4. Mrs. G tells Raymond that the world is "a tough place . . . yet we're called upon to be grateful that we're in it." Do you agree with her? How does this present a challenge in today's world?

5. How do you think it's possible that, after Mrs. G has suffered so much loss in her life, Luis can still say she does not have one bone of prejudice in her body?

6. In one of Mrs. G's conversations, she says that "life gives us nothing outright. It only lends. Nothing is ours to keep." What is she referring to? Do you agree or disagree? If that is true, how does that shape the way you look at your life?

7. From the time Luis is killed, through the trial and the verdict, did you ever feel empathy for the woman who shot him? If so, why? Either way, did you feel the verdict was fair?

8. A recurring theme the author examines throughout the book is what constitutes a life of value. In what ways did this book illuminate or redefine this concept for you?

9. The book examines the concept of privilege and how it can affect the outcome of a person's life. How does privilege play a role in the final verdict of the trial?

10. Before he met Mrs. G, Raymond felt like he didn't fit in and was alone and directionless. In what ways does his relationship with Mrs. G not only change his current life, but shape his future as well?

11. When Mrs. G is the most despondent, Raymond takes her to hear a cellist play. Mrs. G comments on how the cellist says the instrument has the same sad-to-beautiful ratio as life. What do you think is meant by that?

ABOUT THE AUTHOR

Photo © 2017 Laurel Renz

Catherine Ryan Hyde is the author of more than thirty published and forthcoming books. An avid hiker, traveler, equestrian, and amateur photographer, she has released her first book of photos, *365 Days of Gratitude: Photos from a Beautiful World.*

Her novel *Pay It Forward* was adapted into a major motion picture, chosen by the American Library Association for its Best Books for Young Adults list, and translated into more than twenty-three languages for distribution in more than thirty countries. Both *Becoming Chloe* and *Jumpstart the World* were included on the ALA's Rainbow Book List, and *Jumpstart the World* was a finalist for two Lambda Literary Awards. *Where We Belong* won two Rainbow Awards in 2013, and *The Language of Hoofbeats* won a Rainbow Award in 2015.

More than fifty of her short stories have been published in the *Antioch Review, Michigan Quarterly Review, Virginia Quarterly Review, Ploughshares, Glimmer Train,* and many other journals and in the anthologies *Santa Barbara Stories, California Shorts,* and *New York Times* bestseller *Dog Is My Co-Pilot.* Her stories have been honored in the Raymond Carver Short Story Contest and the Tobias Wolff Award and nominated for the O. Henry Award and the Pushcart Prize. Three have been cited in Best American Short Stories.

She is the founder and former president (2000–2009) of the Pay It Forward Foundation and still serves on its board of directors. As a professional public speaker, she has addressed the National Conference on Education, spoken at Cornell University twice, met with AmeriCorps members at the White House, and shared a dais with Bill Clinton.

For more information and book club questions, please visit the author at www.catherineryanhyde.com.